LOVELY BAD THINGS

HOLLOW'S ROW: BOOK ONE

TRISHA WOLFE

LOCK KEY PRESS

The *Lovely Bad Things* Spotify Playlist

Wicked Game - Chris Isaak
Runnin' with the Devil - Van Halen
The Funeral - Band of Horses
Don't Fear the Reaper - Gus Black
Angel - Massive Attack
Sweet Dreams - Trinix
Where is my Mind - Pixies
Running up that Hill - Placebo
Deep End - Ruelle
Madness - Ruelle
Paint it Black - Ciara
Come Back - The Misfits
(Don't Fear) The Reaper - Keep Shelly in Athens
Wicked Game - Jessie Villa

One must cultivate one's own garden.

— *CANDIDE*, **VOLTAIRE**

design swirls along the lower part of his neck. Inked sigils mark his fingers. He taps his thumb ring against the defendant's table in rhythmic succession to the clicking of the A/C vent.

A crooked grin curls his full lips as I take my seat on the witness stand after I've been sworn in to give my testimony.

Judge McCarthy may reside over this proceeding, but this courtroom is Kallum Locke's church. He rules over the eager mass, charming his flock, a magician with a bag of tricks.

His deception is flawless. If you can't see past the handsome, sophisticated philosophy professor with sleek black hair and alluring eyes, then you fail to notice the gruesome crime-scene photos stacked along the wall.

The victim, Percy Wellington, was the fourth in a string of ritualistic murders that ranged across five New England states. I'd been working the Harbinger case for eleven months when I got called to the university crime scene in Cambridge.

Just twenty miles away from the third scene where I was stationed.

Right away, I noticed the differences between the cases. The distance, for one: the Harbinger killer always separated his kills by state lines. The timing: only five days between kills, whereas the killer typically waited at least two months. Which could indicate he was devolving, but then there was the method:

The Harbinger killer performed a ceremony, adorning his victims like the fabled harbinger of death and doom, the death's-head hawkmoth. Once the victim was transformed into the moth with the face of a skull, the killer decapitated the head. This was part of his ritual to try to stave off a doomsday he believed would befall the world.

He always left a letter—written in block letters; no DNA or prints—at the scenes, forewarning about the end of times, a vague event he predicted would occur to wipe out humanity.

First responders recovered no letter at the Cambridge scene.

Rather, the university crime scene was more personal in nature. The perpetrator seemed to either hesitate with severing the head or physically struggle, using a different instrument altogether after a violent attack that left the victim disfigured.

Again, all these findings could denote a devolving offender, becoming increasingly more unhinged and desperate—but it was what transpired my final day at the scene that tipped the scales, and why I'm seated in this courtroom now.

After a brief welcome and introduction, the defense attorney, Charles Crosby, approaches the witness stand. "Miss St. James, you were only on the case for three days, is this correct?"

"Yes, that's correct," I respond.

"And in those three days, how many interactions did you have or interviews did you conduct with the defendant?"

"One," I answer honestly. "As a specialized criminologist, I study the scene of a crime to build a profile for investigators. I rarely have the opportunity to interview suspects."

I regret my words immediately. I can and do conduct interviews with suspects, but it depends on the factors of each case. Like this one, where it was evident within a short period who the suspect was, and I had no reason to delve deeper into my investigation of the scene.

"I see," he says, his gaze fixed on my streak of white hair. "So when you conducted your one and only interview with Professor Locke, how much bearing did that conversation have on your profile, the one that named my client as the prime suspect?"

I incline my head. Instead of answering his baiting question, I pull out my phone and lay it on the witness bench.

Crosby immediately objects. "Not in evidence, your honor," he declares.

I speak up before the state's attorney can argue any point. "Counsel asked specifically for me to explain what bearing my interview had on my analysis," I say. "I think admitting my testimony into evidence is only relevant if that interview is also admitted."

Crosby interjects again. "Boston is a two-party consent state, your honor, and my client did not give his consent to be recorded."

Judge McCarthy calls both lawyers up to the bench. I overhear arguments for federal law consent and expectations of privacy, before the judge dismisses the lawyers.

"Miss St. James," the judge addresses me, "where did this conversation take place?"

"On the campus grounds, in the courtyard near the crime scene, your honor."

"Were there others present?" she further inquires.

"Yes. Local police and federal agents were still

investigating the scene at the time I spoke with Professor Locke."

She nods. "As the conversation was held outdoors on an active crime scene and in the presence of other officials, I'm ruling there was no expectation of privacy, and I'm allowing the recording to be admitted. Let's hear the interview. I'm curious."

I open the voice recorder app and hit Play on the file.

The sound is muffled as it crackles over the small speaker from where I slipped my phone into my back pocket. I was standing opposite Kallum on the university grounds, just feet away from the marked-off crime scene.

The afternoon air was crisp and smelled like burnt leaves. The lowering sun cast the lush grounds in shades of umber and smoky taupe, imbuing a sense of calm despite the unsettling yellow tape strung around the quad.

High, gothic arches framed the central courtyard of the university. Stone benches and birch trees shrouded the crime scene where the mutilated body of Professor Wellington was discovered by passerby students.

The victim had been removed, the site in the process of being cleared, as the dean was anxious to return the university to its stately status.

I had felt Kallum's eyes on me as I walked the scene my last day there. Actually, I had felt his eyes on me the whole time I had been at the prominent Ivy League institution. But this was the first time I looked directly into those eyes—one green, one blue—as he stood before me with a curious glint flashing behind his predatory gaze.

His all-black suit was tailored. Like him, it was stylish and youthful. Quite unusual for a tenured professor with such high accolades. He'd achieved a prestigious reputation by the age of thirty-six, albeit one where he was admired as much as he was regarded dangerous—but dangerous in a dark and mysterious vein.

The bad-boy of academia.

His silent broodiness and blackwork tattoos added to the effect to trigger gossip in the hallways. Yet, as a distinguished professor, Kallum was revered as an expert in all things esoteric philosophy, occult, and antiquity.

I didn't know much about the esteemed Professor Locke at that point, other than a couple of his published research papers I'd previously read—but something in the way he was studying me, like one of his cryptic artifacts, made me wary enough to hit Record on my phone.

His first words to me: "You're an intriguing little thing."

I felt the hairs on the nape of my neck lift away from my skin. When I didn't respond, he said, "You're not a law official."

"No," I confirmed.

"But they trust your opinion."

"Some of them, I suppose."

"And what is your opinion? Halen, isn't it?"

"It is, but it would be inappropriate and unethical to discuss my findings with you, Professor Locke."

"Because I'm a suspect? And please, it's Kallum."

"Yes, because you're a suspect, as are most of the university staff and students. Then there's the obvious fact I won't discuss an active investigation with any person outside of the case."

"That's hardly any fun."

"That's the rules."

"Rules are definitely no fun."

A long beat of silence followed where he drew closer. "Are you afraid of me?"

"No."

"You're trembling."

"I'm not used to the Boston weather."

"You get accustomed to it, just like you get accustomed to drifting below radar, unseen in the shadows, trying to appear unremarkable."

"Is that how you view yourself here?"

"I was referring to you, Halen."

"I'm not sure what you're talk—"

"You know exactly what I'm talking about. All these self-important, big-dick detectives trying to make their case, while here you are, the only one with actual, impressive credentials, the only one who can piece together what happened here, and you haven't spoken a word."

I inhaled an unsteady breath. "I'm not reporting to the local authorities or the FBI on this case," I said, but a sense of dread flared. He had looked into me. "I should leave here now, actually."

He walked right up to me, got close enough I could smell the woodsy scent of his cologne, feel his breath trace a path across the contours of my throat and collarbone in the wake of his trailing gaze. Then he inhaled a deep breath, as if pulling me into his lungs.

"I'd like to know what thoughts you keep silent, what you're so worried might slip past those trembling lips."

I only stood there, staring up into his shadowed face, the sun at dusk a darkening halo behind his head.

"Wellington was the opposite," he continued. "He couldn't shut his fucking mouth. He was a despicable human being. Maybe that's why the killer cracked his jawbone and tore his face in two, split his skull with a tire iron."

I swallowed. "That's very specific."

"One can only presume, of course." His smile taunted me. "If I were his wife, I mean, I'd probably be fucking my personal trainer too and want my husband to shut the fuck up permanently." He winked before he took a step back. "I'll see you around, little Halen."

The recording ends, and I feel the collective shiver roll through the courtroom.

For just a moment, the illusion is broken, and the people seated in the pews glimpse the disturbed monster beneath the handsome veneer of the man at the table.

I felt the same chilling shiver ricochet through my bones the moment Kallum confessed the details of the murder to me, and I knew I was looking into the eyes—no matter how alarmingly beautiful—of a sadistic killer, one with no empathy or remorse.

As tension builds in the room, I say, "In answer to your question, Mr. Crosby, yes, my conversation with Professor Locke had bearing on my profile. The particular detail, that of the object used to dismantle the mandible, that is the jawbone of the victim, hadn't yet been revealed to the public at that time. Professor Locke wanted me to know he had been the one to silence the victim, and he was going to get away with it."

"Objection," Crosby interrupts. "Move to strike. The witness cannot know what my client was thinking, your honor."

"On that, I agree," Judge McCarthy says. "Motion to strike from the record granted. Proceed."

Crosby addresses me again. "Miss St. James, with no expectation of privacy on the scene, is it possible Professor Locke could've overheard detectives or crime-scene analysts discussing this detail of the crime during those three days on university grounds?"

"Anything is possible," I'm forced to answer, as he's using the ruling to admit my recording against me.

"Is there any other element in your report, other than this one brief conversation, that led to your conclusion as the defendant as the prime suspect?"

I roll my shoulders, relieving the itch of the polyester material. My gaze drifts to Kallum, who no longer wears an arrogant grin. His features are sharp and tipped with malice. A prickling sensation webs my nerves, encasing me in cold.

I look at the lawyer. "My analysis was primarily based on the evidence at the crime scene. The defendant meets the physical profile to commit the crime, and he also has a history of discord with the victim."

"But that's not physical evidence," Crosby states, walking

the length of the courtroom to stand near the jury box. "That's considered circumstantial, correct?"

"Circumstantial evidence is still evidence that shapes a crime-scene profile," I say, feeling my hackles rise. I belong in the field, not in a courtroom where my words can be twisted. But this crime is far too important to me not to make myself heard.

The lawyer turns my way. "Shapes a crime-scene profile," he parrots. "But a profile is a theory in itself, not hard, factual evidence."

"Objection," the prosecutor speaks up. "Is Mr. Crosby done questioning the witness, your honor?"

"Sustained." The judge rules in the state's favor. "Counsellor, do you have any further questions for this witness? Let's keep it on point."

"My apologies, your honor," Crosby says, then gives me a leering smile. "Just one last question for Miss St. James. Is there any evidence—any DNA, fingerprints, hair, fibers... anything at all—that points to my client as the culprit of this vicious, heinous crime?"

A lawyer never asks a question they don't already assume they know the answer to. The case against Kallum was built on circumstancing facts. With no DNA, no witnesses, the detectives and federal agents had to take motive into account.

Wellington's wife was looked at hard, but a cheating spouse offing her husband was the weaker motive compared to professional rivalry and revenge. Wellington had insulted Kallum during his keynote speech at the university just hours before his murder.

Then there was Kallum's confession to the knowledge of the weapon—the lug wrench from Wellington's own car. He had been first attacked in the parking lot.

And Kallum had no alibi.

Those key pieces narrowed the scope on him when the state was clambering for an arrest to be made.

Then there's the other, more allusive reasoning.

My gut instinct.

After investigating too many macabre crime scenes, I've walked in the footsteps of many killers to build profiles, and I can sense when I'm in the presence of a killer.

The intense and alarming feeling I get when I'm around Kallum bleeds all rational thought and reason from my mind, leaving me with only one conclusion: "Professor Locke committed this crime," I say, talking around the lawyer and his question. "Physical evidence cannot always be recovered, but the fact is, if you let this sociopath walk out of this courtroom, you'll be letting a killer walk free."

The judge raps her gavel on the block. "Miss St. James, I expect better behavior from a professional in my courtroom. Are you through with your outbursts?"

"Sorry. Yes, your honor."

"Good," the judge states. "The jury will disregard the witness's statement."

A fiery ache lodges in my throat as I meet Kallum's watchful eyes. His mouth tips into a cruel, lopsided smirk.

Crosby rests his palms on the witness stand, drawing my attention. "Miss St. James, you're a crime-scene criminologist, correct?"

I reach for a stable breath. "Yes." *He knows this.*

"You profile, for lack of better terminology, the scene of a crime."

"Yes."

"Then it's fair to say you're not technically qualified to analyze my client's mental state"—he makes air quotes; why, I'm not sure—"am I correct?"

And I realize I declared Kallum a "sociopath" in open court.

"I do hold a doctorate in psychology and a doctorate in criminology," I say, glancing at the twelve members of the jury. "But no, I don't conduct psychological evaluations."

"Do these doctorates allow you to have your own patients?"

My eyebrows draw together. "I don't—"

"Let me rephrase," Crosby says. "Do you have, or have you ever had, patients within your own practice, Miss St. James?"

I shake my head. "No."

"I see. Thank you for your time. No further questions."

I go to stand, and the state's attorney rises. "I'd like to cross, your honor." The judge allows, and the lawyer stays standing at the table. "Just one question, Miss St. James. All credentials aside, why are you certain the defendant is guilty of this crime?"

I remove my gaze from the court. I don't look at the crime-scene images, or the lawyers, or Kallum. I look only at the jury, making eye contact with a few. I'm being *seen*, being

if that scarecrow was a linebacker. He was the first to greet me when I arrived at the police station, regaling me with tales of his high-school football glory days.

He's not a bad detective as far as I can tell, just small-town. As he made detective less than a year ago, the extent of his detecting work has been locating missing teens, who typically disappear for a weekend bender, and lost pet cases.

Which is oddly dull, considering the dark lore this town is steeped in.

Things have been quiet for Hollow's Row for too long.

The town's reputation is why my director tossed the file on my proverbial desk. That, and the fact the locals are overwhelmed and wary of the inevitable FBI invasion.

"This part of the marshland is called the killing fields," Detective Emmons explains. "Local hunters toss the carcasses of their kills out here." He nods down to the skeletal remains of an animal as he steps around the protruding rib cage.

I pause to inspect the sizable, sun-bleached bones. Deer, probably. A stag. Difficult to determine from a glance without the antlers. The hunters keep those as trophies.

Emmons goes to remove a fallen branch to clear our path to the scene, and I hold up my hand.

"Wait." I move quicker to reach him. At his puzzled expression, I add in a less alarmed tone, "Please, don't move anything. I need to keep the scene preserved for my colleagues."

Referring to the FBI as my colleagues is a stretch, but I'm a professional, nonetheless.

Dark eyebrows pinched, he runs his tongue over his teeth,

gaze narrowed. His eyes flit to the streak of white framing the left side of my face, quickly meeting my gaze again before his stare becomes rude. "All right, then."

He starts again toward the scene which has already been marked-off by his colleagues. Yellow crime-scene tape bounces gently in the open air above the reed grass.

I don't take offense to his questioning pause. I understand a man of his stature—both physically and large in reputation —would hesitate before taking an order from a petite woman, and a fed at that.

I give him credit, though, his hesitation was brief. He even made an attempt not to stare at my defect. I should correct him on at least one of his assumptions, though. I'm not a federal agent. The logistics are typically too complicated to explain when I'm called to a scene, however, so I let the assumption ride most of the time.

Technically, the Federal Bureau of Investigation did send me here. But as a subcontractor, I'm not on the government's payroll. I'm a crime scene investigative criminologist with CrimeTech, one of the leading research authorities on criminal behavior and corrections in the country.

But that's still not exactly what I do.

There's a sub agency within the company which specializes in the more bizarre cases. The ones that make most detectives and FBI agents say: *what the fuck.*

Ones like the scene we're encroaching on now.

As I take in the sight boxed-in by yellow tape, I feel the urgent buzz prickle my skin, that anxious sensation which swarms my insides like a nest of relentless hornets trying to escape.

Bizarre is what I do.

The dark and macabre underbelly of the crime-solving world.

If it can't be explained by an investigator or your average forensic psychologist, and it's disturbing enough to make law officials uncomfortable, then my unit is requested to explain the unexplainable.

As a crime-scene profiler, I read motives and clues in what the offenders leave behind in the aftermath of their crimes. Behavior is not just observed within the person; it's observed in the echo of their actions, in the delivery of their violence.

When others look away from a morbid scene, I look deeper.

In truth, I'm here to put people at ease, so they can sleep at night knowing their world makes sense.

What I'm staring at right this moment, however, shouldn't be explained away, or have a label slapped on it like *psychopath* or *mentally disturbed*. We should see it for the gruesome deed it is, for the truth of its existence.

Sometimes, evil things just are.

Detective Emmons can only stomach the sight for a minute before he has to look away, his features failing to mask his repulsion. But I see what he's trying to disguise there: fear. For most law officials, when you come face-to-face with soul-tainting evil, you fear being contaminated by it.

It's like walking a tightrope over an abyss.

"This is just..." The large detective shakes his head,

unable to articulate his thoughts. "God, it's fucking sick, is what it is."

I scan the site, feeling an unsettling touch coast my skin. The fine hairs on the nape of my neck lift away. I let the sensation crawl over me, consume me, because this is the reason the perpetrator went to the trouble of staging his scene. He wants to provoke a response.

As I drop my satchel in the mud, I shift my gaze to the detective. "I've never seen any god have a hand in things like this."

Emmons rubs the back of his neck, measuring my comment with a kernel of disbelief in his eyes. "Seriously? You've seen something like this before?"

I don't hesitate. "I've seen a lot."

He drops his hand and says, "I'll leave you to it, then." As he passes by, he swipes the tall reeds aside, making a point of leaving.

I stare after him and watch the way the tall grass parts for his large form. Then I glance around the crime scene, taking in the techs marking evidence and snapping pictures, the fireflies blinking against the pale backdrop. The silence is loud.

Inhaling a breath laced with the swampy scent of marsh, I face the scene.

Yes, I've seen a lot of things—but this fact doesn't minimize the grisliness before me.

A cropping of thin trees stretch high into the twilight, their branches bare and warped like distorted talons. The trees look dead, mangled. Like they themselves are the victims.

Affixed to the pitch-black bark of three eerie trees are the dissected eyes of thirty-three victims.

The lifeless eyes are filmed over and stare vacantly out over the wetland. The sight chills my blood.

No bodies were recovered.

The eyes have been positioned together, staged. I'd have to measure, but I'm assuming the perpetrator took the time and care to place them the exact distance apart as they were on the victims' faces. Unless he's over seven-feet tall, he would have needed to use a ladder or some tool to reach high enough overhead.

"I don't understand."

Lost in thought, I realize I've been standing in the same spot for too long. I adjust my stance to unlock my knees, and look over at the woman crime-scene analyst who comes to stand beside me.

"It's so damn creepy," she continues, "like, I feel like the eyes should be following me, like they should see me, how a doll's eyes seem to do, you know? But they're not looking at anything at all. Just...lifeless."

"I wonder who they did see," I remark

She turns toward me, her deep-brown skin amber hued in the setting sun. "Let's find out and catch the sick bastard."

Lips rimmed tight, I nod. "Absolutely."

"I'm Devyn Childs, by the way," she says. "Glad to have you here to help."

A smile lifts the corners of my mouth despite our bleak surroundings. She's the first person to welcome me on the case. Not even Detective Emmons offered an official welcome. "Halen St. James," I reply, leaving off my credentials. "And thanks. I really hope I can help."

"I typically wouldn't welcome the feds," she says, "but you seem harmless enough. Halen... That's an interesting name."

An observation I hear plenty. "My parents were big heavy metal fans in the eighties."

She nods, but her tapered gaze conveys she's not quite making the connection. Anyone under the age of forty rarely does. I've had thirty-two years of being subjected to the band Van Halen. I've memorized nearly every song, and know Eddie Van Halen was the "best guitarist ever" according to my father. My mother proudly touted she was first—and always would be—in love with David Lee Roth.

The surfacing memories are bittersweet, and I regret I can no longer listen to the songs.

Devyn gives me a sincere smile. "Well, I'm back at it. Let me know if you need anything while you're with us in Hollow's Row."

"I appreciate that. Thank you, Devyn."

Before I set up my tripod and digital camera, I inspect the reeds around the trunk base of the trees. The grass has been flattened, creating a clearing. No noticeable footprints. As I walk the perimeter, I come up to a blackened patch of reeds. The grass has been singed and burned away by fire to create a pit.

"No remains in there," one of the techs say as he passes. "Already processed."

"Thanks." But I still snap a round of pictures with my

phone and text them to my field manager, Aubrey. Which is an odd title to hold when he never actually enters the field. A point I make often when he rides me on field hours and reports.

A couple curious glances are directed my way from the crime-scene techs, but otherwise, the locals let me work independently in peace. Which, I suppose, is all any of us can aim for in the face of chaos.

I document the scene, starting from a distance and work my way closer. The dissected eyes have been removed from the eyelids cleanly, giving no initial indication of ethnicity to any of the victims, and they all appear a similar silver, grayish-blue due to corneal opacity and the film covering the irises.

I use a plastic probe to reach overhead to inspect one. The whole oculus of the organ is present. The optic nerve has been neatly severed. A medical examiner may be able to identify the exact instrument used, but for the purpose of my preliminary report, I note a general scalpel.

The pupils stare emptily out into the marshland, unseeing. I wonder what horrors they took in right before the perpetrator carved them from the sockets as, based on the cell structure, all organs appear to have been removed while the victims were still alive.

I try to imagine the difficulty, the patience and sheer sadistic brutality one would need to master in order to remove not just one pair of eyes from a struggling victim, but over thirty people.

How did he detain them? Were they drugged? Where were they kept?

Where are the bodies?

I'm impressed with the offender's measure of medical knowledge, if not horrified. The perpetrator was able to extract the eyes so efficiently. No retinal tears or mistreatment.

Every observation is noted and logged in a spreadsheet on my tablet, which is fed directly to the CrimeTech database in real time. But I also keep notes in a basic notebook—my own personal findings no one can access.

Once I've completed my preliminary examination, I move on to what really interests me. The eyes were not just simply tacked to the trees. That would've been sloppy, but also a timesaver. No, he took the time to painstakingly thread lace-weight yarn around the nerves in such precise manner and detail that the thread is almost unseen at first glimpse.

Then he strung the thread to the bark, weaving it in so it disappears around the girth of the three trees. It's clever and well-constructed. The techs will need to cut thread away from the trees and run individual tests. They might even be able to narrow down the age and where the skein was purchased. If it's a rare brand or color, that would be even more helpful.

I highly doubt there will be any DNA retrieved from the yarn or anywhere else in this scene. But, I'm not here to collect and run lab tests. That's up to the techs and detectives to build their case against any suspects.

I'm here to tell the scene's narrative, to paint the gruesome picture of an offender who is methodical enough to dissect thirty-three pairs of eyes and string them to eerie trees in the middle of a killing field.

It's my job to find the killer's story.

When building a profile of a crime scene, I have to consider all the elements. The location, the weather, the wildlife. I have to walk in the killer's proverbial—and sometimes literal—footsteps to uncover evidence the killer may have left behind.

While I'm photographing the intricate detail work on the woven thread, the caw of a nearby crow captures my notice.

Finding the source, I move away from the scene and duck under the caution tape, slogging farther out toward the low-lying ground of the marsh where a murder of crows circle overhead. I don't have to walk far before I see what's drawing their attention.

A fresh kill.

A large stag has been skinned and mutilated and left to bake in the sun.

I get close enough to search for a kill shot before stepping away from the putrid stench. From this angle, I can't determine what was used to kill the deer. But what I do notice is this animal wasn't killed for its meat.

I glance over to the scene to gauge the distance, then look up at the circling fish crows.

If he used a dead animal to attract the birds away from his exhibit, then he knew the area well enough to anticipate the crows pecking at the remains. He didn't want his work destroyed.

He could have buried the bodies out here and simply left

them to decay. The bodies may have never been found. Instead, he made a production of a very specific organ.

He's telling his own story.

The decisive difference is in whether or not the display is for his own purpose or for someone else's. Because if it's a message, why go through the burden of wandering all the way into the deep marsh where there's a chance no one will ever come across his work? Carting all those remains and tools twenty minutes into the killing fields wasn't an easy feat.

Then of course he had to hunt and kill the deer. Skin it, mutilate it. Leave it in a strategic and possibly tested distance away from his display.

The perpetrator could be a hunter.

So why didn't he claim his trophy and take the antlers?

Because those aren't the trophies he keeps.

I look up at the darkening sky, at the crows circling the barren trees. A team is already scouting the marshland in hopes of recovering the bodies.

A commotion of shouts erupt at the crime-scene perimeter as a man with a press badge tries to gain access. He snaps pictures around Devyn as she tries to barricade him from the scene. I start in her direction to help, but suddenly the reporter takes off back through the reeds.

Exasperated, she shakes her head and looks at me. I shrug, because she seemed to handle him just fine.

I'm honestly surprised only one member of the press has found their way out here, considering the history of this town and the media craze this scene will incite once the story breaks.

About five years ago, Hollow's Row was a national hotspot for conspiracy and innuendo when people went missing.

Disappeared.

Thirty-three town residents vanished, never to be heard from again.

As I head back toward the crime scene, I feel it in the dense, marshy air, the whisper too fragile to voice. It's what's not being said in the silence that screams so loud.

Every single person on this scene knows who the victims are—some may even be their family, their friends—even if no one is willing to give voice to that thought. They're just waiting for DNA analysis to confirm it.

Thirty-three pairs of unseeing eyes with a horrific story to tell.

Where have these people been for the past five years? The mystery is far more disturbing than the gruesome scene.

The mystery is the reason I'm here.

Deciding I've cataloged enough of the scene for the first day, I begin to pack up my case and bag the rest of my tools and supplies. I'll return tomorrow when there are less people so I can immerse myself in the scene. I roll off my gloves and stuff them into my jacket pocket as Devyn comes to see me off.

"The trees have eyes…" she mutters beneath her breath.

The fine hairs along my skin stand up, and a fierce shiver races up my spine. "Excuse me?"

"Oh," she says, waving a hand dismissively. "Just

something I recalled from a torturous college class. It's been stuck in my head since I got on-scene."

I give her my undivided attention, every nerve ending flaring with an electric current. "I'm curious," I prod her.

"Chaucer," she says. "My professor was obsessed. Made us read *The Canterbury Tales* without the translated cliff notes. Have you ever tried to read Middle English? Pure damn torture. And I just remember how boring those stories were. Like, I'd rather watch the dullest shade of vanilla paint dry on a wall.

"Anyway," she continues, "one of Chaucer's proverbs was: *the trees have eyes, and the fields have ears.*"

A flash of beautifully disarming blue-and-green eyes…his gaze so arctic and devoid of feeling I can still feel it raking over my body with malicious intent.

Then his final words to me: *"Time and tide wait for no man."*

A quote he delivered from Geoffrey Chaucer.

Twisted apprehension sinks down to my marrow and pits out my bones.

I've tried for six months to bar him from my thoughts, but he's like a dark silhouette caught at the edge of a film flare; some demon affixed to my soul that follows me like a shadow.

"Chaucer," I repeat, the name like acid on my tongue. After Kallum's parting words, I searched the quote, then— with difficulty—attempted to read the author's works. "This was a philosophy class?" I ask her.

She nods skeptically. "Yes, obviously. Halen, what's wrong? You look ill."

I am ill. A deep-seated sickness gnarls my insides like the distorted trees staring down on me, and it's done so since the moment I stepped foot on the university grounds and laid eyes on Kallum Locke.

For three months after the court trial, I obsessively worked the Harbinger case to find a connection, any link, to tie back to him.

"I have to go," I tell her, shouldering my bag. "Thanks, Devyn."

"Sure… See you tomorrow?"

I glance around the scene, wondering how long I have before the techs and officials start removing the remains. "How much sway do you have with your department?"

She cocks an eyebrow. "That depends on whether or not you're going to let me in on whatever you're up to."

"I know someone who can offer insight to this scene," I say. "But, he's not easily accessible." A severe understatement.

Devyn looks at the barren trees. "I might be able to postpone the dismantling until tomorrow afternoon. But I won't push out longer. We have to preserve the evidence, Halen. And the victims could be…" She trails off as she looks at me, an imploring depth in her brown eyes.

"I know," I say, nodding my understanding. "I promise, if it doesn't pan out, you'll be the one I call. Thank you."

"All right. Don't let me down, fed."

I smile, deciding I'll eventually let her in on the whole

truth of my involvement here. She's more assertive than Detective Emmons, and seems to have a more open mind. Something this case will need.

The sky has darkened. Midnight-blue bleeds into burnt umber, hindering my navigation as I maneuver back the way I came through the reeds. My phone chimes with a text, and I dig it out of my back pocket, already knowing who the message is from before I tap the screen.

Aubrey: *You're done already? I haven't received an updated report.*

I call him rather than have this conversation over a text. "I have to make an impromptu trip. I need you to get me a plane ticket."

Silence clogs the line before he says, "You're in the middle of a wetland on an active investigation. Where the hell could you possibly have to suddenly go?"

I wish I didn't have to answer that question. Not for the first time, I wonder what it would be like to work freelance and independently away from the company. There are pros and cons and risks on both sides, of course, and right now, I'd miss the security of the full-time work which keeps me busy.

Placing the call on speakerphone, I light my phone flashlight. I grip my bag strap and sidestep the picked-clean carcass I passed earlier.

"These trees have eyes, Aubrey," I say into the line.

"Yes, I know. That's why you're there," he says, his tone incredulous and short.

"No, not literally. It's a proverb." I drop my gaze to the reeds. "It may be nothing, or there may be some connection. I don't know. Philosophy was never my strength. But that's why I need to find out."

"Wait…philosophy?" His weighted beat punctuates the air with uncertainty. "Halen, don't go there. Don't do this to yourself again." Aubrey's desperate tone bleeds into my own doubts. "I thought this obsession was over—"

"I don't have an obsession," I fire back, my jaw clenched around the words. "Can you find me a philosophy scholar with extensive knowledge in Western esotericism?"

"I'm sure I can," he says.

"One who can also think like a killer?"

He expels an audible breath across the line.

The Harbinger case remains unsolved, a suspect never named. But I know exactly where that likely suspect is right now, and I know he will eventually charm his way to the outside world.

My forearm flares with a heated itch, and I rub at the ink over the top of my shirt, then touch the pendant around my neck to center my diverging thoughts.

Focus on the present.

"This isn't going to go over well," Aubrey finally relents.

I release a cleansing breath, exhaling the tension from my chest. "Look. I'm not looking at him for this…not directly. And I'm not working the Harbinger case. I've put that to rest. But he's an expert in his field—*the* expert—and I need his insight on this."

"And what makes you think he'll be willing to help you?"

My field manager makes a logical point.

Despite the humidity, the evening air drops a degree

cooler, the darkness encroaching. I think about his question in earnest. Not because I don't know the answer—but I'm not sure how to phrase the answer aloud.

Kallum will be all too willing to help. Whether or not his participation will actually *be* helpful...well, that's a risk I have to take.

But he will help me, because he's a narcissistic sociopath who's been locked away for the past six months, and my asking for his help will feed his starved ego.

"I don't know, Aubrey," I say as I come up on the rental car. "But if you get me that plane ticket, once I get there, you'll be the first to know."

I end the call, knowing once the evidence confirms the eyes were removed perimortem, the priority of this case will escalate drastically. The FBI will then take over and may even push me out. Media will descend and congest the town. I have a limited time to work, and I need specific answers.

Answers only a deranged philosophy scholar can give me.

Yes, evil exists.

And I have to look evil right in his beautiful eyes and ask for his help.

3

WICKED EYES

KALLUM

M

ost obsessions start small, harmless. A tiny niggle in the back of your mind, an innocent fixation. The obsessive thought crawls under our skin and we begin to pick and pick until the desire overwhelms and we have no choice but to tear into it, claws raking and drawing blood.

The wound is a form of relief.

All great minds suffer this affliction. A torment that damns us to a monotonous existence.

But what is art and beauty if not pain? Anything which comes too easily is an insult to both the creator and the consumer.

With pain, we feel, we tear ourselves wide, and we allow the wound to heal over. We accept the scar. With obsession, we mutilate the skin until it's destroyed, never allowing the damage to repair.

Blood never clots. We want it to flow, to keep feeding the passion, the desire.

Little Halen St. James didn't start as a tiny niggle. From day one, she flayed my skin wide and buried herself deep.

And I can't stop scratching.

"Locke, you're up."

My name is called over the line of patients in the waiting room seated on a bench. It's dank and crowded in the small eight-by-ten holding area of Briar Correctional Institute for the Criminally Insane. The plain-white walls are dingy with age and neglect. There's a constant reek of bleach with a faint undercurrent of mildew, a stench that can never quite be masked.

The psychotic inmates smell worse.

Donning my neutral patient scrubs, I rise from the plastic chair and drag a hand through my slicked hair. A few loose strands creep over my eye, but the errant stragglers are forgotten when I'm ensnared by the sight at the visitation table.

I allow all five senses to absorb her fully before I step into the room.

Basic heather-gray thermal with three buttons undone at her collar. A simple, delicate white-gold chain drops a one-carat, teardrop diamond in the hollow of her throat. Her dark-brown hair is pulled back in a low ponytail, out of the way. A defiant streak of white frames the side of her unpolished face.

The only makeup she wears is a swipe of mascara to

darken her lashes, and a hint of gloss on her plump lips. But why cover up her natural beauty with layers of toxic chemicals? I appreciate the simplicity, even if those dramatic hazel eyes make me want to draw blood.

As I move into the room, I watch as she observes me just as closely. I like the way she purposely tries not to blink, the way her cheeks tinge the slightest shade of pale-pink. It's deceiving on her part; she's not shy or meek or enraptured by me.

Oh, I know I'm a specimen to behold. There's no modesty in these bones. It would be pretentious of me to fake humbleness. Since I was five, my mother's friends cooed and marveled over my eyes. My high-school girlfriends soaked their panties over my floppy black hair and crooked smile. Come to think of it, so did my mother's friends.

At six-one, my body is leanly cut and toned, honed to wreak havoc on the female mind and body.

Which is one of the many annoyances when it comes to the petite criminologist seated across from me; she never fell into my web. She escaped unscathed, unaffected. More so, she slammed a glass over me and trapped me like a common house spider.

A miscalculation I'm determined to rectify.

My bite has venom.

"Hello, Halen." The gravelly rasp of my voice curls around the syllables of her name. The first tremor of excitement rolls under my skin.

"Professor Locke," she replies formally. "I'd prefer if you addressed me in kind as Dr. St. James."

"This is the first time I've lain eyes on you in months, and here you sit, making demands. Impressive. Once you stepped out of those shadows, it seems you never returned." My gaze skims her composed features, probing for the crack in her armor. I thought I found it once, but I was *un*pleasantly surprised to stand corrected. Amid twelve jurors, no less.

"Am I being recorded?" I ask, not curbing the hard edge in my tone of voice.

"No. This conversation if strictly between us—"

"I thought the last one was."

She tips her chin higher and presents her phone, proving there are no recording apps, before she slips the device back into her bag. "But I'd like it if our conversation remains formal."

"Oh, come now," I say, "we can toss out nominal letters and propriety bullshit. We're both on equal ground."

She arches a fine eyebrow. "Does it rub you raw I won't refer to you as Dr. Locke? Because, given the doctorate in philosophy is the most common in academia, I only presumed you'd find it insulting. Although, I could always tack on the post-nominal lettering if it helps your ego, Professor Locke, *PhD.*"

She's been a busy little bee investigating me to learn how I tick.

Ryder—who I suppose one may consider my closest friend—relayed how she'd been interrogating professional associates and what few friends I have left after this debacle. I may have used him to feed her some interesting morsels.

What tangled webs...

I lick my lips slowly, savoring the burn of her arousing scent as it stokes my senses. A mouthwatering combination of lily of the valley and ylang-ylang, a unique scent well-suited for her.

Poisonous. Toxic, but only if ingested. With a hint of aphrodisiac.

She could market the scent with her own brand: *Lure and kill.*

"Rubbing me raw, little Halen, has all the promise with no follow through." I spin the silver ring around my thumb.

She visibly shifts in her seat, refusing to be baited.

Scratch, scratch, scratch.

"What a waste of your doctorate," I press on, expelling a lengthy breath. "You should be working in academia yourself, fielding your own research. Instead, you're still traipsing around crime scenes, playing chase."

"Keeping tabs on me?"

I smile. "I have loads of time to kill."

Her mouth parts, as if I've said something to confirm a suspicion.

Daringly, I let my hand settle past the midway point on the table. There are no plastic dividers. No metal grates. I could reach out and touch her if I wanted—but I'm not yet ready to tear in and claw that itch.

Her gaze drops to my hand, to the faded inked celestial rose on the back of my hand and sigils that mark my fingers below my knuckles.

"I'm surprised you didn't request I be shackled." I drum my fingers on the surface of the hard plastic tabletop.

When she raises her gaze to meet mine, her resolve is firmly in place. "Should I have? Do you plan to hurt me?"

The vision attacks so suddenly and with startling fierceness—my hands collared around her slender neck; her breathy gasps for oxygen—I have to blink hard and push farther away from the table to escape her scent.

"Anger is an acid that can do more harm to the vessel," I say.

"That didn't answer my question."

"Mark Twain answered it, if you can surmise his meaning. Brilliant writer, horrible businessman."

With a clipped, sardonic laugh, she stands. "I don't know why I'm here. This was a bad idea. Apparently, you really are insane."

On impulse, I reach out and grab her wrist.

A charged pulse ignites a fire beneath my palm. The air, volatile and tense, suspends time for a mere blink, allowing my body to ravenously absorb the feel of her where I've only permitted my eyes to touch.

Our gazes collide on impact of that touch, and I see the conflict in her fearful eyes. I'm not the only one affected.

Her chest rises with uneven breaths as she twists her arm to break my hold, and despite the intense desire to keep her in my grasp, I let her.

My fingertips memorize the erratic beat of her pulse as she slips away. *Bah-dah-bump. Bah-dah-bah-dah-bump.* I want to carve it in my skin.

She crosses her arms, anxiously waiting for my rebound. I flex my hand as my gaze lingers on the visible imprint I left on her wrist. "It must have been difficult for you to come here," I say, sifting her from my thoughts to collect myself. "You should at least tell me why you came before you run away."

"I'm not running." Her strained swallow drags enticingly along the column of her throat to challenge her assertion. Then: "I need a philosophy expert."

"And how convenient you know right where to find one."

She recoils from my insult. I study her soft yet distressed features. I've never witnessed a more emotional creature. Even in her attempt to shield her grief, as she walked the grounds of the university, I could sense her pain. It tasted like the sweetest melancholy, like honeysuckle and cloves, leaving a lingering ache in the back of my throat.

And touching her is like touching the hottest part of the flame, and being unable to escape.

At her prolonged silence, I wave my hand to urge her on.

"What does the proverb, *The fields have eyes, and the woods have ears* mean to you?" she asks.

"It's Chaucer," I say automatically and cross my arms. "From *The Knight's Tale*, the first story in *The Canterbury Tales*. Sit down. You're upsetting the crazies."

She glances around to observe the other patients and their families giving her guarded looks. Then she reseats herself behind the table. "I don't think 'crazies' is acceptable terminology coming from—"

"I'm a professor of philosophy. Not a doctor, as you so clearly pointed out. Challenging political correctness is what I do."

"Among other, more nefarious things."

I crane an eyebrow. "And here you are, still without verifiable proof."

"And here you sit, in a nuthouse."

"My, what dirty terminology from that mouth." I run my tongue along the inside of my bottom lip, sensing the ire brimming beneath her tightly-laced veneer. It's delectable.

After a beat of tense silence, she states, "I know it's Chaucer. I can google. Is that all you have to offer in way of insight?"

I release a low chuckle, thoroughly amused. "You've given me nothing to go on. What it pertains to...is in connection to? Oh, I can spew for hours on end about the boring, mind-numbing tediousness of Chaucer and his overly praised drivel, but I highly doubt that will serve to enlighten anyone."

She tilts her head. "And yet, you once quoted him to me."

Her confession is a small flame teasing my skin, the fiery stroke of pleasure so close yet just out of reach. She catches the slip on her part, her eyes darting away. My remark in the courtroom did more than spark her curiosity; it unnerved her.

She thought about it.

She thought about me.

"I quote a lot of people," I say, my gaze cataloging her every micro-expression. "Once in a while, someone gets it right. Even a cad like Chaucer."

Inhaling a deep breath, her small, shapely breasts rising to attract my notice, Halen relents a degree. She reaches into the satchel she has nestled near her feet and produces a manila folder.

"I was called to a crime scene yesterday afternoon." She opens the folder and angles printed images my way. "I'm exploring an esoteric angle. Possibly a perpetrator with a delusional connection to a philosophy or philosopher." Her eyes catch mine briefly before she returns her gaze to the top image. "Or even a delusional prophetic connection."

Like the Harbinger killer.

But she's trying hard to dance around that angle, though her inability to look me in the eyes gives her away.

"You like that word, delusional." I smirk and lean forward to inspect the images. Her shots are decent, capturing the dark, haunting imagery of the eyes and trees. I fan through them, noting the pictures are more artistic than candid crime-scene shots.

I'm well aware of the scene. I have access to the Internet at Briar, and there's a media buzz surrounding the morbid display of eerie trees with dead eyes. Rumors already circulate around the disappeared people from Hollow's Row, along with whispers of satanic practices.

When fear presents, people can be so boring and predictable. Since the dawn of time, humans have been creating devils to blame for their misfortune. Every generation or so, he's resurrected in a new form and given the power to destroy humanity.

Good and evil do not inherently exist within matter. It's the person, the consciousness, who decides whether or not a deed will serve as either.

"Esotericism is an extremely wide net," I say, disdain evident in my tone. Everything—from ancient Greek philosophy to new age theology—that isn't under the umbrella of the Judeo-Christian religion, scholars have placed within that vague category.

"I know," she says, her agreement surprising me. "It's a catch-all. But it's a starting point, at least."

I use the tips of my fingers to nudge the images back in her direction. "That's one hell of a leap from dissected eyes to Chaucer. But that's your specialty, isn't it? Leaping to a suspect based on no real evidence at all."

"A crime-scene tech made the connection," she says, decidedly ignoring my scathing sarcasm.

"And I came to mind. Should I be flattered, or insulted?" I sit forward, palms braced on the edge of the table. "I'll go with insulted, seeing as the reason you're really here is that you assume I'm somehow involved."

She shrugs, unapologetic. "I didn't discount the notion when it came to me."

I smile wickedly, giving her the full, panty-dropping wattage. "Then maybe I should be flattered you think of me at all. But the last time we spoke, I wound up in a straitjacket. So I'll take a hard pass this time around."

"You approached me, Locke. I didn't force those damning words from your mouth." As I start to rise, she says, "Wait—" She points to a particular section of an image where it appears there was a fire. "I need to know if any of Chaucer's works parallel with the scene."

I smile and push to my feet. "Dr. St. James, you can

google, as you've said. Get the cliff notes." I wave my hand to summon the beefy bouncer of the visitation room.

"Right," she says, slipping the images into the folder. "Chaucer's not the only overly praised drivel in academia."

Despite the obvious dig at my ego, I rise to the challenge. "Chaucer is way off course. You have to go back further than him to find any tenable esoteric correlation."

Her gaze snaps to mine. "How much further?"

"Start with antiquity, and go from there."

She shakes her head. "That's...vast. You're fucking with me."

Her crass words are nails raking my back. Oh, how I can't wait to fuck with her.

I spin my thumb ring as I meet her suspicious gaze. "He who sees with his eyes is blind," I say, the quote slipping coolly off my tongue like water over ice. "Just a guess. It's a starting point, at least." I give her a wink.

I start to turn away, and an ember of panic flares behind her hazel eyes. "What do you want?" she asks.

As the psych tech approaches, I ask for a moment longer, then meet the eyes of the woman who had me committed to an insane asylum. "First, I'd like you to use my first name. Second, I want what anyone in confinement wants. My freedom."

She stands opposite me, her stature that of a sprite, her temperament just as volatile. "No window views or stocked commissary for the great Kallum Locke, I see."

"Naturally."

"What you're asking for is not within my power."

43

I lean across the table, inhaling a punishing lungful of her arousing scent. "You have no idea what's within your power, sweetness."

This time, the pretty pink hue dusting her cheeks isn't a ploy.

A satisfied current of pride ripples beneath my skin as I push away from the table. "Short of my freedom," I say, "I want you to fuck off, Halen. Good luck on your case."

I exit the visitation room with the tech, leaving Halen staring after me for dramatic effect.

Once I return to my room, I close the door and stalk to the wall of art I was given *permission* to hang…with adhesive putty, since there's a fear of using tiny thumbtacks as weapons. I could do more damage with the cheaply printed poster by inflicting paper cuts.

I remove the tacky, mass-produced print of a Nietzsche watercolor portrait and flip it over, retrieving the photo I placed there earlier this morning before Halen's arrival.

Granted, had I known she'd come to me, I wouldn't have wasted one of my favors from a nurse. Trust—or more aptly *faith*—is a process. Once the sigil was charged, I tried to purge all traces of it from my mind—but relinquishing control is an even harder practice.

I touch the image of Halen standing in the killing fields, her intense focus on the crime scene. I had the nurse pay a gross amount of my money to one sleazy reporter to capture the picture.

I mean, I do have a vivid imagination. I could have simply imagined her there, let my mind run wild as I envisioned her gazing at the trees, doing her little deduction dance as she pieced together the clues. Her pain a sonnet to the crime gods.

But there's no comparison to having the feel of something tangible in your hands, to touch it, to know you're so close.

I bring my hand to my nostrils and inhale deeply, breathing in her delectable scent, before I reach down and adjust myself.

Such sweetness, like the tastiest peach—one I can't wait to sink my teeth into and feel the juice dribble down my chin.

My obsession didn't start small. It rushed me like a tsunami. Watching this docile little thing walk the university. Seeing her nibble her lip, tuck the white strand of hair behind her ear every time it fell loose.

A flurry of chaos swirled around her like a vortex, yet her pain was so profound it stilled her amid the storm, a heavy anchor not even a tidal wave could uproot.

I was so fucking awestruck, I gave in to the demanding itch to scratch her surface—to unravel the enthralling spell she bewitched on me.

She was an unhealthy craving I had to have.

I curl my hand into a fist, feeling the echo of her staccato heartbeat against my fingers.

She was like gravity. The moon goddess herself controlling my tide.

Then she became the spider.

And she spun me right into her web of pain.

4

BAG OF TRICKS

HALEN

Y*ou have no idea what's within your power, sweetness.*

Kallum's words taunt me like his woodsy scent of clean sandalwood, like a secret confession, as if he deliberately baited me with a veiled implication of what he knows.

Which, admittedly, could be nothing at all, and he's simply using me and my case to his advantage. Like a true sociopath, he's mastered the art of manipulation.

Realistically, Devyn quoting Chaucer at the scene could be a coincidence. Which would give credence to Aubrey's claim of my obsession with Kallum.

Maybe I've worked in this field too long, have seen too many cryptic things. The rational psychologist within me fights to be heard over the irrational sentiment that nothing is ever coincidence.

Just a guess, he said.

Men like Kallum don't guess.

He saw something in those images. He knows more. I feel it in my bones the way I felt he was connected to the Cambridge murder, and I have to follow my instinct, even if it leads down a path of ruin.

I have to—because while working the Cambridge scene, I wasn't at my best. I wasn't sleeping. I was sidetracked with painful memories, furious that yet another piece of my past was being tainted. I made mistakes…I know I did…otherwise Kallum would be sitting in a prison rather than this cushy hospital.

This is my chance to rectify that.

Just six months ago, I knew of Kallum by reputation only. You don't work in my field without stumbling across the major contributors to the hidden topics of the world. The fact Kallum was a highly regarded philosophy scholar hid him well within academia.

It wasn't until Kallum was taken away to Briar that I really began to dig. I interviewed previous colleagues and contacted ex-romantic partners. One of Kallum's assistant professors stated Kallum's alchemic research bordered on obsessive, as evident in the runes and sigils tattooed on his body. A previous lover witnessed his fixation with the dark arts, his often "unsettling" research reaching as far as their bedroom.

I scoured the web for all mentions of him. I avoided active

cases in pursuit of the truth, which nearly cost me my career, but what I unearthed was a disturbing history of violence and deviant behavior.

As Kallum touts, I may never uncover the physical evidence of the Cambridge murder. I've learned to accept this fact. That case is closed. If not for the personal nature of the murder, Kallum may have never been caught.

Initially, I was of the mindset that the Cambridge murder was a crime of passion that Kallum then attempted to disguise as a Harbinger copycat killing. At the time, the murders were all over the media. It was a sound theory.

However, once Kallum was locked away, a curious thing happened.

The Harbinger killings stopped.

Kallum Locke is far more sinister and unhinged than a one-time crime of passion killer, and I now have the chance to prove it—to comb through the dark chasm of his mind and uncover his connection to the killings.

The devil is in the details, and the details are inside that devil's head.

And I'm about to throw the doors of hell wide open to let him roam free.

The literal door before me opens, and I straighten my shoulders. "Dr. Torres." I address Briar's head psychiatrist as he grants me entry to his office.

"Miss St. James. It's a pleasure to have you. Please, be seated."

The office of the man in charge of a ward for the criminally insane doesn't look how I visualized: with textured gray walls, cherry oak furniture, and framed pictures of Freud. I even presumed there'd be a trace of cigar smoke in the air.

Dr. Torres has published three papers on the treatment and correction of dangerous offenders with mental disorders, he's highly regarded in the medical community for his innovative methods, and his office is a wreck.

Pages are strewn across the desk and falling to the floor. Folders lie open and article clippings pepper every available surface. There's even a half-eaten club sandwich hanging out in a parted Styrofoam container on a bookshelf.

He, himself, is not quite put together, either, with crooked wireframe glasses, a mop of messy, thinning gray hair, and a half untucked Polo button-down.

And the office smells like cheese.

I glance around for a seat, and he waves a hand apologetically before he clears clutter away from one of the leather chairs in front of his basic wood desk.

"Please excuse the mess," he says, offering me a seat again. "I'd like to say this is rare, but I find I'm always occupied with a task and in a state of disarray."

I smile. It really doesn't bother me...for a short period, knowing I'll soon leave. I grew up with an ADHD mother who sprinted from one hobby to the next, like she did with occupations, always leaving a chaotic mess in her wake. But her chaos was often the result of a selfless love, and that was the trade.

The surfacing memory weighs heavily on my chest.

"No worries at all." I set my canvas bag on the only clear

space on the floor. "All genius comes with a dash of madness, so they say."

He chuckles as he seats himself in his desk chair, flipping his askew tie around. "Yes, so they say."

"Hence why you're the leading authority in the treatment of the criminally insane."

He cocks his head, a suspicious gleam in his narrowed, faded-brown eyes. Dr. Torres might appear distracted and dull-witted, but he's earned his reputation for a reason. He's no fool, and apparently, ego-stroking won't win him over.

"You came here to visit my patient, Kallum Locke," he says, diving right in. "I typically require a psychiatric technician to be present when law officials want to conduct an interview with a patient—"

"I'm not a law official," I say, clearing that right up.

"Which is the reason as to why I waved the rule...this time." He makes sure to stress this last part.

My smile falls. "Which I appreciate, but I wasn't conducting an interview."

Dr. Torres regards me closely. "Then what can I help you with, Miss St. James?"

Straight to the point. "I work for a specialized department of investigation, and Kallum may be of use to us on an active case."

My comment seems to amuse him, as he steeples his fingers together and flashes a smile. "Kallum won't be of any use to you."

"Why is that? Because of his mental state?"

"No, because you're the reason he's here, Miss. St.

James." He grabs a pen off his desk and shuffles to locate a leaf of paper. "In my opinion, it would be a stretch to trust Kallum would help anyone in authority, but especially you and your division. He may lead you on some entertaining tangent, but he has no desire to see justice served."

I nod slowly, reevaluating my approach. I actually appreciate his frankness. But I also don't have time to debate the ethics, which is one of the reasons I chose my career path over the medical field.

"I wouldn't think you'd want to impede this investigation, Dr. Torres. Because, despite any vain professional desire to analyze a mind like Kallum's to further your research, I'd assume you'd rather be helpful, and in doing so, get more acclaim." I smile chastely. "Briar's patient, under your direct care and supervision, helps authorities solve a crime."

His features pinch in serious deliberation before he erupts in laughter. He rubs the creases along the corner of his eye. "Oh, I have no desire to impede your investigation, and I also have no desire to be a part of the media show, or the fallout."

Maybe I took my bad-cop persona a bit too far. "Thank you, then?"

He sobers, readjusting his glasses. "As much as I want Kallum removed from my facility, I'm afraid that isn't my call to make."

"I understand," I say. "Kallum should've been locked in a penitentiary and not a hospital." Out of the two-hundred and fifty facilities nationwide, which are all overpopulated and understaffed, Briar is a retreat in comparison to a prison.

"Then you should have done your job better."

Now I'm offended. "If you don't think he belongs in your facility, then why is he still here? If he's not actually mentally ill, that is."

"Oh, he's absolutely fucking insane."

I raise an eyebrow. "Is that your professional opinion?"

He makes a throaty sound of amusement, then jots a note on the page. "Miss St. James, there are many gray areas where the legal system is concerned. I'd dare say that, obtaining a judgement of not guilty by reason of insanity is the most difficult judgment to obtain. But if one is highly intelligent and knows the system, it's also the easiest to manipulate."

My head throbs at my temples, impatience raking my nerves. "Wait, I'm confused. Now you're saying he's not insane? Which one is it, Dr. Torres?"

He holds out the sheet of paper. "The mind is the most powerful force in the known universe," he says. "This, at least, we can all agree on. If the mind believes a thing to be true, then the mind makes it true. And a brilliant mind can be the worst affliction."

I open my mouth, but the words stall on my tongue. Instead, I accept the paper and glance at his scribbled writing.

Get this demon out of my hospital. Call Joseph Wheeler.

A phone number is listed below the name.

My heart rate climbs, reminiscent of the last day in court when I waited—breath bated—for the verdict on Kallum's hearing. The man across from me has the same bated hope welling in his eyes many of the jurors had in that moment.

Honestly, I'm not sure how it happened, or why the judge allowed the verdict to be upheld. When I asked the jury to do their job and put Kallum away, this is not what I intended. The only logical explanation is that, with no physical evidence, the jury knew a guilty verdict could be appealed. By sentencing him to a hospital, he's at least barred from the public, unable to harm anyone else.

Or…maybe not, according to Dr. Torres's note.

"To have a patient transported out on official FBI business," he says, "you would need a court order, of course. Wheeler can make that happen."

I lace my arms over my chest, suddenly more than suspicious. "And I'd assume the patient would need medical supervision, like from their doctor."

We lock gazes, and after a moment of strained silence, Dr. Torres straightens his tie again. Apparently stalling, as he's proven he's not one to be concerned with his unkempt appearance.

"I could refer a psychiatrist to the case," he says, adamant on his position.

I nod, even though I feel there is no one who can control that monster. "I'll try for a court order through my own division first, then we'll see what else can be done."

"Try, Miss St. James, is unacceptable." He grabs his shirt cuff and rolls the sleeve, thrusting the fabric the rest of the way up his forearm.

Second- and third-degree burns pock the skin of his arm in horrific, disfiguring patches. My stomach drops, and I stare, aghast, at the sight.

"How did that happen?" I ask, my voice having lost its edge.

He slides his sleeve down, not bothering to button the cuff. When his gaze settles on me, I see what Dr. Torres was trying to disguise beneath his apparent eccentric nature. The stench of his fear permeates the room.

"I'm a man of science," he says, tactfully avoiding my question. "I'm a man of logic and rational thought. Yet, I'm not too obtuse in my vain, professional pursuits"—he tosses my slight back at me—"to admit when I'm out of my depth with a patient. There is something deeply disturbed in Kallum's psyche, and I am not the doctor to help him."

I feel for his plight, but he still hasn't directly stated what torture Kallum has subjected on him. I have no doubt Kallum is wreaking havoc on this man, and Dr. Torres probably already weighed the ethical dilemma on how to be rid of him —but as a woman of science myself, I need the facts stated loud and clear.

This time, I need the evidence.

"Is there anything I should be aware of in the event Kallum is remanded to a doctor and released from your care?" I ask.

Collecting himself, he considers for a moment, then: "Late onset mental illness isn't developed later in life. Most of the time, as I'm sure you know, the illness has simply gone unchecked until it worsens and becomes evident. Kallum was previously diagnosed with brief psychotic disorder in his youth. A diagnosis revealed during his trial."

Which was curiously suspicious. Was that really a surprise reveal, or did Kallum's lawyer leak the diagnosis in order to sway the jury toward an insanity defense without having to change the plea after my testimony?

Like Dr. Torres stated, Kallum is intelligent enough to work the system, but it just seems too much of a risk, even for him.

Proof of the diagnoses was presented, but the details around the violent moment in history were only provided to the judge and kept from the jury and witnesses. As the file is a juvenile record, it remains sealed and inaccessible. Even to me.

"As I'm sure you also know," he continues, "recurring bouts of violent psychotic episodes tend to be triggered by obsessive thoughts. I have noted a high level of obsessive behavior with Kallum. I would be cautious, Miss St. James, seeing as you're a likely focal point for his obsession."

My gaze drops to his covered arm before I meet his eyes directly. "I appreciate your concern." He nods solemnly in reply. "Do you actually agree with the diagnosis?"

His smile is forced. "You may have to decide this for yourself, *Dr.* St. James. You have the credentials, after all. I would even go as far as to suggest you as the doctor to oversee Kallum in the field."

"Absolutely not," I say, my walls erecting. "I appreciate your endorsement, but I don't want that responsibility."

"Yet, you're willing to risk others in order to have his expertise on your case."

"We should all be willing to risk something for the greater good," I say as I stand, hoping Dr. Torres appreciates his own sacrifice in keeping Kallum away from the public.

"One last thing," he says, halting me. "If you do happen to use Wheeler, all I ask in return is there be a stipulation placed that Kallum is remanded to a *nicer* facility upon his discharge from the case."

I hold his gaze, understanding passing between us. "Of course," I say.

"I hope you find what you're searching for, Dr. St. James."

"Thank you for your time." I turn to see myself out.

His parting statement feels oddly phrased, and it festers in the back of my mind as I exit the institution. The only thing I'm searching for are answers.

The greater good requires sacrifice, and I'm willing to risk making the biggest mistake of my career to get those answers.

The designated hotel for visitors sits adjacent from Briar. I stand at the window of my hotel room, watching the grounds as the sky darkens and the lights of the facility blink on to cast distorted shadows along the grass.

Earlier, I placed a call to the Hollow's Row Police Department and was put through to Devyn. She promised to keep the scene intact until this evening, and I had to make her aware I wouldn't be returning in time.

"Thanks for trying to wait for me," I said to her, "but I won't be back today. Maybe tomorrow, and possibly, I'll be bringing help along."

"Another fed?" she asked. "Because, the suits descended today. I don't see how this town can hold any more."

"No. Not a fed," I assured her. "A psychotic philosophy professor."

She laughed, but when I didn't join in, the line went silent.

"Oh, you're serious," she said. "Halen, are you helping, or are you bringing something worse to my town?"

I try not to lie to those I respect. "Honestly, I don't know."

After I ended the call, I contacted Special Agent Wren Alister, who's been appointed lead on the Hollow's Row task force. He's the one I need to gain approval from in order to bring in an expert consultant on the case.

My division has a lot of sway, but I can't push Kallum through as a consultant with my director. Aubrey made that clear when he reprimanded me about this trip.

I check my email on my phone. Still no confirmation from Agent Alister. I've already completed the pile of required paperwork. I've put everything in place. And I'm still not certain this is the right course of action.

Anxiety tightens my chest, and I glance at the slip of paper Dr. Torres handed me.

Peering out the window, I touch the pendant at my neck, seeking some semblance of comfort and maybe even guidance.

"I'm making a very bad mistake," I whisper.

Dr. Torres's words haunt me, and I'm not entirely sure of my purpose, or intent.

I accused him of using Kallum to further his career—but

am I just as vain in my endeavor to prove Kallum is the Harbinger killer?

Who am I risking if this goes horribly wrong?

Then I picture the gruesome crime scene, the eyes staring vacantly, the tortured bodies of the victims still lost.

Bodies that may still be, in fact, alive.

It's the one thing no one said at the crime scene, but it's what the silence screamed.

It's why the FBI has been called to Hollow's Row.

If there's a chance these victims can be found alive, and that chance rests in the ruthless inked hands of a killer...

I grab my phone and open the web browser. I type in *he who sees with his eyes is blind* and hit Search.

The quote pulls up right away, citing Socrates in Plato's *Allegory of the Cave*. I click the link and dive in, immersing myself in the reading. My basic understanding of the interpretation is it's a metaphorical play about the theoretical difference between intelligence and ignorance.

I rub my forehead, trying to stave off the forming headache. Philosophy—especially ancient Greek—was not my strength in college. I'm too rational, too grounded in practicality to ponder the meaning of the universe.

The further I delve into my research, the more I gather a dominant theme. For the most part, the dialogues allude to most people being happy without a muse, living without divine inspiration, as they have no access to higher perceptions of reality.

In simplified, cliché terms: Ignorance is bliss.

After clicking through links and reading definitions and

interpretations of epistemology, I find myself on the back end of the Internet on some philosophy forum, where I've lost all track of time and reason, and I can't even recall what I was originally searching for.

"Shit." I blow out a frustrated breath.

I glance at the window, as if I can feel Kallum's derision, his mockery of my attempt to piece together this lead. A lead or a tangent, like Dr. Torres warned? Either way, this is exactly what he wanted.

I'm questioning everything.

Risk, like philosophy, presents a danger outside of ourselves. The only way to mitigate the danger in risk is to have control over the variables.

Rationally speaking, I need to gain control over Kallum Locke.

I've put myself in the mind of many sociopaths and killers over the years. I know how they think, how they behave, respond to stimuli—and how they need to be the smartest, most powerful force in the room.

If a wilting rose is what Kallum desires, then I will show him my withered petals.

I click out of the sites and grab a bottled water from the mini-fridge. Then I make the call to Joseph Wheeler, the agency lawyer Dr. Torres referred, to make the deal.

5

DEAL WITH THE DEVIL

KALLUM

"Two visits in as many days. I'm honored, Dr. St. James."

Halen sits in the same seat she sat in yesterday at the visitation table. Only today, she seems a little less on edge. Her hair is down. The rich layers drape her shoulders and stop right below her natural, pear-shaped breasts.

I have the sudden, destructive urge to sweep the white strand behind her ear, or wrap it around my fist. I curl my fingers toward my palm on the table to curb the impulse.

She's freshly showered, and I inhale the scent of generic shampoo and soap. She packed in a rush to get here; she didn't bring along her own brand of cleansers and fragrance.

Without a retort, she removes documents from her satchel

and lines the forms in a row on the tabletop between us. She's all serious business.

"This is the offer, Kallum," she states. "You can't barter or hold out for a better deal. This is time sensitive. This, or nothing at all."

I don't look at the documents. I hold her silvery gaze. The overcast sky threatens bad weather, and her irises reflect the stormy atmosphere outside the windows, making her look more like an ethereal fairy creature.

"Before you give me your pitch, I have a request."

She braces herself with a fortifying intake of air. "Go ahead."

"The white forelock…?" I use my finger to motion around the side of my face in mirror of hers.

"Poliosis," she answers straightforward. "The harmless, genetic kind. My mother also had it." Her rough edges sharpen around the mention of her mother, and her defensive walls erect higher as she avoids my eyes.

"Seems we have a commonality," I say. "My heterochromia is also a rare pigment condition passed through the genes." I blink and flash her a smile with my eyes.

"No underlying conditions?" she probes.

She's fishing for more than the reason behind my striking eyes in my gene pool. "Not unless you count smoldering genius….no."

With a hard nod, she glances down at the documents. "For the record, we're nothing alike, Kallum. Now, let's go over the specifics—"

"Just tell me the offer." She's using my first name, one of my terms. From the tightness rimming her pouty lips, she's not thrilled with the concession.

But she is desperate.

"There is no judge in the state of Boston who is going to grant you a full release," she says. Her features soften as she delivers the practiced half of her speech. "But, you will have a measure of freedom while you're participating on the case. You'll be required to wear an ankle monitor, and assigned a psychiatrist to supervise you. Then, when the case is closed, provided your help is deemed valuable, you'll be relocated out of Briar to a less restrictive facility."

I link my hands together on the table, interlacing my fingers. I hold her unwavering stare for a beat, then glance down at the scripted ink on my forearm. One line in particular, a quote from Plato: *There will be no end to the troubles of state, or of humanity itself, till philosophers become kings.*

"And what do I get from you out of the deal?"

Her dark eyebrows draw together. Her emotions are so transparent, it fills my head with a buzz, like I'm drugged. "I don't understand," she says.

"What are you offering me? Not the state, the judge, or the FBI. *You.*"

She doesn't respond immediately. The sounds of the visitation room become louder. The scrape of chairs against the tile floor and conversations press in around us. As she considers her answer, I see the same obstinate certainty she wore in the courtroom drape her like a cloak.

"I know what you've done to Dr. Torres," she says.

I crane an eyebrow. "Is that so. And what, little Halen, have I done?"

"I saw the burns," she says, dropping her voice low. "You tortured him."

Elbow braced on the table, I cover my mouth with my hand. "That is quite the absurd theory coming from you."

She pushes in closer, all pretense lost from her features. "Are you saying you aren't the cause of those burns? That you didn't torture Dr. Torres?"

"He tortured himself," I say with conviction. "And stop trying to psychoanalyze me. I can't be the scapegoat for everyone. At some point, Halen, the niggling itches become an inferno that must be snuffed out."

She shakes her head, her eyes searing where her gaze touches. "You once asked me if I was scared of you."

My breath stalls, the sinew in my body corded tight. I'm way too anxious to hear where she's taking this.

"I am frightened of you, Kallum," she admits, her voice a sensual, breathy cadence that slinks beneath my skin. "If that's what you're capable of doing to someone you find a mere irritation…" She trails off, her teeth catch the corner of her lip. "Well, I already know what you do to someone you feel deserves revenge."

My whole body is fire. If she's not careful, I might drag her into the blaze. Her confession is a wicked tease, daring me to show her real fear, to make her scream. If little Halen glimpsed the images filling my head right now, she'd shred that paperwork and flee this building.

But for her—to get what I need—I have to behave like a good dog. No biting. No scratching. No humping. And definitely no marking my territory.

I expel a breath, releasing the wound tension from my muscles. "Why are you saying this to me?"

The vulnerability in her features is raw and aching, and if we were alone, I'd lap it up while making her mascara streak her pretty cheeks.

"Because," she says, voice hitching. "I'm the focal point of your obsession."

A chuckle escapes. "You have quite the obsession brewing yourself." I lick my lips, tasting her fear, the most fragrant and intoxicating flower. "Don't worry. I don't hold a grudge against you. You're safe from me."

She doesn't believe me. Her eyes shimmer with her cresting trepidation, and the tremble of her lips damn near makes me come undone...before she finally reins in her emotions. I'm becoming exhausted from holding myself back, my knuckles white as I grip the table.

"What is it that you want from me?" she asks. "What do I have to give you to make you accept this deal, Kallum?"

Her question flays the last layer of my restraint. I drive my hand through my hair, turning away from the table. *Just give me a goddamn pen.*

A heavy beat of silence stretches, then she says, "If it means some good comes out of this deal, then...within reason, I'll give you whatever you want."

A vicious spark ignites my blood. The current races to my heart, and anticipation licks my spine with a forked tongue. I lower my hand to the table. The craving to feel her heartbeat thrums against my veins.

I don't suppress my crooked smile, and I like the way that makes her shift in her seat. "What would your good do if evil didn't exist?" I say to her. Bulgakov's words are so aptly appropriate for this moment, I could've written them myself.

She touches her forearm with purpose, and I'm curious to scratch away all those layers to find out what lies beneath.

"No games, Kallum," she says. "I will comply within reason, but that means your help must be deemed *valuable*."

"And what would be within reason? A hamburger? A phone call to a friend? A midnight walk on the beach?" I shrug playfully, rather enjoying *all* of our games. "Maybe all I want is you worrying about what I have in mind so I can watch you squirm."

"You're sick," she says, letting her guard slip.

"Perhaps, but you're the one who needs my sickness, sweetness."

She reaches into her bag and produces a pen, but holds it just out of reach. "We have a *contingent* deal, then?"

I nod once.

She offers me the pen. "Sign your name."

As I accept the pen, I rest my index finger alongside hers. A charged current arcs between us before she pulls away. The slightest touch stirs a primal yearning within me to snatch her hair and shove her down against the table.

Jaw clenched, I grip the pen, damn near cracking the plastic. I have to work on keeping these urges in check.

Patience has never been a virtue I deem valuable. I'm

something of a hedonist, I admit. And the dark energy pulsing between Halen and I wants to drive me mad, wants to make me tangle her up in my web and bleed her until I'm gorged.

Pen poised over the page, I glance up at her. "I wonder which one of us is the devil, and which one is selling our soul?"

She shakes the loose waves of hair from her face. "You first have to have a soul to sell."

Before this is over, my little Halen will look into the eyes of her devil and know fear.

With a satisfied smile, I sign my name to the forms. As I set the pen in front of her, I say, "When I solve the case, I expect the terms to be renegotiated."

She releases an amused breath. "And why in the hell that spawned you do you think that would ever happen?"

I cock my head, letting my gaze lower to the diamond sitting in the hollow of her throat, before I find the alluring silver of her eyes once again. "Because this matter is far too urgent for simply locating bodies and naming a suspect. I'll be the savior of thirty-three lives, Halen. I'll be a hero. And a hero can ask for any-fucking-thing he wants."

She doesn't need to say a word. Her sobered features confirm the veracity of my statement.

Instead, she makes a production of packing away the forms before she stands over me, satchel in hand. "Pack lightly, Kallum. Your ego will need the room."

My gaze admiringly lingers on her backside as she leaves the visitation room.

My muse confessed her fear, opened herself wide and

allowed me to wade around in her depths.

Now the yearning to delve deeper is hungrier than ever.

6

THE INSANE ROOT –
SHAKESPEARE

KALLUM

Dr. Stoll Verlice is a lanky, middle-aged man with ultra-white hair who looks more like a politician than a psychiatrist. One well-timed *boo* will have him quaking in his cheap loafers and scare him off the case.

From the way Halen is apprising him with guarded glances, she also considers him a poor choice to be assigned as my field psychiatrist.

But here we are, in the heart of Hollow's Row, all three of us ready to make history. If only I could intone sarcasm in my thoughts.

Halen hands me a room key, careful to keep our fingers from touching. I turn the key over; it's an actual key. Not a plastic card. The bronze is dulled and worn, much like this gothic hotel and town. Although there is a certain macabre charm, like the deathly murmur that creeks in your bones and whistles threats through ancient trees, it's mostly a dilapidated pile of ruins.

Regardless of my appreciation for all things ancient and mysterious, I still prefer new, clean, and contemporary when it comes to where I lie my head.

"Be content it's not Briar," Halen says, reading my aversion. "Your room is connected to Dr. Verlice's, and the conjoining door is to remain open and unlocked. Put your stuff away. We're meeting up with the feds to head to the scene."

"I all but inked my name in blood," I say. "I'm yours to command."

Dr. Verlice doesn't take offense to this statement the way Halen does, but he ushers me toward the stairwell, making sure I know who's in charge.

Once Halen confessed to the urgency of the case, admitting the potential was high the victims may still be recovered alive, events moved swiftly. My meager personal items were approved, packed, and taken to an airport, where an agent cuffed my ankle with a monitor.

I'm able to roam within the approved areas of the town, such as the crime scene, hotel, and main street vicinity, but one step past the figurative town limits, and I'll be hunted like the FBI's most wanted.

The rundown of the rules have one major overlap: if I fuck up, I'm sent back to Briar.

"Your actions will be on me," Halen said on the flight. "I won't let you fuck up."

I got a deviant thrill out of her vow.

By the time the major players of the unit are assembled in a caravan of giant, gas-guzzling SUVs, I've gotten a feel for the dynamic of the town. Admittedly, I'd already done my homework years ago when news of the disappearances first went viral.

Hollow's Row has a reputation for bad things.

Our vehicle lurches forward with Halen seated in the passenger seat, Special Agent Wren Alister behind the wheel, and me and my watch dog psychiatrist taking up the two backseats. Agent Alister has one hand on the wheel, the other tapping the keyboard of his console computer. Halen and Dr. Verlice both stare at their phones.

I'm the only one without a device to distract me from the scenic view as we cruise through the narrow, timeworn streets. It's like a shadow has been cast over small-town USA, as if a dark shroud has fallen over the once-white picket fences and smiling faces.

The gothic revival homes are ancient themselves, some dating back two-hundred years. They appear to have been restored at one point, but where time couldn't break the structures, loss and pain have chipped away at the classic veneer.

People drift like ghosts on the sidewalks. They are extensions of the dead houses, bound to the skeletons by memories, unable to depart their haunts.

My expertise is not in the social sciences, but even I can appreciate what hardship the disappearance of so many people from a tight-knit community can cause. Many family units lost at least one loved one. Thirty-three members of a family-focused society vanished from existence.

And now, as news of the discovered remains airs through the town's corpses, these people lurk like animated zombies, their bated breath a death rattle waiting to exhale, to hear the names of those loved ones announced.

They wait for closure.

As our SUV coasts close to a freshly worn trail in the marsh, I look at Halen. "When are the DNA reports being made available?"

She turns my way, a curious furrow notched between her brows. She glances at Agent Alister, and I dislike that she feels she needs his permission. At his affirmative nod, she says, "The DNA of five remains were confirmed to be town locals."

"That sets a very dark but redundant tone," I say, and Halen frowns disapprovingly.

Five positive IDs should be all that's needed to draw a likely conclusion to the rest of the eyes belonging to the missing. Let's just refer to them as that from now on, for simplicity's sake.

"I think referring to them as victims is preferable," Halen remarks, and I realize I must have spoken my thoughts aloud.

I have to be more mindful of that. Spending six months isolated in my head, flushing antipsychotics down a toilet, has the ability to wreak havoc on one's mental state.

Before I exit the vehicle, I reach down and rub at the irritating itch caused by the ankle bracelet. Agent Alister opens my door, and the pungent marsh scent smacks my face.

As I allow my senses to acclimate, I notice another faint odor wafting through the tall reeds.

Death.

The townies call this area the killing fields because hunters discard their kills here.

But the town didn't get its reputation because of the great hunting. After the mass disappearance, the past few years have been comparatively quiet. Before, however, Hollow's Row earned the very clever nickname *Hollow's Death Row* from neighboring cities due to the high fatality rate.

But that's another story.

I trail behind Alister as he walks the well-worn path. Dr. Verlice stays behind with the SUV, catching up on "patient work", but I suspect he doesn't have the stomach for this part of the deal.

Halen stalks a short distance behind me, as if she's fearful I'll pull a Houdini and vanish right here in the killing fields.

"When I give my word, I honor it, Halen," I say, stepping around the bleached bones of a stag carcass. "I'm not sprinting off into the forest to live off of berries and brambles. Don't let my presence preoccupy your mind and deter your focus."

"I'm capable of multitasking," she says. "You just focus on the scene, Kallum. What you're here to do."

And as we come up on said scene, I remove my hands from my jacket pockets, letting them hang loosely at my sides. Caution tape wraps the trunks of several spindly trees, designating the crime scene within. Or what's left of it.

"Would have been better if I could've viewed the scene

before the uniforms and techs disassembled it." I flex my fingers, picking up on the lingering energy of the site.

Halen moves to stand beside me. The hum of her nearness vibrates in my bones, distracting me, overpowering me. "Had you not been such a primadonna, you would have," she says. "Yesterday."

"Everything has a price, sweetness." I give her my devilish smile before I duck under a tattered section of tape. "Especially brilliance."

Her strained exhale reaches my ears as I move closer to the crop of dead-looking trees. A few straggler techs and officers are conducting useless tests on the trees and grass, but I push them out of my mind, trying to see only what was here before.

I locate the burnt reeds—the area of Halen's interest—and stalk to that spot. As I crouch down to get a better look, Halen removes a tablet from her satchel.

"Analysis from the lab workup logged a substance on the reeds containing calcium carbonate, potassium sorbate, sulfur dioxide, glucose—"

"Sugar," I say, touching one of the sooty reeds. I draw my fingers up the blade, and a smudge of sticky residue adheres to my fingertips. "Wine."

"That's what the lab concluded." She scrolls the report. "A tawny mixture, most likely homemade. The analysis states—"

"Halen." Her name is a guttural command that gains her full attention. "I'm not law enforcement or a lab geek. And neither are you."

After a heated second where our gazes stay locked, she

lowers the tablet. Understanding lights her hazel eyes, and she pushes the escaping white streak of hair behind her ear to break the intensity of the connection before she directs her focus on the fire pit.

"Just talk to me," I say, my tone yielding. "Why did you first leap to an esoteric connection?" I wipe my fingers off on my black jeans, spreading the residue thin in search of any defining substances, such as blood.

Blood is to rites and ritual as lead is to alchemy. One claims to produce gold, the other to strengthen life force. But when both are present, it's typically to provoke something very dark.

"The intricate yarn work," Halen says, interrupting my thoughts and surprising me. "The craftsmanship feels ritualistic in nature. Why that particular thread? Why not rope? Or some other simpler, logical means of adhering the oculus? It's almost ceremonial, ornate, like the act itself is sacred, and the exhibit is an offering or…"

"A sacrifice," I say.

She pulls her bottom lip between her teeth briefly. "He took a lot of care with staging the eyes. He spent time here. Around a fire. Pouring wine. Weaving thread."

Becoming docile, contemplative, she disappears somewhere inside herself. I'm again tempted with a famished hunger to explore that inside chasm, that part of her psyche she keeps hidden.

I want its secrets.

Inhaling a lungful of swampy marsh, I rise to my feet and

shift my focus to the trees. "The alchemy of the soul is transforming pain into creative genius."

I'm not aware I've said this aloud until I catch Halen's tapered gaze directed on me. Her guard lowers a fraction, allowing a suspended heartbeat where her ache becomes mine, before she reins in her unruly emotions.

"And which one of your philosophers said that?" she asks, voice clipped.

Me.

"Some writer. I don't recall," I say. "But along with the intricate thread work, your suspect makes his own wine. There's a certain alchemy to the vinification process, going as far back as Hermetic Egypt. His method or signature"—I use her terminology—"could be as simple as that. His signature."

"None of this feels simple." Tension layers her voice. "You're going to have to narrow the scope."

I rub the back of my neck. "Where are the images of the eyes?"

A printed image is slipped into my hand, and I look down. "These are the crime-scene photos taken by first responders," she says.

I hold one of the photos up against the overcast sky, and just as I felt the day before, it's useless. I lower the image. "I need close-ups. Pictures of the eyes, the thread."

Halen briefly touches the diamond at her neck, a subconscious habit, before she drops her canvas satchel to the ground and digs out a digital camera. She hands it up to me.

"I didn't have time to print off all the images," she says.

"But I wanted closer shots. To see if the perpetrator had doctored the eyes at all."

A knowing smile curls my lips. Figures my little unseen seer would be the one to look beyond the obvious.

Flipping through the digital photos on-screen, I stop on one pair of eyes and use my fingers to zoom in on the glazed-over iris.

"I looked for any puncture marks," she says, crossing her arms. "There are none as far as the images allow us to see."

A frantic bat wings to life in my chest at her inclusive *us*. I glance over to catch her turn her head away, seemingly aware of her slip. But I don't mind. As far as I'm concerned, we are the only two here in this field of death and decay.

I pan over a few sets of eyes on the camera screen, focusing on the pupils. "If he did, he'd likely go through the pupil, making it more difficult to determine. Maybe your lab geeks can get you a report. But he wanted the pupils in a particular way." I point to three sets that appear to all align.

A *caw* sounds from above, and I momentarily glance up at a row of crows perched on a thin branch.

"The perpetrator used an animal to deter the birds from the crime scene."

"He hunted it himself?"

She nods in confirmation. "Possibly. I assumed as much."

Interesting. "Likely because he didn't want the scavengers picking at his exhibit." They would ruin his work, steal the sacrifice. But where is the blood? He's either the least practiced...or the tidiest little OCD freak.

"I know where you're going with the pupils," she says,

77

bracing her hands on her hips. "The unis already combed the marsh looking for the bodies. The eyes weren't staring at anything, Kallum. There are no bodies in the fields."

A light breeze tosses her lock of white across one eye, and a violent need to sweep it aside, to let my fingers taste her skin, stirs heated embers in my veins.

I swipe my tongue across my bottom lip, watching as she gracefully tucks the hair behind her ear.

Scratch. Scratch. Scratch.

I unclench my hand from around the camera and return her device. "Law officials are limited in their thinking." I turn to stare out over the gray-washed marshland. The reeds gently sway in the slight breeze, carrying the scent of death.

"That may be, but it's their case to solve." Anxiety leaks into her voice. "I need you to look for any philosophical correlations, that's all."

I could tell her what she needs, but she's not yet ready to hear. Instead, I start off in the direction just left of the beaten path.

Little Halen follows, leaving Agent Alister behind, and that brings a smug smile to my mouth. She's not one of them.

"You haven't said anything about the scene itself other than a wine recipe and signature." She sidles up beside me, her mud-covered rain boots requiring two quick steps for my every one to keep up. "I need more to go on, Kallum."

"Your suspect chose three trees on purpose for his exhibit."

"Because…the philosophy of trees states three is the magical number?"

I chuckle, nearly alarming myself and her. "Something like that."

I can sense her wariness drifting, becoming less intense. Which opens a portal to a glimpse of Halen before her grief. She was witty, and charming, and made people laugh. Those who knew her then must miss her, and it's probably why she lurks in the shadows now, trying to be unseen.

I'm not interested in restoring her.

"The site is very well organized," I say, my pace slowing as we head deeper into the soggy earth. "It's clean, practiced. Which makes you wonder if it's his first one, doesn't it?"

She's silent as we wade through the marsh reeds, careful our steps don't land on a reptile. But I can hear her thoughts shouting above the caws and insects.

Then, she finally says, "Five years is a long time to practice. If he's been torturing these people for all this time..." She trails off. "There could be many more crime scenes buried in these fields."

"What kind of space would a suspect like this need?" I ask, prompting her.

"Somewhere assessable to him, but a place he feels safely hidden." She marches alongside me now, her curiosity superseding any hesitancy or trepidation.

I carefully swat at the reeds the deeper I verge into the wetland. Mud forms a suction to the soles of my boots. If the canine squad was utilized to comb the area, the dogs didn't direct them on this course. The water could've hindered their smell or, more likely, the noticeable scent of citrus I catch a whiff of every time I fan the reeds.

"What's that smell?" Halen asks.

"Lemon."

She doesn't respond right away. I imagine she's processing the fact there are no lemon trees out here.

Ground water seeps up over the toes of my shoes, and when I see the starburst blooms, I halt and hold my arm out, preventing Halen from walking any farther. My arm grazes her chest, and her breath hitches before she pushes away on reflex.

"I don't need your protection, Kallum."

I look over, my eyebrow craned. The irony is amusing. The woman who set out to destroy me—my life, freedom, reputation, career—believes I have concern for her safety.

I take a step closer. My towering height casts a shadow over her slight figure.

And then we're both instantly aware of the silence, of the very aloneness of our state.

Her snap of anger is a poor concealment tactic for the fear I see banked behind her large hazel eyes. She doesn't want to be afraid of me, but she can't contain her strongest emotions. She's afraid of so much she doesn't understand, and I reflect that fear back at her. I sense little Halen hasn't been in control of her world for some time.

I wonder how often she gives in to the pain, lets herself spiral out of control.

"I'm not really the protecting type," I say, "but you definitely need something from me." I step toward her and close the distance between us.

She doesn't retreat. She raises her face toward mine, her

chest rising and falling with controlled breaths. I reach out, and she starts to lean away…

"Don't move—"

She freezes.

Shock is an electric jolt to my adrenals as her gaze locks with mine. She doesn't move, doesn't breathe, as my command hovers between us. I could wrap my hand around her throat and choke the life from her tiny body before she eased out a squeak.

I force a swallow at the thought. A fiery ache claws its talons down my throat as I use the cuff of my jacket to detangle a stem from her ponytail. She angles her head slightly to peek at the sprout of white flowers held aloft by my covered hand.

"Hemlock," I say.

She exhales. My stomach tightens at the tantalizing caress of her breath along my neck. She's so close, I can taste her dread. It leaves an aftertaste of her sweet lily of the valley.

"Water hemlock," I clarify. "The kind that grows in marshes and wetlands. Although—" I glance around "—it's not really native to this part of the country."

"Someone planted it here." Her voice is breathy, stirring a visceral reaction that ignites my chest.

The closer I am to her, the more her pain is sweet agony, a torment so fucking raw I have to grit my teeth.

I take a purposeful step backward. "I'd say that's an intelligent assumption, considering this person also planted the ears."

A confused expression draws her features together until

she turns to see the shriveled human ears strung to the stems of the hemlock shrubs.

"You can hear no evil...if you have no ears."

Her little sprite features seethe, indignant. Admittedly, that wasn't my best pun.

She immediately drops her bag and digs out her camera to start taking pictures and cataloging the crime scene. "How did you know this was here?" She turns incensed eyes on me. "You better start explaining what the hell is going on, Kallum."

The accusatory tone of her voice crawls under my barely restrained composure. "Or what?" I ask, my voice dropping to a lethal decibel. "Most field agents carry some form of weapon. You have no gun, no Taser, no baton. Not even handcuffs, which is just a shame."

The rapid shutter click of her camera halts. Her body stills as the sounds of the secluded grove encapsulate us.

"I'm not sure if it's arrogance or stupidity," I continue, situating my jacket cuff to occupy my hands, "why you choose to walk around unprotected."

"I've never had use for a weapon."

And then I catch what she realizes instantly.

Until me.

I lick my lips and smile. "You've never had use for a weapon...until me." I gauge her body language, the defensive draw of her shoulders. "If that's what you're thinking, I'd say it's a little late." *Far too late.*

"There are agents and officers out here," she says, trying to rationalize with me. "Would harming me...physically harming me, be worth risking any chance you may have at freedom? Would that satisfy your compulsive need?"

Not even fucking close.

She rises to her feet slowly. Camera in hand, she faces me like she's not aware she's half my size. "I understand what you're feeling."

This intrigues me—everything about her is intriguing. "You understand?"

She nods. "I am a psychologist. You can talk to me, Kallum. Whatever is torturing your mind, I promise, I'll understand. I can maybe even help you."

How tempting to split my mind open right here and let her take a tour. How would little Halen react to the visual of her pressed up against a tree, her wrists bound to the rough bark. Blood coating soft skin in the most enticing dark-red.

The image has my teeth sinking into my lip until the metallic trace of blood hits my tongue.

She chances a step closer, as if I'm a wild animal she fears startling. "If there's something you want to talk about… anything from your past that you've done. Anything I can do or offer—"

"Stop." The sharp edge in my tone halts her.

With contempt, I wrangle the frenzied thoughts into a dark corner of my mind and lock my hands together before me, proving I have no intention of harming her. "You should be careful how you word things, Halen." Keeping my hands bound, I lean in closer, just to absorb the fragrant scent of her terror. "You do happen to have some powerful weapons at your disposal." My gaze tracks over her agonizingly slow, making my point.

Her scent, those intense liquid eyes. That pouty mouth and dangerous body. All lethal when she wields those assets with grave intent.

Her mouth parts, the intensity of her eyes damn near flaying me as she senses my waning restraint.

"But you should also carry a weapon," I say. "Just in case."

With a sideways step, she removes herself from my proximity and pulls out her phone. "Agent Alister, we found something."

Then, before there can be anymore revelations between us, she departs the scene, leaving me and the shriveled ears to listen to the hollow sounds of the marsh.

7

INTO THE ABYSS

HALEN

Dusk settles over Hollow's Row like a widow's veil. The texture is silky and fine to the touch, a fragile darkness you can just see past, but shields you from the bright world of gawkers.

The young waitress sets a cup of warm chamomile tea on the unsteady table in front of me. I thank her as I submerge the tea bag with a dull spoon.

I imagine the local diner is normally busier at this time of day. Early bird special-seekers mingling with high-school kids just letting out of class. But today, as news circulates of the second crime scene discovered in the killing fields within seventy-two hours, there are far more open bench seats than patrons.

The morose atmosphere thickens with wary glances and whispers our way. The town is curious about us. More so about the two strangers than the two obvious FBI agents seated three tables behind.

"I'll have the ribeye. Extra-rare. And baked potato with all the dressings."

I look up from dunking my tea bag to witness Kallum ordering from the waitress. I must wear a puzzled expression, because his mouth quirks into that heart-stopping grin of his.

"Might as well enjoy the local specialties," he says as the waitress silently ambles off. "I haven't had much say in what I've eaten for the past six months, and my appetite is...particular."

Ignoring the baiting comment, I refrain from mentioning that this luxury may soon be taken away again. With what transpired at the second scene, I'm questioning whether Kallum can be contained on this case.

Either way, my attempt to comb through his mind was obvious and sloppy. If I had any sense at all, I'd glean what I can from him about this case and then send him away. *Far away.*

"Don't you eat?"

His question interrupts my thoughts, and I remove the tea bag and set it on the napkin. "I don't eat with colleagues." *Or unhinged serial killers.* "This isn't a—"

"Date?" he supplies, his smirk slanting mischievously. "I have no delusions of that fact, little Halen." He winks.

A tendril of alarm wraps me at the action, inducing a foggy sensation of being outside myself. A sliver of panic coasts through me before I'm able to brush the eerie feeling away.

"What's wrong?" he asks.

I sip my tea faster than I intend, and my eyes water as I choke back a cough. "Fine."

Ignoring Kallum's smug expression, I send a reply text to Aubrey, resuming normal behavior. Kallum will only feed off my unease. He said he wanted to watch me squirm. I'm giving him exactly what he wants.

I have to curb my responses to him. I'm a wilting flower, yes—but how much of it is an act on my part? He makes me feel unstable.

Another text from Aubrey pops up, and I reply, explaining why I'm sitting in a diner as part of my investigation notes. Company phones and GPS aside, I do value my job. Maybe value is the wrong word—*need* feels more appropriate. What I *don't* need is the stress of having to explain my methods— sometimes unorthodox—when I want to explore a lead.

I admit, I stepped way out of bounds when I circumvented CrimeTech and presented Kallum as an expert consultant to assist the FBI. I needed their authority to expedite the process, and I did so in spite of any potential consequences.

Which is unlike me.

I don't exactly play by the rules, but I also don't all-out break them.

I used to care more about what Aubrey and my supervisors thought, whether or not I was surpassing expectations, following procedures to keep from disturbing the balance.

I know the exact date those cares faded, and I know everyone in my life is waiting for me to "get better," "snap out of it," "be the old Halen"—but I also know that's more for their comfort level than mine.

Pain makes people uncomfortable.

Strangely, today, that burden didn't feel as heavy. Even with my guard erected, I found myself falling into an ease with Kallum at the scene I don't experience with others. I don't have to force a smile. Place technical labels on my thoughts. Censor my humanity for his comfort...because he has no humanity to comfort.

It's easy to forget, while staring into his divine beauty, the brutality and sadistic manner in which he kills. Charismatic smiles and quipping dark humor with the face of an angel— yet a devil lurks beneath, his depths a purgatory stained in red.

This is what I must remind myself when I feel his draw reeling me in. I'm feeling at ease with a sociopath who is adept in manipulation, whose very nature is to set mine at ease before he breaks my face with a tire iron and severs my head.

Perspective.

I sip my tea slowly.

"Where were you just now?" Kallum questions.

Setting the cup down, I link my fingers around the warm porcelain. "I was contemplating how to work with you and keep my distance at the same time," I answer honestly.

He pushes back in the seat and tilts his head, assessing me seriously. "That's going to be difficult for you. Is there anything I can do to make it easier?"

"Yes," I say, locking gazes with him. "Stop calling me things like *little Halen* and *sweetness*. Stop undressing me with your smoldering eyes. Stop the flirty banter. For one, it's disturbing. Two, I know you're doing it to unnerve me. But we're not colleagues. We're not even rivals. We have a deal. One that will be honored on my end if you honor yours. That's all."

His mouth tips into the faintest, knowing smile. "You think my eyes are smoldering?"

"You know they are," I say. "You're very aware of your attractiveness, and you use it to disarm people. Your ego is bigger than this entire town."

A text from Aubrey flashes on my phone screen and I turn the device over.

"Need to check in with the parents?" he asks, his tone baiting. "That must suck to have a curfew."

His callous remark punches past my defenses, and I look away to drag in a fortifying breath before I can reply. "Kallum, I need to hear you say that you understand me."

Gaze probing, he says, "I'll try my best. But you don't make it easy, either. With your pouty sprite mouth and infuriatingly intoxicating scent. You're fucking mayhem on the senses."

The way his gaze darkens, the defiant spark of hunger igniting within the flinty shadows, makes me question how much of it is an act on his part, also.

"Please stop," I demand, tamping down the reactive flame curling in my belly.

"So you're the only one allowed to be brutally honest, then."

I glance away. "You're right. Your thoughts are valid. I'll…try to smell less appealing."

He chuckles unexpectedly, and the deep sound hits my chest, unfurling a light, fluttering sensation.

This is why I don't have a partner. Human nature distracts from the work, the purpose. And Kallum Locke is a huge distraction. Besides my body being highly responsive to his, the Harbinger case keeps resurfacing to taint the current case, and it's increasingly maddening to separate the two when Kallum is purposely trying to put me on defense.

I take a long sip of tea and refocus my thoughts on the second scene, where I'm assuming we're still dealing with body parts from the same group of victims.

The ears were a degree less difficult to classify and label based on initial observation. The offender severed the entire ear with precision, shaving it cleanly away from the cranium, possibly with some sort of straight razor.

The same thread and weaving technique was used, denoting the same offender.

Kallum drums his fingers on the tabletop. I finally look him directly in his eyes.

"You're agitated again," he says, then spins the saltshaker three times.

"That's because my time is supposed to be spent at the crime scenes, building a profile of the actual scene."

Instead, I'm seated across from a dangerously delusional philosophy scholar who claims that, in order to further analyze the scenes, he needs to learn the town philosophy.

On the ride into downtown, Kallum suggested our best

way to interview the townies was to start with the local restaurants and watering holes. Socialize, blend, become accustomed to their customs. Observe their philosophy, so to speak, before asking the difficult questions which usually shut people down. Like the feds have been doing with their interrogations since they arrived.

Agent Alister wasn't impressed.

"This town is one whole crime scene," Kallum states. "When do you think we'll uncover the tongues? Maybe we can make flyers of those little monkeys to hand out—"

"I'd hate to think this was a stall tactic," I say, cutting him short. "There are—"

"Yes, I know. Lives in peril. It's all very dramatic. But let's consider this…" He leans forward, his height and large persona crowding the small table. "I'm only here for my own selfish need. Which includes this town being my only taste of freedom. There's no incentive for me to work quickly, is there?"

"I'd say you have that brutally honest thing down." I pivot back to his earlier comment.

He wets his lips, suppressing a smile. "People waste their lives lying, concerned with what others think." He swipes a lemon wedge from his glass and squeezes the slice into his water. "Once you realize everyone you know will die—even your helpless victims; if not today, then in just a short matter of years—there's no reason to care about much of anything."

I lower my gaze, my throat constricting. "Is that your life philosophy, or someone else's? Do you have any original philosophical opinions?"

"Interesting you should ask," he says, smearing the lemon wedge along his fingers. "Considering it's your perpetrator's philosophy. I just tend to agree with that aspect of it."

"How can you know his philosophy? We don't know anything concrete about the scenes yet." My tone echos the frustration starting to unravel me. "Matter of fact, how did you locate the second scene? Can you even give me a straight answer?"

"The only true wisdom is in knowing you know nothing." His mismatched blue-and-green eyes widen, revealing the unstable current drifting below his smooth surface.

He licks the lemon juice from his finger, triggering a wild flutter in my belly. Incensed, I drop my gaze to the plain-white cup. "Obviously you can't."

He reaches across the table and grasps my wrist.

My heart batters my chest as I fight his grip. "Let go—"

"Listen."

His command hits my body like a crash of thunder. I go still, my heavy breaths the only sound between us.

The whole diner fades away as Kallum's long fingers circle my wrist, his heat bleeding into my skin. Then, with his other hand, he places the lemon to my knuckles. Applying delicate pressure, he slides the peel down the back of my index finger, setting off a riot of heat and frenzy to my nervous system.

As he moves to my middle finger, dragging the slick pulp over my skin, I stare at his hand wrapped around my wrist, at the inked sigils stained into his fingers. They're unique to him. The designs don't pull up on any rune chart that I've searched.

I feel every slippery pass of the lemon over my heated flesh, and I know he feels the tremble in my body.

"Lemon has amazing cleansing properties," he says, "making it a natural disinfectant."

My throat tightens. I swallow past the ache lodged at the base, trying to control my breathing. My rapid heartbeat pulses in my veins, fighting against the press of his fingers.

"Those same cleansing agents hide aroma," he continues, "masking most scents for at least a while." He reaches my pinky finger and pauses, forcing my gaze up to lock with his. "Your guy masked the scene to hide the scent. He covered the perimeter. Maybe before, or even after the first scene was discovered."

I find my voice. "That doesn't make sense. Why hide one scene and leave the other out in the open?"

He turns my hand over, commencing to apply the lemon to the underside of my fingers. The sensual feel sends a shiver up my forearm, and I struggle to keep my eyes open. The rush of blood sears my veins.

"Psychology isn't my department," he says, setting the wedge on the table.

As I try to pull away, Kallum maintains his firm hold on my wrist. He draws my hand toward his face and, for an alarming moment, I fear he's going to lick my fingers…and what havoc that will wreak on my composure, until he brings my hand to his nostrils and inhales.

"No more traces of Halen." A sly smile crooks his lips. "If

I bathe you in lemon, we can solve at least one of our dilemmas."

He lifts his fingers one-by-one, letting me slip free. As my agitation ebbs, I rub my hands together to remove the excess lemon juice, effectively removing the tingling, lingering sensation of his touch.

"It's not that he's worried about being caught," I say, making an effort to sort the offender's logic. I retrace our conversation at the killing fields, about the perpetrator having a site he used for practice. "He just doesn't want to be caught before he's done."

"But done with *what* is the question." Kallum eases back against the bench, a defiant gleam behind his shadowed eyes. "I'd also wager uncovering his practice site will make him desperate."

"Don't ever do that again."

"What? Answer your questions? Help tease the answers from your mind?"

"Touch me."

In response, Kallum's teeth clench, feathering a muscle along his sculpted jawline.

The waitress arrives with his order and places the plate in front of him, severing the tense connection. She leaves without inquiring if we need anything, turning away before I can get a read on her expression.

I shake my head, further clearing my thoughts. "These people are victims themselves," I say, wondering if she's related to one of the missing locals. "Questioning them directly won't work. We need a different approach."

Kallum unrolls a cloth napkin and lines up the silverware, then selects the steak knife. Placing the tip of his finger to the knife point, he inspects the serrated edge. "Don't you think it's strange she's not questioning us?" he says. "Wouldn't she be curious about the victims? Who they are, their names?"

I twirl the tea bag string around my finger and glance at the waitress taking an order from the agents. She's maybe twenty-four. Heavily lined eyes, wearing a thick, trendy headband. "People are untrusting," I say in answer. "Especially after the way this town was spotlighted in the media years ago. The judgement, the rumors. Their guards are up."

I turn my attention to Kallum, who's staring at the steak knife with too much interest. And I realize how easy it would be for him to pocket such a weapon—to lose control of his barely contained urges, as he so clearly demonstrated earlier, and use it on Dr. Verlice, or on me...

He chuckles and wipes a hand over his mouth. "Halen, if I had something diabolical planned, I wouldn't make it so obvious." He picks up the fork. "At the institution, I wasn't even allowed to have thumbtacks. I'm acclimating to my new surroundings."

His gaze darts to my arm and the long-sleeved thermal before he cuts into the steak. "Besides, you can't make good on what you owe me if you're dead," he says, and way too casually for my comfort.

I push my arms under the table. "As long as you cleared that up, I feel much more at ease," I say, my tone heavy with sarcasm.

He chews the bite of steak, then: "Even if you can't trust the person, trust their intent."

"And what is your intent for me?"

He waves the fork. "My intent involves you very much alive."

"All right, since we've thoroughly beat around the vagueness of that bush, I know you have some theory about the hemlock."

"Nice punning segue. But can I enjoy my dinner first?" he asks. Then, as he looks at the overcooked meal: "Enjoy might be too generous."

"Talk while you eat."

"Savage." But the dark twist of his mouth implies how much he embraces being just that.

I watch as he uses a butterknife to slice the baked potato with dexterous movements, as if he relishes the way the tight skin splits at meeting the steel.

"The hemlock is more mysterious," he says. "I need more time to work it out." He takes a bite of potato and pins me with an amused look, suggesting he's not talking about the hemlock at all.

"As I've said, we don't have time."

He sets the silverware on the plate. "You want conjecture?"

"I want conjecture, theories. I want everything rattling around that demented brain of yours. That's why you're here. An expert to give an expert interpretation. It's not up to you to solve the case, to be a hero." I stress; there will be no renegotiating his deal. "You explain the philosophy and theology to me. Then I explain it to the FBI in a workable profile so they can find a suspect."

He regards me with tapered eyes. "I have another request."

I expel a slow breath and push back against the bench seat. "Fine." I relent. "But then I get a request."

"Tit for tat. This game could get interesting." He cuts a bite-sized section of steak. "While we're together, dissecting this town and spinning theories, I'd like it if you didn't refer to me as delusional. Demented. Deranged. Or any other demeaning terminology, but especially those that begin with the letter D." He pops the steak into his mouth, watching me expectantly.

I nod slowly, running the tip of my finger around the rim of the cup. "I can accommodate that request."

"See how easily we're acclimating," he says, pushing his plate aside. "Now, what can I do for you?"

My gaze drops to his fingers interlinked on the table. "What are the meanings of the sigils?"

He holds my stare a beat too long before he looks down at his hands, flexes his fingers. "Unfortunately, I can't say."

"That's not how this works." I push my cup aside and raise my hand to flag the waitress.

"You don't understand," he says, and I lower my hand. "I can explain the concept of sigils, the theology, the history. But every sigil is unique and, once charged, should never be thought of again. I've purged the meanings from my mind."

I watch as he flattens his palms on the table, then I glance up to gauge the candor of his expression. I believe him. I believe he believes himself. Dr. Torres made a comment about the mind being the most powerful force, and how Kallum's belief system, his obsessions, rule him.

I wet my lips and fold my arms on the table. "If you need to forget them, then why tattoo the marks on your skin? Wouldn't that be a constant reminder?"

His face breaks into an easy smile. "Such a logical mind," he says.

"Is that an insult?"

He shakes his head. "Not at all." He turns the silver ring around his thumb. "The sigils are neither names of demons nor angels. They're neither good nor evil. The psyche is more powerful than any manmade deity, and the subconscious can be invoked to obtain our most coveted desires."

I'm hyper-aware of how his heated gaze drags over me, stopping on the pendant around my neck.

"Every sigil is personal," he says, "and I find permanently etching my most coveted desires into my skin satisfying. It helps with the unhealthy cravings."

The air charges between us. The psychologist in me wants to probe further, to uncover the desires he obsesses over and how much control they harbor over his actions. Whether or not those sigils parallel with the Harbinger killings, and if he forced himself to "purge" his actions once carried out.

I hold Kallum's intense stare, sensing a dare, some challenge—but knowing I was shutout the moment I tried to push at the crime scene.

He covers his mouth as he leans on his hand. "It also helps curb envy in the academic realm, knowing you have an edge over your rivals. Put your wants, your aspirations, even your fears, into the sigil, then release it. Far healthier than spite."

Suppressing my own desires for the truth for how that spite ended in his rival's murder, I change course. "You answered my question."

"But you have more."

"I know you have some initial theory on the hemlock. I'd really like to hear it."

He drapes his arm over the seat back. "At the first scene— what we assume is his exhibit—it's not about the shocking display of dissected eyes. The symbolism is not art, or representation."

"But it was important enough that he arrange them precisely."

"Precision...perhaps. I'll leave the psychological profiling to your expertise. I'm more interested in the number. Three trees. Three rows of thirty-three sacrifices. Three, three, three. Do you see the pattern?"

"The perpetrator likes the number three. So what...an OCD tic?"

He shakes his head slightly, his dark hair drifting over his forehead. "You're thinking too much like a psychologist. Think like a criminologist. You know, that career you gave up major accolades for."

"This isn't a test, Professor Locke. You're not here to quiz me."

He licks his lips, dragging his tongue between the seam of his mouth as his invasive gaze pushes against me. "Three is the sacred number. Three is the triad, the trinity. The beginning, the middle, the end. Body, mind, spirit." He cocks his head. "Every civilization, every religious sect has some reference to the number three. Not to mention, just about every secret society."

A strange awareness crashes over me as he says this last part, some element of the crime scene trying to link together. I look down at the table, letting my thoughts drift.

"Secret society...hemlock..." I say aloud, attempting to fit the puzzle pieces together.

"Good girl," he says. "There are a few societies, some public, some hidden, that mention the insane root. But I think what you'll find is your guy is very much hidden. Let's try out your favorite research tool. Google 'hemlock,' and see what fascinating details pull up."

With a resigned breath, I flip my phone over and, swiping away the many messages, perform the search. A description with an image of the plant pops up, and as I scroll farther down the page, I see a familiar name.

"Socrates." I blow out a puff of frustration. Kallum stated the answer already with his vague wisdom quote earlier. "Why do you find it difficult to say things clearly?" I set my phone on the table and look at him expectantly.

A gleam flashes behind his eyes, and he smiles. "How is that any fun?"

"None of this is fun."

"Then why do you do it?"

At my obvious loss of patience, he concedes. "Hemlock and Socrates go together like small-town USA and apple pie. Ironically, I think, in this case."

I rub my forehead. "Shit. I've already fallen down this research hole once. Socrates, Plato, Aristotle…"

"But that was before you acquired my services," he says. "*The* philosophers of Western esotericism. There are others, of course, but all schools of thought circle back to the three masters."

"Explain it to me clearly, without veering off on tangents with pantheons and mythology. Just the historical facts." I finally succeed in gaining the waitress's attention and ask for the check as Kallum delves into the details.

Apparently, Socrates was tried in ancient Athens for moral corruption of youths and impiety—that is, sacrilege against the gods. The charge claimed he tried to introduce new deities into society, and this has always been deemed blasphemous across most religions.

Found guilty on both counts, the jury sentenced Socrates to death by execution, where he was forced to commit suicide by drinking a hemlock concoction.

"I could expound for days just on Greek philosophy alone but," he says, "as you've so adamantly declared, you don't have days. And I'm guessing the cliff notes version won't impress the feds."

"Can you surmise it in one word? Just…give me some base to stand on."

His smile stretches, making a slight dimple pop in his cheek. It's a cruel sight.

"Nietzsche," he declares.

By the time I've paid for Kallum's dinner on my company credit card and we exit the diner, the sun has completely set on the town. The chirr of crickets are too noticeable with the lack of vehicles on the road.

The street lights glow against a black, moonless night sky, illuminating the stretch of sidewalk. As I start toward the hotel, Kallum turns back toward the diner.

"I forgot something," he says.

"You don't have anything."

While the agents watch Kallum, I light my phone screen and scroll through the missed calls and texts from Aubrey. I frown at the device. I don't remember turning my ringer off.

Kallum returns wearing a sexy grin, his ego on full display. "Let's walk," he says. He glances back at the agents before he slips a folded piece of paper into my hand. "I agree with your assessment that this town's guard is too high, that we need a stealthier approach."

"That's not how I worded it."

"And then I remembered… I'm a college professor."

I discretely unfold the note. It's an address with a girl's name: Tabitha.

"Kids use any excuse to party," Kallum says. "Especially tragedies. This town needs a lubricant, and a party full of young, gossiping locals might reveal some insight."

I raise an eyebrow, admittedly impressed. "How? She wouldn't even ask if we needed refills."

Kallum turns smoldering eyes on me. "I winked and showed her my ankle monitor."

I stop walking. As Kallum turns my way, I stare at him, look deep into the beautiful blue-and-green stormy seas of his eyes—eyes that wound as sharply as they captivate. Suspicion crowds the small span of air between us, and I question his true motivation for helping.

"Be careful," he says as he dips close. His warm breath fans my lips, and my own breathing shallows. "You know what Nietzsche said about gazing into abysses."

He backs away, leaving me with the lingering sensation over my lips. As I watch him walk off, I finally inhale.

The abyss gazed into me the day Kallum first laid eyes on me and, if I'm not careful, he'll pull me right into the pitch-black void of his soul.

DIVINE MADNESS

KALLUM

A rapid knock jars me from sleep.

My first thoughts are groggy and laced with violent tendencies toward nurses, until my eyes adjust to the dim light bathing a foreign room.

The frantic knock sounds again. I drag my body out of the hotel-room bed and pull on a T-shirt. As I swing the door open, I find little Halen on the other side.

She's wearing tight black leggings and a long-sleeved, fitted nightshirt—one that makes it painfully evident there's no bra beneath. My gaze lingers on the enticing oval outline of her nipples a moment too long before I find her face.

She's all soft features and heightened vulnerability at this hour, and I feel her all the way down to my fucking marrow.

Thrusting a to-go cup of coffee toward me, she says, "Get dressed and wake Dr. Verlice." Her gaze tracks over my chest, searing my skin where her eyes touch the exposed ink of my neck and arms.

She averts her eyes as I accept the paper cup. The warmth against my palm induces a fierce hunger. "Why?"

"We're going to the crime scene."

I take a sip of black coffee, savoring the hit of caffeine as it rushes my system. "Why?" I ask again.

Impatience creases her sultry mouth into her pouty expression that drops right to my dick. It's too damn late—or early—to guard my bodily, carnal reactions from her.

"Nietzsche," she says, leaning against the doorpost. "You brought up a good point before. You're a professor. So you're going to teach me, Professor Locke."

Goddamn. I don't even try to curb the wicked smile that tugs at my lips.

"Don't say anything," she warns. "Just get your shit."

It's three a.m., the iconic witching hour, in the middle of the killing fields. The marsh is wet and stagnant, making my clothes cling to my skin like the air of a damp cellar. The sounds of restless insects vibrate against the reeds as the two tagalong agents set up a spotlight.

As the light flicks on to illuminate the eerie trees of the first crime scene, Halen turns off her flashlight. She's staring at the ring of burnt reeds, lost in her thoughts.

"Take your podium, professor," she says, turning her gaze on me expectantly.

A devious thrill surges my blood. The way she says *professor* does something dangerous to my ego. Makes me want to teach her all about the bad things that go bump in the night and make her scream.

Her hazel eyes reflect the spotlight like a deer caught in a headlight. The cliché analogy suits her well right now, as I imagine her poring over research into the late hours, adrift and consumed with panicked frustration, trying to puzzle together the association to Nietzsche.

The dark circles beneath her flashing silver eyes look like bruises, and the sight tugs at some foreign feeling inside. My desire to help her grasp more than just this concept grips me fiercely.

I place my coffee on the supply table left behind by the techs. "Where do you want me to begin?" I don't try to mask the exasperated edge in my tone.

"From the top," she demands.

I gift her a strained smile. "Three thousand B.C. it is, then."

Dr. Verlice groans into his cup, and I bask in his torment. I need to get rid of him soon.

I spin my thumb ring around three times before I dive in. "Good girls in my class take their seats."

Halen doesn't appear amused by my sarcasm as she clears off a space on a cooler to use as a bench. "Walk me through every thought you had when you first saw this scene." She sets her phone to record, but also breaks out a pen and her notebook.

I lean back against the table, palms braced on the edge. I'm not one to pass up the opportunity to impress with my mind—but I'm far more tempted to lure Halen out into the marsh and sinfully feast on her until my bones ache from gluttony.

I rub the back of my neck and breathe out the tension from my muscles. "First, a history lesson," I say, my gruff voice raking the air. "Everything connects. When you delve down one rabbit hole just to end up in another identical hole, and experience that unsettling sense of *déjà vu*, it's simply the history of the world repeating itself. We humans like to think these correlations are mysterious insight. When really, everything connects, because it's all been done before. Only one mind, one consciousness, is observing those histories for the first time."

"In psychology," Halen says, "we call that Beiner Meinhof Phenomenon."

"In philosophy, we call it synchronicity," I fire back.

She jots down a note, and I'm agonizingly aware that the only thing in nature separating her skin from mine is her flimsy shirt. I fist my hand and shift my attention to the barren marsh trees.

"The number three," I state, "is a spiritual number, as we established. Nearly every society in history references a devotion to this number in order to ascend. Be it to heaven, or to an enlightened plane of the mind. And, Halen, you'll appreciate that it's even referenced in modern psychology.

The law of three stages suggests that your sociology is the most advanced science humankind has left to discover before we are to become a fully enlightened species."

She listens with rapt attention, revealing the side of herself made of raw, naked vulnerability. This is an area out of her comfort zone. I can mold and shape her with a selective delivery of information, and I'm so fucking tempted...

"There are two histories," I say to her, leashing the terrible compulsion. "Public knowledge passed down through the generations, and secret knowledge passed down to the elite few."

Her eyes alight on me as the connection dawns. "Secret societies."

The way she says it, so cavalier, so accepted and logical, lets me know she's done her research thus far and has no personal reservations. Not the way the feds will have when she tries to feed this theory to them.

"Yes, a hidden wisdom. Otherwise referred to as mystery schools. Let's follow the evidence." I walk toward her. "You've already established your link to Socrates." I sweep my hand out to encompass the scene. "The removal of the eyes denotes searching for an enlightened wisdom unable to be seen by the physical realm, an unseen knowledge."

After she writes a note, she promptly curls her fingers toward her palm in a gesture to urge me on. I can't help but smile at my eager student.

"Socrates' student, Plato, initiated"—and that word is crucial for later—"the Platonist school of thought, which was the very first academy. We'll skip the boring topics of this institution and jump right into the celestial. Theory of Forms, metaphysics, body of light—"

"Which is…what?"

"Astral projection." I nod toward her cooler bench, and she only hesitates a moment before she clears her satchel to allow me to sit.

Progress. I seat myself next to her, and even though I keep a good six inches between us, our bodies hum at a high frequency, a charged current snapping like a magnetic force to draw us together.

"Plato and his student…" I trail off, waiting for her to fill the blank.

Her weary sigh fans my cheek, eliciting a violent craving. "Aristotle," she answers.

"They taught us that the stars are composed of an unearthly matter. According to the masters, the spiritual element of the mind, the psyche, was made of this mystical material. Hence, the reason why the stars govern our lives."

"Astrology," she surmises with an air of logic, but it's the dewy glow of her eyes that conveys I'm touching on something divine within her own soul.

I smile. "Which is why they believed the psyche could be projected out into the universe."

"Okay, Kallum. I understand the basis of the theology." She angles her body toward mine. "But how does any of this parallel to Nietzsche?"

"I offered you the cliff notes. You're the one who wanted to take the scenic route through philosophy."

She presses the end of the pen to her lips, and I've never

been more envious of an inanimate object. "Proceed," she allows.

"All of the above is to preface what is not recorded in history," I say. "We only know of the unwritten doctrines because Aristotle cited them once in a dialogue. These doctrines were highly secretive, passed down orally to only the most trusted philosophers. Such teachings centered around the primeval wisdom of ancient sages, such as Hermes Trismegistus."

Halen regards me seriously. "An example of such teachings?"

And here is where the tide turns. "The divine ability to deify man through knowledge."

The night clings to the silence as it wraps us, a cool embrace to suppress all other sounds, an absence of the senses. Now it's just the two of us in the darkness.

Dr. Verlice has drifted off to my lecture. The stalker agents have lost interest in monitoring me and have inserted earphones to watch their devices.

Halen and I exist in this moment on a plane of our own, where—if I reach her, touch her—she might let me break through.

"So to recap," I say, resting my palms on my thighs. "Aristotle was the father of Western esoteric religions. The poet Dante even claimed he was 'the master of those who know', giving credence to the existence of mystery schools and their hidden wisdom. And the god Hermes gifted this divine, hidden wisdom to man to be passed down from sages to philosophers, and so on and so on. To those deemed worthy."

"So all the—" she makes air quotes "—divine wisdom was just handed down to select sects. And for thousands of years, no one ever accidentally let the secrets to the universe slip to a wider audience."

It's a difficult concept for a student of psychology and logic to grasp. "Here's a rational construct. Ivy League colleges and their elite alma matters. Their code of initiation and inside secrets, all passed down from generation to generation, all stemming back as far as Aristotle's first institution of higher learning. The academy wasn't established for the public, though over the years it did evolve. But the architecture is still in place in every elite school. Only the select few are initiated, and those few go on to become presidents, leaders, CEOs of fortune 500 companies—"

She nods and holds up her hand. Then jots a sloppy note. "Got it. Conspiracy theories…"

I chuckle. "Call it what you want, it doesn't offend me, Halen. But the people who believe, believe wholly. They believe in this hidden wisdom and its power so fiercely that entire religions have been founded upon its teachings."

A serious expression traps her features, and I swear she's made of ethereal matter herself. "And one such person who believed was Nietzsche," she reasons.

"Thus concludes our intro into philosophy," I say, stretching my neck.

"Kallum…" She taps her phone to display the hour. "I don't have any more time for the scenic route. I have to give a detailed update to the FBI in less than three hours."

Pivoting my body toward her, I move in a little too close. Her breathing shallows, her gaze wide and anxious as I reach down between us. My fingers graze her thigh as I touch her phone to kill the recording app.

A wary edge frames her delicate features as she studies me, waiting for what happens next. The demanding impulse to sweep the stray lock of white behind her ear thunders through me.

"Before we make our final descent into the abyss of philosophy…" I stand and motion for her to join me. "We need to take a walk in your perpetrator's footsteps."

A moment of hesitation, then she sets her notebook aside. As she gets to her feet, she crosses her arms and casts a look at the distracted agents in the SUV.

"You can ask them to join us," I offer. "If that will make you feel safe."

She wraps her arms tighter around her midsection, shielding herself from the early morning chill. I remove my jacket and hold it open for her in offer.

Dark eyebrows draw together over cautious eyes, her walls erecting to shut me out. I grasp the collar and dangle the garment out to her instead. "Don't make me watch you freeze, Halen."

Resigned, she accepts the jacket and slips her arms inside the sleeves, forgetting about her fear of being alone with me. I suppress a smile at how my jacket dwarfs her, but some other intense feeling licks my insides at seeing her petite body in my clothes.

Halen pushes her hands into the pockets and looks over

the jacket. "It's comfortable, warm," she says. But her drawn features reveal the distress trying to crack her surface, and how hard she's pushing back against that emotion.

The yearning to scratch her surface burns through my veins, a threat to consume—but I tamp down the urge. Patience may not be one of my virtues, but delayed gratification is far more appealing than any virtue.

Leaving behind the safety of the lighted crime scene, we start out into the marsh, where the dark is absolute and presses against us like an entity.

"The new moon denotes new beginnings," I say, tilting my head up toward the moonless sky. "If you believe in that sort of thing."

Halen treks deliberately beside me, careful of her steps. "I'm not sure what I believe anymore." Her confession is as vulnerable and transparent as the sky in the open field. "But what I do care about is snake bites."

She goes to light her phone, and I say, "Leave it off." She can't confront her snake, her underworld, if she's never bitten. "The cosmos are viewed more clearly in the dark."

"Snake bites," she stresses, even though she's wearing mud boots.

Our fear of the unknown, of what we can't discern in the dark, is an inherent fear. It teases out our universal fear of death.

"The light won't protect you from snakes." I glance over at her. "Or any other devils of the night."

Halen stops walking, forcing me to halt and turn around to face her.

Suddenly, she says, "Before, when I said you frightened me…" She trails off, gathering her nerve. "You don't scare me the way you want to, Kallum."

The illuminated crime scene frames her silhouette, transforming her into a celestial creature of myth, the moon goddess Selene incarnate. I have to stalk closer to make out her eclipsed features, and I don't stop walking until I'm towering over her, so close I can hear her uneven breaths.

She looks up into my face and, this time, I don't deny myself what I want.

I raise my hand and trap the defiant lock covering her eye. Sweeping my fingertips across her soft cheek, I guide her hair behind her ear, letting the pads of my fingers linger on the delicate curve of her neck.

A violent tremble racks her body. Her lips part, her breath a tease against my mouth, her sweet scent a fiery lash across my senses, as those silvery eyes glisten with starlight and fear and so much want it spears my rib cage.

As I drop my hand, I lower my mouth to her ear. "I think I scare you exactly how I want to, sweetness."

She takes a reflexive step back, putting distance between us. "You said you wouldn't touch me."

"I said I'd try…and I also said I'd try not to call you endearments." I eat the steps necessary to bring us together. "But we can't always resist our most coveted desire."

Her eyes burn as hot as the stars. "Carve it in a sigil on your skin and never think of it again."

She takes off then, marching past me and heading deeper

into the marshland. I follow, because I have no choice, and I'm also not sure if she realizes where she's going.

I'm not far behind when I see what Halen doesn't. I capture her around the waist and draw her back against my chest before she can take another step.

The burn of her fear tunnels down my throat, practically setting my insides on fire, as she tries to fight free of my arms. "Let me go—"

"If I do that—" I band my arms around hers, trapping them against her sides and her body against mine "—then you'll never get the stench of death off you."

Confusion stills her fight until she looks down, then she instinctively pushes back against me to escape the mutilated remains of the deer.

"Why didn't they mark this area off?" Her tone has gone from panicked to incredulous as she relaxes into the arms of her perceived killer.

And I'm not above feeling—greedily, wickedly—every inch of her warm body pressed against me.

Awareness settles over her as the silence thickens. The air turns electric, enfolding a heated current around us. As she begins to turn, I loosen my hold and allow her to face me. She doesn't look up as she presses her hand to my chest. I let her touch sink through me before she pushes out of my arms.

"How am I supposed to trust your intent here, Kallum," she says, "leading me into the deserted marsh on a new moon…?" Her questioning voice quivers, either from the chill or our proximity, I'm not sure. But my jacket is of no more use, and I have the sudden, fierce desire to strip it away.

She inhales a steadying breath and finally drags her gaze upward to meet mine. "I think your intent is to maliciously toy with me," she accuses.

I remain silent. I won't justify any of my actions.

"Say something now, Kallum...something that will change my mind, or I swear I'll file the paperwork to send you back."

"Do you want a clever lie? Or the truth?"

"The truth," she says with no hesitation.

A deep chuckle booms from my chest. Her eyebrows knit together. I'd think the crease between her brows was cute if her statement wasn't so untruthful itself.

"We are base creatures, little Halen," I say. "We can pretend to be more evolved than our heathen ancestors, but we're just flesh and bone. Carnal desires and the need to be sated. Even the enlightened masters of antiquity caved to their fleshly desires."

She shakes her head. "That didn't answer my question at all. Are you *fucking* with me, Kallum?"

I drag in a lungful of sodden air, detesting that we're doing this here in a swamp. "Nothing has changed for me since that day I approached you at the university," I say, setting the truth free.

"You approached me to glean information on the case," she says, all logical accusation.

"I approached you because I was curious about you. Because your hypnotic eyes and your goddamn perfect, alluring body punched me in the gut, and I've never felt such sweet pain."

117

She looks down at the reeds, then her flashing eyes pin me. "None of this… Nothing you say makes sense."

A defeated smile pulls at my mouth. "That's because you're so lost."

Even now, her pain clouds her reason. She's fighting for a rational grasp on the moment, on her life, and her bottom has all but fallen out, leaving her suspended in an abyss.

I want to be the one to find her. I want to be the one to descend with her to the depths.

I want to be the one to devour her pain.

She swallows hard, tugging my jacket around her tighter. "Did you kill Wellington?" she demands. "Did you commit the Harbinger killings? Did you mutilate those victims, Kallum?"

I appreciate her finally dropping the pretense and asking me outright.

This time, when I move in close to her, I don't plan to let her escape. "You want the answers so badly it's driving you fucking mad."

She raises her chin in answer, a manic hunger waging war behind her eyes. "Yes."

"I'll tell you the truth," I say. "I'll give you every answer you seek."

Something in my expression must convince her, because she doesn't deride me for being delusional or lying. Her features open, urgently willing me to say more. "Okay then. Tell me."

I lick my lips. "Are you ready to honor your end of the deal?"

She's indebted to me for more than a desperate deal struck at a visitation table, but let's start there.

Her silent acceptance of our bargain infuses the stagnant marsh air. As she relinquishes her control, a thrill courses my blood, and the glass lifts to free the venomous spider.

"This is what I want, little Halen." I trail a finger over her forearm. "Trust my process, my methods. Don't question the course. Let your reservations go, and when the case is closed, I promise you, I'll hold nothing back."

Her eyes search my features, trying to discern the truth or uncover a loophole, but there is only us and the darkness that surrounds us.

"If you give me this," I say, dropping my hand, "then I'll reveal every dark truth to you."

Washed in the pale light of the marsh, she holds my gaze with a measure of uncertainty.

She wants the answers so desperately—how much is she willing to surrender?

After a weighty stretch of contemplation, she extends her hand, as if striking a deal.

With a wicked grin, I accept her hand and pull her to me. I bring her hand to my mouth and place a lingering kiss to the back, my gaze trapping hers.

"You're going to tell me everything," she demands.

"I'll be an open book to you." A threat, not a promise. "Now, ask me anything you want about Nietzsche."

Once I release her, she hesitates before making her decision and turning toward the deer carcass. "I have an FBI briefing soon," she says. "If I can't give them a profile to narrow down a suspect, then I have to give them a useful lead."

I rummage around the reeds until I find a decent stick. Then I lower to my haunches and probe the mutilated deer. "Did the local department or FBI process the stag?"

She glances back at the crime scene briefly. "I didn't see any reports, but I can check. I'll go grab my tablet."

"No need," I say, lifting a section of the shredded shoulder. "Light your phone."

She does, aiming the flashlight on the decaying flesh as she covers her nose with my jacket from the stench. The remains have been picked over by the crows, making it difficult to discern, but amid the torn flesh is the distinct imprint of a bite mark.

Made by human teeth.

Halen says nothing as she takes pictures of the mark. As she inspects the rest of the mutilated carcass, it becomes evident there are also claw marks from human fingernails. What we don't uncover is a kill shot. Not from a bullet or a bow.

"What am I looking at, Kallum?" Her low voice echos the brutality of this scene.

"The stag was torn apart by hands and teeth," I say. "Then consumed." A primal act that, admittedly, excites me as a scholar as much as it horrifies Halen as a criminologist hunting an offender.

"*Sparagmos* was part of a secret rite," I explain. "The Greek translation is to tear or rend a living animal to pieces.

Sometimes, even a human being. The primal act itself, of being dismembered, is a sacred sacrifice."

She takes a moment to accept this knowledge, then: "You said you agreed with me that leaving the deer here was a forensic countermeasure to protect his exhibit."

"That was before I saw the engravings." I glance up to lock gazes with her. "And now that I have confirmation here" — I nod to the stag—"I can confidently conclude this scene is not an exhibit." I stand and look at the trees.

I hear the music, the pipes, the drums.

I smell the earthy notes of wine and taste the copper in the blood.

I sense the energy as the thyrsus impales the earth to mark the damp soil.

I feel the frenzy, the madness.

"This is his ritual ground."

Halen moves to stand before me. Her expression conveys her surging annoyance. "*What* engravings?"

It takes longer to reach the hemlock crime scene in the near pitch-black. The darkest hour is just before the dawn, or so Thomas Fuller once said, making the trek difficult until we spot the caution tape.

"You said at the diner your guy wasn't concerned with getting caught, that he didn't want to be caught before he was done. Add that to your profile today. Even though he tried to methodically remove all evidence, he left evidence of the ritual at the scene with the stag during the height of frenzy."

"Suddenly you're all terminology and level-headed deduction skills," she says, and I hear the tangle of exhaustion and impatience creep into her voice. "And I don't follow any of it."

As we duck under the yellow tape, Halen pans the area with her phone light, careful of the clusters of white, poisonous flowers. "Where?" she demands.

She follows me farther past the marked-off scene to a giant black willow tree. I sweep aside the low-hanging sprays. Along the thick girth of the trunk is an engraving. "The symbol for Socrates."

She uses her phone camera to capture pictures as I circle the trunk. On the backside is another engraved symbol. "The herd," I tell her. "Which is the symbolism most associated with Nietzsche."

Once I saw this, I made the connection. But there is a scholarly glut of conflicting interpretations when it comes to Nietzsche's doctrine.

Halen snaps a picture of the carved symbol, then pins me with a severe gaze.

"The engravings have been seared into the bark, branded," I say. "I'm sure the lab geeks can discern what was used."

"That's not important right now," she says, tone accusatory. "You've known about this since before the diner, and you didn't say anything. You've known the whole time we've been talking—"

"I didn't know anything confidently." Making the

association to Nietzsche means nothing. Nietzsche lambasted the master philosophers of antiquity, and he's often associated with Socrates for this reason. There are several of Nietzsche's works that parallel to the ancient gods and philosophies.

It's like trying to pick a needle out of a haystack, only the picker sees a stack of needles instead of hay. Philosophy is interpretation. I need to see the needle and the hay through the suspect's eyes.

Releasing a heavy breath, she returns her attention to the symbols. "Then what do you now know confidently?"

I lower myself next to her. "A serial killer covers his tracks. He hides his kills. Performs forensic countermeasures. All because he doesn't want to be caught, because he has a compulsion he needs to continue to feed."

She turns wary eyes on me, and I can hear her speculative thoughts, questioning if I'm speaking from personal experience.

"Your perpetrator has no worries of being caught in the long run," I continue. "You realized this. Matter of fact, he wants the world to know. He is bringing people a gift. He is coming. If he doesn't believe he's already arrived..." Then I consider the lemon he used. "No, he still has more to achieve. That's why he backtracked to mask his practice site."

"Kallum," she interrupts, "what the hell are you talking about?"

I glance around, trying to locate the third symbol. There has to be a third—there are always three.

"The stag," I say, pushing aside willow sprays as my search becomes frantic. "It was hunted and torn apart during a ritual by a man who practices very specific alchemy." My voice falters as I uncover the third engraving.

"The symbol for Dionysus."

A dark thrill sets my blood aflame as I run my fingertips over the Greek symbol for the god of madness and frenzy.

I found the needle.

And the haystack just went up in flames.

"Socrates. The herd. Dionysus." I tick off the symbols on my fingers as I turn toward Halen. "The order of his ascension."

She's lowered her camera, no longer concerned with cataloging the scene. Her eyes are wide and flashing like a scared and wounded animal caught in a trap.

My blood is fury and blisters my veins as it rushes every artery. She has no comprehension of what we've uncovered, of what this entails.

"Pleasure. Madness. Frenzy." I climb to my feet and brace my hand on the tree for support.

Halen mutters a curse and latches onto my wrist, forcing my palm to scrape down the bark as she scolds me about evidence. But I'm tunneling too far down, my mind delving to the depths, to where Dionysus dwells in the underworld.

Only Halen's fragile, distressed voice pulls me from the brink. "Kallum, please…"

I drive my hand into my hair as I draw close to her, tearing down superficial boundaries to be near her, to feel her energy and feed off her pain. Her sweet scent of honeysuckle, the searing echo of clove that clings to her fear and scorches my throat. She could drug me with one touch.

Sheltered under the weeping limbs of a swamp tree, where Nietzsche himself would feel at peace, I find Halen's beautiful and alarmed gaze, and I breathe in her maddening scent.

I push in so close, her back hits the tree, and I can't stop. I clasp her face, ravenous for a taste of her.

My peripheral catches movement as she reaches out to grab hold of a stick.

I smile down at her. "We already talked about the weapons you possess, sweetness. I won't be stopped with a twig."

Her strained swallow presses against my palm, and she releases the branch. But something else—something dark and frightened and aware—sparks in her gaze, and I wonder what mental images are flicking through her mind.

She licks her lips, drawing my deviating thoughts to her alluring mouth. "I want you to release me."

"Is that what you want?"

Nodding against my hands, she forces out, "Yes."

With severe difficulty, I break away. I set her free, but only for this moment. She took hold of me from the very first instance and has cruelly kept me bound with no intention of releasing me.

Every step I take away from her, the turmoil attacking my mind lessens, until I finally inhale a breath not laced with her scent to cleanse my lungs.

"The divine madness," I say to her, pointing toward the symbol.

"What does that mean?"

"The power to become deified through wisdom." I widen my arms. "To become a fucking god."

Real fear crests in her pale eyes. And I know that fear is directed toward me, not her suspect—but she has no idea how close she is to the abyss.

"Your suspect is the *Übermensch*."

9

DEITIES OF FRENZY

HALEN

S leep deprivation can cause disorientation, impaired judgement, and memory loss. But suffer this ailment long enough, and it's the strain on the heart which inflicts the most damage.

I'd like to blame my disjointed presentation to the FBI task force today on my lack of quality sleep—but I've worked off of less; I know what my body and mind can tolerate. I know my breaking point.

And the need for sleep has nothing to do with the palpitations attacking my heart as I watch Kallum stalk toward me on the sidewalk.

Dressed in an all-black suit, his leanly cut form slices the night like a razor. He's the devil of every ailment come to inflict damage to my heart.

This is the first time I've seen him since his manic episode at the scene last night. And I'm unsure if it was that episode or what came before that has me so unnerved.

As he and Dr. Verlice approach the entrance to Pal's Tavern, I touch my chest and clasp the solitaire diamond, distractedly returning my attention to the revised profile on my tablet.

I've been reworking it since Aubrey relayed our director's dissatisfaction with my report. Agent Alister's initial briefing with my unit expressed as much with my performance.

I've had to deliver more bizarre and far-reaching profiles to authorities before, but trying to deliver a ritual ground crime scene where the unnamed suspect tears apart animals with his hands and teeth and consumes the flesh has its own unique challenges.

Then there's the added layer of difficulty when explaining the associations to secret societies and mad philosophers to outline a suspect who aims to ascend into a super human.

Besides the obvious credibility issue, the profile gets no one any closer to locating the missing victims.

When Agent Alister pulled me aside and reprimanded me about withholding the evidence of the engravings, all I could do was nod and chew back retorts.

Alister's admonishment was fair and even warranted. Using Kallum's eccentric methods as an excuse wasn't an option. I was the one who requested his participation on the case. He's my responsibility. He's my problem to contain.

And as his blue-and-green smoldering gaze drags over me deliberately, stoking embers long ago doused, I know it's not just the urgency of the unusual case affecting me and my ability.

Something is wrong with me.

Dr. Verlice glances at the wooden sign above the worn door of the local townie bar. "This doesn't seem like an ideal method of investigation," he says.

"There isn't much of a nightlife in town," I reply. "This is the only place still open. I'm almost finished..." I toggle between documents on my tablet.

In an effort to condense the overabundance of information in my report, I presented my quickly hatched profile in bullet points to Agent Alister's team:

• Suspect will display fixation with ancient Greek philosophy. Will feel strongly connected to the three master philosophers, but especially the philosopher Socrates. Will show disdain toward his teachings i.e. preaching mediocrity, but covertly believes Socrates passed down a hidden wisdom to worthy scholars to ascend to a celestial plane within the mind.

• Friedrich Nietzsche: German philosopher / *Übermensch* - rough German translation: overman. Suspect harbors delusional belief in a supreme, god-like being. Believes the philosopher Nietzsche constructed secret instructions within his doctrine that document his discovery of the masters' hidden wisdom to ascend into an enlightened being he dubbed the overman. Nietzsche's hidden wisdom cited as the Philosopher's Stone (fabled alchemic substance to convert base metals into gold): a psychological alchemy concealed in the depths of the subconscious which one reaches to ascend to a higher, enlightened state of consciousness.

• Dionysian Mysteries / ritual / ascension. Nietzsche's doctrines centered around the Greek god Dionysus (god of madness and frenzy) and metaphors of invoking the god himself. Dionysian Mysteries were a secret rite of the Maenads (followers). Not much is known about the rituals other than cryptically written dogmas that cite a ritual of animal and/or human sacrifice, orgiastic sex, wine, death, and rebirth in order to invoke Dionysus into one's "spirit". The suspect will display extensive knowledge of the Dionysian Mysteries, along with knowledge of Nietzsche's philosophy incorporating Dionysus.

• Hemlock / Suspected use of poisonous plant to either mimic Socrates and take own life in event suspect is discovered before goal is realized (ascending into overman) and/or overman philosophy is rejected by society (i.e. Socrates' introduction of new deity).

My finger hovers over the remark about the hemlock. An ill feeling coats my stomach, and I feel as if my assessment is still off. I'm tempted to delete it. I'm tempted to delete the whole profile.

There are other descriptors such as likely age, gender, education level, behavioral traits—but those are vague and pale in comparison to the extreme belief system of the suspect. Which is the main reason Agent Alister dismissed my first profile to begin with.

I hit Send on the email to Alister with the revised profile attached. Then, with a resigned sigh, I tuck the tablet away in my bag. I'll either wake up tomorrow with a suspect list, or jobless. Most likely the latter.

Turning toward Dr. Verlice, I hold out my bag. "Can you please put this away in your room for now?" I ask. At his perplexed expression, I lift the hem of my dress to reveal the bandage around my ankle. "I injured myself in the field. I'd really appreciate the help."

He pushes his wireframe glasses up the bridge of his nose and glances at the hotel across Main Street. "That's why I didn't go gallivanting in the dark last night."

When he accepts my bag, I thank him. "A wise choice. We'll wait here for you."

As I watch Dr. Verlice cross the street, I feel Kallum's consuming presence pushing against me. I finally meet his narrowed gaze, and a flash of something primal and starved registers there.

"You lie so pretty," he says with a crooked grin.

Choosing to ignore the comment, I turn toward the bar entrance. "Let's go."

We had agreed that, in order to infiltrate the house party without drawing negative attention, we'd have to ditch Dr. Verlice, and find a way to keep the two special agents out of sight.

But that was before last night. Before his unhinged episode. Before he said what he said...and before I was even more wary of being alone with him.

Despite my rational reservations, the temptation to unravel the mystery of this case is too dangerously strong.

I want to locate the missing residents before something

extremely bad happens, yes—but beneath my desire to do good is the dark and seductive lure to unravel the mystery of Kallum.

I need the answers only he can give me.

As we enter the dimly lit interior of the bar, we're engulfed in a smoky pit where a few pool tables crowd the center. The twang of folk music drifts through the sullen atmosphere. We pass the small bar top with a handful of patrons and too many feds to count. Apparently, this really is the only nightlife.

Moving quickly, we make our way toward the back exit. Once we hit the street, Kallum checks the directions I wrote down for the party location.

I toss a purposeful glance at his ankle. Without my need to point out the obvious, he says, "Don't worry. The house is safely within bounds of the monitor."

We veer off the road toward the destination, and I glance back at the trailing agents.

Before I left the hotel, I made the agents aware of our destination and goal, with a *please hang back* unless needed. I have no authority to give them a directive. But I'm hopeful the *please* stressed this scene will not be FBI friendly. No one will talk if the agents are spotted anywhere near us.

The directions lead us to an aged Gothic revival home with a steeply pitched gable roof and castle-like tower. The arched dormer windows have a touch of classic tracery, utilizing a swirled black, ornate design. It's gaudy and elaborate, denoting old money.

Like every other house in town, the siding is chipped and

peeling. The worn appearance reflects the sad tone of the people that inhabit these houses regardless of status.

The heavy thump of bass escapes the open windows as we draw near. Before I approach the slender columns of the wrapped porch, I bend down to remove the bandage from my leg.

"We should start by locating Tabitha the waitress." I toss the bandage in a shrub and start toward the house. "Since you have a rapport with her, we can ask her—"

"Wait."

Kallum's stark command is delivered in a deep baritone that resounds in my chest. I linger near the concrete steps as he advances, the sliver of moon cast in the pale hue of his eyes. I brace myself for some mention of last night...

"This is what you decided to wear to a party?" he asks, his gaze absorbing me. "The plan was to blend."

Relieved, I glance over my black maxi dress. It's the only semi-formal outfit I ever pack, yet this is the first time I've worn it. I also put my hair in a high ponytail and sported dangly silver earrings.

"Let me guess," he says, "you googled current fashion trends and found out funeral-chic was all the gen-z rage."

His words summon a blistering ache to my chest, snatching the breath from my lungs. An image of a funeral dress rises up from the trenches of my mind to try to drag me under.

I force my voice steady. "As opposed to your choice of goth chic?" I say, refusing to let him see his effect on me.

"Were you going for nineties emo-kid, or Anne Rice vampire groupie?"

Kallum runs his tongue along the ridge of his teeth. "Vampires prefer to see a little skin."

I shake my head and turn away. "No one will care—"

I make it a single step before his hand wraps my arm, drawing me to a stop. My gaze drops to where he touches me. My heart flips inside my chest as he grazes his hand down to the tapered hem of the sleeve.

"What are you doing…?" A shock of fear strangles my breath as he rolls the sleeve to reveal an inch of skin.

"Your part of the deal is to trust my methods," he says, tone casual, as if he's not causing my heart to tear through my chest wall.

"No… Please." I manage to free my wrist and shove the sleeve down.

"Do you even know what you're pleading for?" His question leaves me speechless, but he doesn't wait for the answer. "Either you hold up your end, or—"

"Anything…else." I swallow the ache clogging my throat.

He cocks an eyebrow, then rakes his gaze over my dress. A sinful gleam alights behind his gaze to make me regret my words and then, with a groan, he drops to his haunches.

He grasps the flare of my hips, igniting a searing heat that threatens to burn me to ash as his palms travel painstakingly slow down my thighs. His fingers bunch the fabric, driving any rational response from my mind.

His hands stall above my knees, and I feel the pressure of his fingers…then cool air touches my skin as Kallum tears my dress down the seam. He grunts as he rips the material, leaving me with half a dress.

Mortification envelops me as I stare down. He discards the shredded lower half of my dress in the same shrub as he stands.

I grab the torn hem, a raw ache burning my throat.

Features shadowed by the dark, he inspects his handiwork appreciatively. "You do care," he says. "And I care." He moves in, and I'm unable to escape him before he clasps the back of my neck.

He pulls the hair tie free, letting my hair fall loose around my shoulders. Then, trailing his fingers up the curve of my neck, he touches one of the dangly earrings. "These distract from your eyes." After he removes my earrings, he says, "Natural beauty should never compete with decorations."

He places the earrings in my hand as he steps around me.

I stare at the silver jewelry in my palm, unable to move, feeling as if I've just been stripped naked by Kallum—and my body is betraying me.

Curling my fingers over the earrings, I give myself a moment to let the infuriating mix of emotions sear through my veins, then I throw them in the bushes. By the time I've caught up with Kallum, he has the front door open and reaches behind to grab my hand.

A shocked second where his fingers lace between mine, then he pulls me over the threshold and into a throng of undulating bodies.

Multi-colored lights strobe and pulse with the beat of the raging house music. The dense body heat coats my skin in a balmy wrap, making me partially grateful I'm not suffering the full coverage of the dress. Shouts and obnoxious laughter bleed over the music, and as we head deeper, the dim lighting obscures my vision.

But none of the distractions are enough to remove the heightened awareness of my hand in Kallum's.

As we weave through the gathering in the main room, I'm met with bloodshot eyes and slack features. Despite crashing into several intoxicated dancers, no one really notices us. But I notice a familiar face on the edge of the crowd.

I tug at Kallum's hand, and he looks back as I nod toward Devyn. "I'm going that way."

Brow furrowed, he releases my hand. "I'll find drinks."

I won't be ingesting anything from here. However, I refrain from telling him as much, using the much needed space away from him to breathe, even if it's laced with vape smoke.

Devyn spots me, regarding me curiously as I weave a path toward her. She's wearing civilian clothing. Jeans and a cropped blouse. Her hair is pulled back in a thick headband. She's attractive and stylish, and she could pass for one of the teens.

I lean in toward her ear. "Are you undercover?"

She laughs. "In this town? That'd be impossible," she says, her voice pitched over the music. "I'm helping cover for a friend on the force. Someone called in a noise complaint."

Eyebrow arched, I glance around. "Your approach doesn't seem to be working."

Her throaty laughter makes me smile. "This is the Lipton

house," she says, implying a common local knowledge. "The Liptons pretty much do what they want, and so do their entitled asshole offspring." She nods to a tall blond guy who looks like he was DNA-coded to be a star quarterback. "I'm just here to make sure no one gets hurt and nothing burns."

I nod toward her plastic cup. "And the incentive to babysit the prom king doesn't hurt."

"Oh, you're a funny fed." But her voice is playful, and when she laughs again, she holds up the plastic cup in mock toast. "To whatever gets us through the day."

As I'm empty-handed, I tap her cup with my knuckles.

It's been a long time since I was able to actually make a joke, or be around anyone I wanted to joke with. A familiar twinge blooms in the center of my chest, reminiscent of homesickness.

Shoving the sensation aside, I cast a look around the scene. "I haven't seen Detective Emmons around town. Is he avoiding the feds?"

She lowers her cup as her features fall. "DNA on one of the remains was matched today," she says. "Came back a positive ID to his brother."

"Oh, my god." I shake my head, not knowing how to respond. I recall his hostility at the crime scene, his reluctance to be there, and I now understand why. "I'm sorry," is all I can manage.

She waves her hand, relieving me of the burden. And I wonder who went missing from her life, who she's thinking about—hopeful, or dreading the outcome—every time a match is announced.

"So I take it you *are* undercover." She switches the topic as she scans my wardrobe with interest.

"The sick dress gave me away, huh?" I lift the torn hem for emphasis.

"Look at you with the hipster lingo. You won't stand out at all."

A full laugh slips free, and my head catches a tiny buzz from the effect. Then, as an electric current zips across my flesh, I feel his eyes on me. I can sense him drawing near, and like a droplet of ink clouding water, Kallum's presence permeates the air like a dark vapor.

"Want a drink?" Devyn asks, but then she spies Kallum circling back with a bottle in his hand. "Oh, this must be the consultant, and I think he has you covered…in more ways than one. Damn." Her voice drops low as she makes an obvious point to check him out. "Well done, Halen."

I should object, but my mouth goes dry at the way his heated gaze traps me.

"You made her laugh," he says to Devyn, his eyes never straying from my face. "A difficult feat to pull off." He then turns his attention on Devyn. "I'm Kallum."

"I know who you are." Devyn apprises him with a smirk. "I've heard rumors."

The panty-melting grin he pulls off should be illegal. "Well, rumors are entertaining, but only Halen and I know the truth." He winks at me, and the frantic need to escape and find fresh air assails me.

Before I can devise an excuse to leave, he leans in and

whispers, "You sound like a pixie when you laugh. It's fucking adorable."

I put space between us and say to Devyn, "Can you do me a favor?"

"Feds and favors." She *tsks* teasingly. "This time, you'll owe me one. And tomorrow, I want a full update on what the feds have. No one is getting anything done around here."

"I promise, I will," I assure her. "Actually…" I go to grab my phone and curse. Realizing I left it in my bag, apprehension grips my chest. I never forget my phone.

"Are you okay?" she asks, worry creasing her features.

"Yeah…yes." I shake my head. "I was going to send you my profile, but I'll have to send it later. But I will. Then you can help me narrow down a suspect."

This seems to persuade her, and her expression turns serious. "All right. What can I do?"

I nod in the direction of the arched hallway. "There are two very obvious special agents stationed out front," I say. "Keep them from crashing the party?"

She downs the rest of her drink. "I have practice marking my territory with the feds."

After seeing her handle the reporter, I believe her. "Thanks."

I'm not sure why I'm just now realizing she really can help on the case. Devyn is a local. She knows this town, its people. Having her read over the profile would garner more information then observing a party full of wasted youths.

"Nice to meet you, Professor Locke," Devyn says to

TRISHA WOLFE

Kallum, then touches my arm, leaning in conspiratorially. "I want intel on more than just the profile tomorrow."

As I watch Devyn clear a path through the mass, I push farther into the corner, trying to put distance between me and the bad boy of academia. Since his confessions last night, it feels as if every barrier has been stripped away, and I can't re-erect my walls fast enough before he's tearing them down again.

I lean my back against the cool wall and drag in a breath, letting my gaze roam the clustered groups. Every single person here is too young to be a real, potential suspect.

"Stop trying to force it," Kallum says, disturbing my thought process.

He pushes in too close, his body blocking my view of the crowd. I have to angle my head back to see his face. "What am I forcing, Kallum?" I can't mask the panic bleeding into my unsteady tone.

I haven't thought about taking anxiety meds for months, didn't even take them when it was necessary, and suddenly I wish I had access to them.

Something is wrong with me.

"This is a small town." He pushes in even closer, strangling my air. "They're curious. They'll talk. Let the answers come to you."

This corner is suddenly too tight, his body heat an invasive touch against my skin. My clothes are too binding. His clothes are too abrasive against my now-bare thighs. As if he realizes I'm about to flee, I feel the chilled glass of the wine bottle against my palm.

"The Liptons have decent taste in wine," he says, his deep voice carrying over the music.

I drag a hand through my hair, then push the bottle back toward him. "No thanks. I'm good."

"I can grab an unopened bottle," he offers. "Open it right in front of you. But drugging you unconscious would hardly be any fun, Halen."

This time, he forcefully places my hand around the bottleneck, pressing the issue without verbally reminding me of our agreement.

"Trust your methods," I say beneath my breath. Trusting Kallum's methods is a deliberate descent right into his fucking madness…this case's madness…and once I fall, I'll never crawl out of the dark void.

Not this time.

I don't have the strength to crawl out twice.

Reminding myself I'll be unemployed by morning, I bring the rim to my mouth. *Fuck it.* "And we're drinking straight from the bottle."

"Just like heathens."

I turn up the bottle and slug back a generous sip. The red wine is bitter and robust, and goes straight to my head. I breathe out the fumes to clear my teary eyes. The lights flash with the swelling tempo of the song, and the crowd responds. Hands thrust into the air, bodies roll in a seductive wave.

Kallum's warm hand covers mine around the bottleneck. He draws closer to me, his proximity overriding my anxiety, his scent as intoxicating as the wine. Keeping my hand pressed to the bottle, he brings it to his mouth and drinks. I watch the way his Adam's apple dips, stare at the tattoo swirled along his smooth skin. It's entrancing.

He then places the bottle rim to my lips.

"Heathens," he says, eyes flashing in time with the pulsing beat. "Like the Maenads, let all your reservations go, Halen."

I tilt my head back farther and let the wine flow over my tongue. Face flushed from the alcohol, I lick my lips, savoring the tingling effect. I decide wine works well in place of anxiety meds.

Kallum removes the bottle from my hand and places it on a side table. Then he slips his hand around my waist and palms the small of my back. The intensity of his stare pins me to the wall.

His other hand cups the side of my face, his fingers rest along my jaw. He uses his thumb to tip my face up toward his. I suppress a shiver at the feel of his cool thumb ring along my skin.

A roar fills my head as we stand still amid the heaving party. The music fades into the background, the flashing lights slow to a hypnotic beat, inducing a trance-like state.

"Relax," he coaxes. His pinky settles over the pulse point in my neck and, as he begins to sway us away from the wall, my heartbeat throbs violently in my veins.

It's too dark, too loud, too crowded and isolated all at once.

And I'm too aware of the feel of him—of every overstimulated spot his body touches mine.

I'm struck with the reckless impulse to push onto my toes and link my arms around his neck. Blinking hard, I turn my head away to break his hold. I place my hands on his chest to force space.

"I'm not well," I hear myself say.

His hand covers mine, and the furious beat of his heart thunders beneath my palm. "I disagree. I think you're getting better."

His statement clouds my thoughts as much as his inebriating, woodsy scent.

"My jacket still smells like you," he says, a lopsided smile slanting his mouth. "It tortured me all day."

"And where were you all day?" I ask, avoiding his remark.

"Waiting for my muse to return," he says without missing a beat.

"You never answer my questions."

"I always answer them. You just refuse to hear."

I release a strained breath and drop my gaze. "And this isn't accomplishing anything. No one is approaching us. We're not getting any answers."

"You're too anxious."

A humorous laugh tears free. "And you're too...close." I push against his chest. "This isn't what we agreed on."

When I meet his eyes, a flicker of heat sparks amid that soulless darkness, and I'm livid with myself for how easily I give in to him. How easily he can charm and manipulate.

What I am is too exhausted after taking today's licks, and I need to regain control over this situation and my senses.

Kallum finally releases me from his penetrating gaze as he

lowers his mouth next to my ear. "Alister doesn't respect your profile," he says.

It's an observation. As I was working on the profile tonight, Kallum can determine the logical outcome of the briefing.

"He doesn't understand it." I correct his assumption. "I don't really understand it," I confess.

"Then let's make you understand it."

I shake my head. "Visualizing a scene in the middle of this chaos—" I wave my hand at the raucous party "—with an erratic consultant isn't really how I work."

"Don't limit yourself," he says as he starts to sway us. "Sometimes, to connect with your suspect, you can't just walk in his footsteps. You have to dance in them."

There's a moment of urgency, one second where I have control to stop the descent, but I falter. I've already stepped off the ledge.

The sensation of falling pitches my stomach as Kallum carves a path through the dancing throng, then he draws me against his solid chest.

As he wraps his arms around me, the gauzy feel of webbing coats my skin and, too late, he catches me.

And I'm caught.

10

DANCE WITH THE DEVIL

HALEN

If you dance with the devil, expect to get burned.

Kallum is fire and brimstone and every salacious dark dream. I'm embraced by the arms of a killer, and this reality should terrify me, his touch should repulse me—and somewhere below the heady rush of wine and intense chemical attraction, a kernel of logic fights for dominance.

Only sometimes, a whisper is louder than a scream. The tendril seductively curls around us, the soft murmur luring us into the flames.

As the slow and seductive music infuses the overcrowded house, every nerve in my body is lit up like a live wire seeking a grounding connection. The feel of Kallum's hand at the small of my back attacks my nervous system, and just the sweep of his thumb over my jaw sparks across my skin.

His heated gaze holds mine captive as he stares down at

me, our movements so subtle we're barely dancing. His thigh eases between my legs, sending an arousing throb to my core, and I shut my eyes against the sensation.

This is wrong.

I'm wrong.

My obsession to name Kallum the Harbinger killer has mutated into a gross form of transference. It's the only rational thought I can grasp as I fight to maintain a level of composure over my senses.

As his hands wander my body, exploring me like I'm some precious artifact, an internal alarm flares. He continues to coast upward until he has my face between his palms. His fingers tormentingly sink into my hair past the nape of my neck, his hold preventing me from escaping.

Forced to stare into the void of his beautiful eyes, I sense the floor shift beneath my feet, losing gravity. "How am I supposed to visualize the scene when you're staring at me like…" I stop myself, unwilling to finish that sentence.

He licks his lips, savoring my unease. "If you starve an animal, that animal will make a mess of its meal."

"I'm not the meal," I say, my voice edged in anger to control the tremble.

His captivating smile sinks through me. He doesn't force the subject, and instead says, "This is your crime scene, Halen."

He spins me around and brings my back to his chest, hands fastened to my hips. "Look around at all this wild debauchery. This is what you need to visualize, to see"—he grinds obscenely into my backside—"to *feel.*"

His fingers coast across my pelvis, setting off a riot of tremors. "Kallum—"

"Can you still taste the earthy notes of the wine?" he cuts me off, ignoring the plea in my voice. "The tawny mixture, thick and heady with tannins?"

The taste of the cabernet still lingers on my tongue. I swallow and nod against his chest.

"Close your eyes. Hear only the drums. Envision the reeds. The dark trees. The night. How the moonlight spills over the marsh. It's all a part of his sacrifice."

"Dance in my suspect's footsteps," I say, suspecting this is a very bad idea.

I have nothing to lose.

"Feel the heat of the fire on your skin," Kallum encourages as he rocks us, our bodies fused together amid the strobing lights and pulsing music. "Smell the charred reeds. Taste the smoke. Let it infuse your body. The only way to connect with him is to give yourself over to the frenzy."

I know what he's trying to do, to make me submit to—and yet, being aware of his tactic doesn't make it any less effective. It's so tempting just to give in…to let myself fall away.

I clasp his wrists, my heart drumming so hard in my chest I can barely breathe.

Kallum sways us faster as the tempo increases, the music drowning out the frantic thud of my heartbeat. He overpowers me, his hand snaking across my belly, leaving a searing trail beneath my dress in his wake.

I seal my eyes closed, letting the wave crash over me.

"Tell me about the Dionysian ritual," I say, succumbing to the feel of his hands manipulating my body.

His forearm tenses around my waist. He sweeps my hair away from my shoulder, resting his mouth near the curved slope of my neck, his breath hot against my skin.

"How deep to you want to go?"

His question infuses my blood with a shot of panic. I'm wilting for him so I can snare him like a spider in a Venus flytrap. Only, my body makes my betrayal all too believable, even to me.

I force my words bold. "Make me feel it."

His low groan vibrates against my back, sending a shockwave of arousal through my system. "You wouldn't be fucking with me, Halen?"

Making Kallum question my intensions bolsters my resolve, and I swivel my hips provocatively, rubbing against him until I feel his stomach tense. Raising my arms, I link my wrists around the back of his neck as I grind against him.

"I want to know what you know," I tell him. "You know more than any search engine or FBI analyst."

The press of his erection along my backside ignites a flame in my belly, and a sliver of anxiety slices through the carnal heat—but I push back against the uncertainty.

"Be careful what you ask for, little Halen," he says, his voice thick with restraint.

Then his hands are touching me, testing me. His thumb skims the bottom of my breast, his fingers probe downward, tracing the seam of my panties along my pelvis.

I swallow the fiery ache, keeping my eyes closed against the flashing room. "Tell me everything," I demand.

"Pay attention." He clamps his hands to my hips, his fingers drawing the torn hem of my skirt upward. "To become as wild and uninhibited as the Maenads, one must pass an initiation."

"So the suspect was testing himself—"

Kallum threads his fingers in my hair and tugs, effectively silencing me. "My job is to regale you. Your job is not to think, to only feel and let the answers come." His mouth brushes over my neck, and my mind empties, unable to grasp my previous thought.

"They were feared yet envied," he says, swaying our bodies to the rhythm. "They were the raving ones who lived fearless and donned fawn skin and adorned headdresses of bone and ivy."

The mutilated stag appears in my mind. I imagine the suspect wearing the skin, his body drenched in blood. He's standing where the fire pit will be; that's why he set the fire— to offer the blood and wine in sacrifice. None of it was a countermeasure.

"The Freemasons recorded that this aspect of the rites was passed down to the Dionysian mystery school," Kallum continues. "Initiates wore a purple robe, and were crowned with ivy."

I try to think past the distracting feel of his hands roving my thighs, rough fingers grazing too dangerously close to the inside seam of my panties. An uneven breath slips past my lips. "I can google that," I say, making my voice firm. "Tell me what no one else knows."

His deep laugh thrums through my chest, digging in with an itch I can't scratch.

The swarm of bodies infest the energy of the room, and my body hums at a high frequency in response. Kallum curls his fingers beneath the shredded fabric of my dress, his thumb ring scraping my skin and eliciting a shiver.

"Possessed by the god's frenzy, the initiates gave in to their base, carnal desires," he says, his voice a husky rumble against my ear. "They danced freely, partook in wild orgies, gorged on wine, and entered a state of madness, where they reached an altered, primeval state of being." His mouth presses behind my ear. "They went mad with pleasure."

I mindlessly dance against Kallum, lost in a sensory of images as I visualize the offender in the throes of a passionate ritual. It's evocative...primal. Like a beast, he let himself go feral.

"Once this state was induced, they hunted. Animals... humans... In their frenzy, they tore apart their prey. They invoked and manifested Dionysus in the bestial form. They became the Horned Hunter, and they devoured and fucked like beasts."

My core clenches, and I involuntary roll my hips, seeking friction. Each pass of Kallum's hands over my body stimulates every erogenous zone, wreaking havoc on my nerves. I suppress a whimper as he grips my inner thigh.

"Then the initiates entered into the night journey, descending into the depths of the underworld. When they reemerged, when they *ascended*, they had been gifted the wisdom of the gods. Above man, above even the gods themselves, they possessed the clarity of the universe, empowered to obtain their every desire."

Immersed in the scene, the hoard of people disappear, and I no longer care about what they see, or any guilt or judgement. I'm all flesh and craving. I'm a lightning rod seeking the flame of his touch, desperate to sate the throbbing ache between my thighs.

"The frenzy is pure seduction," he whispers near my ear, and I can feel the lure, the corruption, to be drawn into the hedonistic pleasure.

Wrapped in Kallum's arms with the hypnotic music and raw, depraved hunger, it's the temptation to forget—to become something or some*one* other, with no past or history.

Stepping into the offender's shoes is always a form of escape.

Isn't that why I lose myself in the job?

To escape…to feel something other…

Yet, there's a line I can't cross.

Kallum is too intelligent not to discern this. He knows the precise buttons to push to entice me right over the line.

My head falls back against his chest, my mind adrift in a lurid haze, my body succumbing to his primal touch.

As his hand coasts higher up my inner thigh, his thumb abrasively grazes the sensitive folds shielded only by the sheer material of my panties, and I suck in a shocked breath. My body pulses in time with the flickering lights.

I clamp my thighs closed, trapping his hand. "Keep

going," I say, my voice shaky and barely registering over the climbing music.

I feel his growl rip from the deep trench of his chest. "You want me to keep going," he says, a taunt. "Or keep going..." He parts my legs and splays his fingers over my clit and lips. "How the fuck am I supposed to focus when you're soaking my hand through your fucking panties, Halen?"

His admission does something dangerous to me, and I feed off it, lost in a heated tangle of lust and uninhibited yearning.

Somewhere in the background of my mind, I register a sprig of regret. But the atmosphere is too intoxicating, and Kallum is too persuasive—and the desire for oblivion is too fucking irresistible.

I thrust my hand between my thighs and cup his fingers, undulating my hips to push against his palm with shameless urgency.

"Goddamn." His growl gathers my muscles tight before he sinks his teeth into the soft junction between my shoulder and neck.

The sharp pain spirals through me, and I moan as it invokes emotions that have lain dormant, dulled by heartache. The piercing of his teeth overrides the blunt ache, and my body flares with the insatiable need to be touched—desperate for the fiery alchemy to meld pain into pleasure.

Kallum teases the frenzy from my soul, like a sorcerer cloaking us in a storm of licentious fury and madness, and as his fingers erotically knead between my thighs, I whimper, pulled under by the salacious feel, my body starved for what I've denied it for so long.

His mouth touches the shell of my ear, breaths heavy and sawing over the throbbing bite mark. "I'm going to tear through you like a ravenous animal."

His dark groan resonates in my chest, urging my hips to heave in the most tawdry taunt as lust burns under my skin. I'm so close to losing control.

Surender the pain.

Feeling pain is a choice.

The realization comes with a stark epiphany, the ability to choose to be lost to my pain, or to surrender to pleasure. The maddening chaos delivers clarity.

"Oh, my god," I say, shuddering as Kallum's thumb ring sweeps over my nipple, causing me to almost break. My core clenches, my lower back arches, and I sinfully spread my thighs as the intense pull steals my breath.

But the fight to maintain clarity burns through the haze. "I know why he's stalling," I say, "why he's not done."

Kallum's hand winds into my hair and grasps at the roots, and the feel is so seductive, the pleasure so addictive that I realize…

The offender is lost to pleasure. He seduced himself into a state of perpetual frenzy.

"Why suffer a painful ascension when you can fulfill every desire, experience every pleasure?" I ask aloud. Nietzsche claimed the path to ascension was through pain. That's why the worthy are so few.

The suspect is questioning his worthiness.

As Kallum rocks our bodies in sync, I mentally comb over my notes. "He's been seduced by the herd," I say, following the logic. "He has to overcome his bodily desires, but if he can't..." I trail off at the sensual feel of Kallum's hand collaring my neck from behind.

The eyes. The ears. The dismembered body parts appearing in the marsh.

He's working up to his ultimate sacrifice.

Kallum's violent growl proceeds the stab of his rock-hard cock against my ass. "Save it for your profile," he says, then he twirls me around, bringing my chest flush against his. His hand captures my face in a commanding grip. "I want to taste your frenzy."

Desperate to see his eyes, to see something past the bottomless abyss, I lift my gaze to his.

The room vibrates around us. As if in slow motion, our gazes collide. His penetrating eyes ensnare me, and I can't hide from him—I can't pretend what's happening between us isn't affecting me, changing me.

Kallum tips my face up. The cool press of his thumb ring against my chin clashes with the searing heat beneath my skin, and when he thrusts his hand under my dress and his fingers graze the seam of my panties, my teeth sink into my lip.

The coppery taste touches my tongue, and a growl unleashes from deep within his chest.

He smears his thumb through the blood on my lip, then brings it to his mouth. An uncontrollable tremor attacks my belly as he pushes against the barrier of my panties and licks my blood from his thumb at the same time.

"I knew your pain would taste sweet."

"You're a monster," I say.

His tongue sweeps his lips, and the volatile intensity I glimpse there—the insatiable hunger—nearly levels me as his gaze drops to my mouth.

"Whoever fights monsters should see to it they don't become one," he says, paraphrasing Nietzsche's infamous line. "But in my little Halen's case, I think you crave the touch of the monster as badly as the fight."

I push away from him, making it as far as staggering into a dancing couple before he seizes my wrist. I resist making a scene, letting him draw me back into his arms. My breaths tear through my chest as I restrain the urge to claw his skin.

My nails sink into his forearms, but this only brings a devious smile to his face.

His arm binds my lower back and he dips me low. Holding me angled beneath him, he devours me with wicked eyes.

Breath trapped in my lungs, the pressure builds until I'm forced to release it, a moan escaping as Kallum's hungry gaze consumes me. He brings his lips so close to mine, he inhales me right along with my breaths.

His eyes flick over my face, tracing a fiery path over the contours of my neck, then he slips his finger under the pendant resting against my throat.

"Tell me," he says, staring at the teardrop diamond. "Did he make you feel this alive?"

The air vacates my lungs.

As if falling in a dream, the terrifying sensation prickles my skin, then suddenly I wake up before hitting the ground. The party crashes around me, reality snapping into focus, vivid and clear.

I push against Kallum's chest. "Let go—"

"I can't do that."

I wedge my knee between us and, before I actually hit the floor, Kallum catches me and brings me upright.

With a forceful spin, I windmill my arms and break out of his hold. I shove through the crush of bodies, unsure of which direction I'm going, but I get far enough away from people and music and the panic ripping me apart.

The hallway is dark and lined with locked doors. I try three before I find an open room, where I slam the door and press my back to the cool wood. I'm able to steal two unobstructed breaths before the door drives me forward, and Kallum's towering form fills the doorway.

He shuts the door, barring me from escape and muffling the music. The *snick* of the lock sliding into place detonates through the room and my body.

For every step he takes, I retreat a step backward, until my back lands flush against the wall. This is someone's bedroom. There's a bed and pillows and a desk—but there is nothing within reach to use as a weapon.

The dark is smothering and complete…except the blinking red light on Kallum's ankle monitor.

He takes another step forward.

His hands come up on either side of my head, barricading

me against the wall. "We're not done." His voice drops low; too deceptively calm.

"We're absolutely done," I say, instilling strength I don't feel. "I'm filing the paperwork. My private life is off limits."

He slams his hands against the wall, making me flinch. My breaths tremble past my lips on a whimper. "We're not *done*."

The dark pits of his eyes shut down any argument.

"When he died," he says, "did he take you with him?"

"Fuck you."

"No, sweetness. Fuck you." He takes hold of my hips and yanks my ass off the wall.

I drive my fists into his arms, but Kallum has my dress ruched up past my belly before I can put up a real fight. He grips the back of my neck and holds me in place as his other hand flattens against my stomach.

"Your fucking pain strangles me every day," he says, resting his forehead to mine. As the backs of his inked fingers graze my sensitive skin, my stomach seizes with uncontrollable tremors, my whole body succumbing to the violent attack.

"Please…" I try to reason.

"What are you *pleading* for?" He growls the question, his demand provoking reactive tears to my eyes. "What do you want?"

I don't know.

Pushing his mouth against my ear, he says, "Before I even saw you, I felt your pain. It called to me like a siren, my muse of heartbreak. I wanted to taste it, to feast on it, your pain is that irresistible. All I wanted was to drop to my knees and devour every last drop of you just so you could breathe…so I could fucking breathe."

My breaths are ragged, choking my voice. "You're fucking sick if this is what gets you off." Anger sears my insides, rising through the debilitating fear. "A soulless demon like you could never understand what I feel."

He slams his hand against the wall, so close to my face I feel the force ricochet through my bones. I shake from the force of it, tears spilling over my eyes. I'm angry and frightened and yet I want to *scream.*

"There it is," he whispers over my lips. His frenzied gaze hungrily tracks the tears, then he pushes in against me and drags his tongue up my neck and jaw, tasting my emotions, lapping my tears.

"I can taste your anguish like the spiciest curry," he says. "It's so goddamn delectable, it's driving me fucking crazy. I want to sink inside you and rut out the pain."

His admission stirs a visceral reaction, and my body responds against my will. I feel the heated wetness pool in my panties, and I press my thighs together to offset the throbbing ache.

Kallum moves aside and leans his forehead against the wall, his body corded tight around me. He plants the heel of his hand to my chest, fingers trapping the solitaire pendant— the diamond from my engagement ring.

On instinct, my hands go to my belly, trying to control the tremors racking my muscles. My knees buckle. The only thing holding me upright is Kallum's grounding touch as the unwanted memory cruelly breaks through.

The sound of grinding metal. The flashing lights of the ambulance. The doctor's stoic face as she delivered the news of Jackson's death and the loss of our unborn baby.

"Stop—" I say the word aloud, but I'm not sure who it's directed toward; me or Kallum.

He releases a laden breath as his hand travels to my stomach. He grasps my hand and pins my wrist to the wall with an unspoken command before he skims the backs of his fingers across the sensitive plane of my abdomen, provoking another hard shiver.

"Here's the truth of your pain, sweetness." His fingers tease the flesh of my pelvis. "Nietzsche believed the only way to achieve our desires was through suffering. Anything that comes easily is measured as mediocre. Any art, any passion, any great love"—he pushes away from the wall to capture my gaze "—is attained only through pain and struggle. Your beautiful pain is divine, and you still have no idea how much power you possess."

"You're not making any sense," I say, my voice trembling.

His chuckle slips over my flesh in a sensual caress, and he grabs my face in a brutal grip. His thumb swipes the tear tracks from my cheek before he moves to my mouth, clearing away the remnants of blood staining my lips.

"One taste." His gaze is on my mouth, and fear stabs my chest, knowing I will not survive if his lips touch mine.

Kallum drops to his knees. His mouth delicately brushes

my belly, trailing to my pelvis, before his teeth capture the border of my panties.

"Oh, god…"

"I will make you see god for damn sure." He drags my panties down around my ankles and notches his arm beneath the soft junction of my knee, spreading my thighs.

The feel of his mouth surrounding me, tongue delving between my slick folds, buckles my knees. He pins me to the wall as he tastes me. Fire blazes up my back as his teeth scrape over my clit before he sucks my lips into his mouth.

A broken breath escapes past the aching pressure in my chest and, losing my mind, I fist my hands in his hair. I buck against him, my body detached from all rational thought. I'm so close to falling over the edge…

Then suddenly the feel of him is gone, cool air caressing my bare skin.

I chance a look down to see him staring up at me with those clashing eyes, hellfire and maddening desire swirled within the depths.

He drags my panties up, slowly sliding them in place, then pulls my dress down. He braces his forehead to my belly, feeling the tremble of my body, before he stands. He backs away, his heated gaze still causing havoc to my body.

The red light of his ankle monitor flashes in rhythmic pulses, chasing the acceleration of my heartbeat, then sounds with a *beep*.

A smug smile pulls at the corner of Kallum's mouth as he places his hands behind his head. And waits. His eyes never leaving mine.

"We're far from done, little Halen." He licks his lips in warning.

The bedroom door breaks open, and three FBI agents tear into the room. Kallum's gaze stays on me as they apprehend him, cuffing his wrists behind his back. One of them asks if I'm all right, but I can't take my eyes off him. If I look away, if I let the spell break, whatever transpired between us tonight becomes real, and I can't face that yet.

Flames engulf me as Kallum is taken into custody and, despite my every attempt to cheat and deceive the devil, I danced with him. I wasn't just tempted by the flame, I stoked it into a roaring inferno.

Then I begged for the burn.

WILL TO POWER

KALLUM

The alluring sight of Halen's tear-streaked mascara tracking her beautiful face keeps me from completely losing my mind in the holding cell.

Apparently, Dr. Stoll Verlice didn't take too kindly to our ditching him. The monitor was already out of bounds, and along with his tattling report, the feds decided to make good on their threat to hunt me down like the FBI's most wanted.

It was worth it.

I bring my knees up to the bench and lean back against the wall, savoring the mental image of Halen. A fucking vision of my muse in ruin as she confronted her grief.

Goddamn delectable.

Her sweet taste clings to my tongue, and I'm not sure how I willed myself to stop when I was so close to tearing into her, to seeing her break…but stamina is a virtue I do value.

TRISHA WOLFE

You can't spoil your dessert with a hastily devoured meal out of famished desperation.

And *one taste* only whet my insatiable appetite.

Letting my thoughts roam, I probe the ankle bracelet. Tampering with the device sends off a signal. But like any manmade apparatus, there are always flaws in the design.

The loud *click* of the holding-cell door grabs my attention, and I drop my feet to the floor. Dr. Verlice shuffles into the room, followed by a rookie agent who looks too young to be out of training pants.

"Professor Locke," Stoll starts. "We have the matter of your misconduct to address—"

"Where's Halen?" I demand.

A faint, derisive smirk registers on his pale face. "Miss St. James is none of your concern," he says, setting binders on the only chair. "But I believe she's been removed from the case. She'll be leaving soon—"

I'm off the cot and in front of him before the rookie can make a move to restrain me. I have Dr. Verlice backed against the wall, my hand clamped around his throat.

"I won't be leaving this case." My voice drops to a lethal decibel. "Which means, we'll be roomies again real soon." I smile, my eyes drilling into his as he trembles. "And you saw how quick it can happen. They'll never even hear your neck snap."

The agent grabs my wrist, but not before I'm able to retrieve a necessary item from Stoll's jacket inseam. I allow the agent to remove my grip on Stoll and, as I back away, I lift my chin, my features carved in stone.

I keep my gaze aimed on the quivering doctor, waiting to see what he decides.

He touches his throat and coughs, but it's the wet mark pooling on the front of his slacks that makes me smile.

I glance over at the agent, then look at Stoll. "No one has to know," I say to him.

Humiliation blisters his face. Hurriedly grabbing his binders, he covers himself before he rushes from the room.

Smart choice.

I then look at the young agent, who is suddenly aware we're now alone. "Take me to the guy who thinks he's in charge."

The briefing is still underway when Agent Training Pants leads me into a room full of suited feds and team leaders from the local departments. A giant whiteboard is covered in a distressing amount of false information.

As I pan the space, I recognize Detective Emmons, the crime-scene analyst Devyn, and the two generic feds that have been shadowing me since I arrived.

Then my gaze lands on Halen.

She's seated in the back, out of sight, hidden away. As if she's already distanced herself from the case.

Agent Alister stops mid-sentence to look at me, his face bracketed in sharp angles to stress his annoyance. When

Halen glances up at the interruption, she's all I see—and I discern what's sheltered behind her twisted uncertainty.

Fear and lust.

The two most powerful, primitive emotions.

She hasn't had much sleep, as evident by the dark blotches under her widened hazel eyes. Temptation tenses my muscles, making it painful to simply stand here, when the urge to gather her in my arms and take her straight to bed is so damn demanding.

"Locke." It's Alister's displeased tone of voice that steals my attention away from her. "This meeting is for officials only. I'll deal with you momentarily."

Deal with me. A smirk slants my face at his condescending reprimand, and I tic my head in the direction of the whiteboard. "Satanic practices," I say, the sardonic question implied.

Alister casts a look at the board, then crosses his arms over his shoulder harness as he faces me fully. "Do you have something relevant to say, Locke? Something helpful? Because, as far as I've seen, none of your expertise has been particularly useful. In fact, since my team was able to interpret the symbols without the need of your *expertise*—" the derision in his voice, by gods "—the FBI is no longer in need of your or Miss St. James's services." He directs his attention on the agent beside me. "Remove him from the room."

The agent hesitates, giving me time to call Halen out of the shadows. "Do you agree with this bullshit, Dr. St. James?

After all, you did point out a huge oversight on the feds' part with the mutilated stag."

As all eyes turn to her, Alister levels the young agent with a warning glare. He doesn't like being called out on his oversights. "Get him out of my room—"

"I'd like to hear what Dr. St. James has to say." Devyn stands in the middle of the room. Surrounded by the members of the local department, she addresses Alister. "And, no offense to the feds, but this isn't your room or building. It's town owned, paid by our taxes."

Alister has gone furiously silent. Then, aiming a narrowed gaze on Halen, he says, "We have a lead in a neighboring town on an occult practice that delves into satanic rituals. This is where we're focused, and the profile only derails."

Devyn shakes her head. "I read the profile," she says. "As did my colleagues and Detective Emmons. We have three suspects—"

"The FBI still has jurisdiction over this case," Alister snaps. "No one is conducting any interviews outside of the Bureau's investigation."

"If you look for the suspect anywhere other than Hollow's Row, you'll waste precious time." Halen remains seated, but her voice carries over the room. She glances at Devyn and gives her an appreciative nod.

Devyn follows up. "No one is pissing around jurisdictions, but the feds questioned everyone in this town except the actual suspect pool." Her features draw together, conveying the weight of her next words. "And the fact is, Agent Alister, this is our family out there. Our friends. Our town. Our department should clear our suspects before crossing town lines. And for that to happen, we need very clear answers on what we're looking for. Not vague parameters based on data and speculation."

Hands anchored to his hips, Alister only nods once at Halen, giving her permission to respond to Devyn's request. My hand curls into a fist at his disrespect toward her.

Devyn seats herself and breaks out a notepad, clicks a pen loudly. "What about the occult link? What do we look for?" She directs her questions toward Halen.

Tablet in hand, Halen stands. "It's my opinion that the occult shouldn't be a focal point. Occult practices aren't sinister by nature. They're merely hidden from general society." Instead of giving this lecture to Alister, she turns her focus on Devyn and the locals, where it might resonate.

"The occult can delve into magick, Witchcraft, Wicca," she continues, "or it can even explore Satanism. However, it's man who's flawed. Man can take any spiritual concept, any higher wisdom intended to enlighten, and in his selfish vanity, greed, and desire for power, corrupt absolutely. We've seen it throughout history with world leaders and tyrants who destroy and kill in the name of a higher purpose or god. But it's man who is evil, not the practice itself."

Alister opens his mouth to interrupt, but Halen pushes on, undeterred.

"As far as the profile, the offender is twisting an ideology for his own vanity. He perceives Friedrich Nietzsche as something of a prophet, treating his philosophical work, *Thus Spoke Zarathustra,* as a guide and instruction manual, written for those deemed worthy to decipher the three stages of ascension into a higher being. The overman."

As I start walking toward the back of the room, Halen visibly stiffens, like my nearness causes her physical discomfort. I don't stop, and neither does she.

"The offender may be a loner, a recluse," Halen says. "Someone you don't see enter town often. He keeps to himself. He may not even live here full-time, keeping a temporary vacation home. This is because, as he identifies with Zarathustra, he's spent months or even years in solitude 'meditating' to become enlightened. He'll be friendly if approached, but it will feel forced, contrived. He views small-town life as mediocre, its people as lesser humans, because they're content to live without the suffering and struggle to obtain a higher purpose in life."

She's dug into the archives. While I was sitting stagnant in a wrinkled suit for hours, Halen was poring over research, tying up connections—connections she formulated while embraced in my arms as she submitted to our frenzy.

"He will be intelligent," she says. "Book smart. He may or may not have attended college, but he didn't graduate. His knowledge of Western esoteric sects and philosophy is self-taught. Somewhere in his life, someone important made him feel inadequate. He has a superiority complex, but loathes intellectual debates. He feels a strong link to the master philosophers and may even believe he's a reincarnation of one or many of them.

"But the most troubling aspect, and the reason apprehending the offender is crucially time sensitive is that, while he believes he is worthy of ascension into the overman, he has weaknesses holding him back." Her gaze darts to me briefly where I hover at the end of the row, and everything left unsaid and unfinished blazes between us.

"His doubt is manifesting into a delusional state," she continues, "where, if he can't conquer his fear, if he cannot overcome his weakness of the flesh, out of desperation he may turn toward a primeval alchemy, one incorporating human sacrifice, to achieve his goal." She takes a steadying breath as the weight of her words bears down on the room. "By sacrificing his victims to Dionysus, he will make himself less human, thereby separating himself from his mortal aspect and allowing himself to ascend and become other, divine."

But that's not the full scope of what she's come to realize. I can sense her holding back.

If we take into account the literal vein in which the offender is interpreting the metaphors, then it's not a huge leap from sacrifice to cannibalize.

Actually, it's not a leap at all—it's a bridge.

Zarathustra could only find characteristics of the overman among the herd. He sent those he referred to as "higher men" to his cave where he proclaimed these men were bridges to the overman. Then they feasted.

With the way Halen is avoiding eye contact with the locals, it appears she's drawn the conclusion that, maybe the offender is weary of feasting with his chosen higher men and he'll soon feast *on* them in order to take their overman aspects within himself.

"So this sick fuck is carving off pieces of people because

he's a weak pervert, is that what you're saying?" Detective Emmons asks. The sharp edge in his tone cuts through the tense room. He runs a hand down his unshaven face in an impatient manner.

Halen lowers her tablet, her expression somber. "Essentially, yes."

"And you're positive the victims are alive?" Emmons presses.

Halen's lips pinch together in a tight grimace. "I'm not the one to answer that question, Detective Emmons. I'm sorry."

While Alister directs the chief medical examiner to confirm his findings, I close the distance between us, sensing the muddled emotions within her. Today, her confusion is stronger than her grief, and it's draining.

I move to stand beside her and notice the suitcase on the floor. "You're not leaving."

Without acknowledging me directly, she slips her tablet into her bag. "I am officially done here." She delivers her point by slinging my words from last night back at me.

"No, you're not done. You're running. There's a difference."

Frustration seizes her petite frame, and she drops her satchel on the seat of the chair. "You're right. I am running. I'm running away from you, Kallum. Is that what you want to hear? Well, I admit it."

The accident report detailed Halen as the driver in the car wreck that claimed the life of her fiancé. I wasn't aware of her other loss, of her miscarriage, until last night. She didn't have to say it aloud; I read the painful truth in the way she touched

171

her stomach, the devastating pain that racked her until she could no longer hold herself up.

She's been running from that grief since the day she was released from the hospital. Concealing her scars. Hiding from her life, reality. Immersing herself so far down in her cases to escape the pain.

And now, to escape it once more, she's even willing to sacrifice the truth she so desperately craves.

"You're leaving without your answers," I say to her. "But we both know why that is."

When she finally looks at me, the depth of her resentment damn near flays me alive. I made her *want*. I made her *feel*. But my worst offense: for a brief moment, I made her *forget*.

And that truth hovers in the tense space around us, adding weight to her own self-deprecating feelings where, if she scrutinizes what happened between us too closely, she'll have to face the frightening realization of what she's capable of.

How will she rationalize getting off with a killer?

I hurt my doctors. I kill my rivals. I'm a delusional, psychotic serial killer. I'm a disturbed practitioner of chaos magick.

All she accepts as fact in order to reckon how she was manipulated into feeling a sick attraction to the villain.

I'm okay with being her sickness. I can even be her antidote.

Leaving all of it unsaid, she gives her attention to the front of the room, where the loud disturbance of Detective Emmons scraping his chair back gains everyone's notice as he pushes to his feet.

He straightens his wide police hat. "Then why the fuck are we just sitting here, listening to bullshit theories instead of interrogating every single possible suspect right now?"

Emmons makes his point by storming out of the room. A number of his colleagues silently follow after him.

Agent Alister regains control of the room and proceeds to update the whiteboard, then starts handing out personalized assignments. The whole while, I refuse to release Halen from my gaze, studying the way she blatantly avoids my presence.

"That was impressive, Professor Locke." Devyn stands opposite of us, a row of metal chairs before her.

"On your part, too," I say, still keeping Halen in my sights. "I thought I was the only one who got under Alister's skin."

I catch her smile in my periphery, then she directs a serious look toward Halen. "Based on what you said, I think we have a main suspect," she says to her. "There's this hermit guy who lives in a creepy gothic mansion on the outskirts of town. I know, not politically correct, but that's actually what people call him. Hermit Guy who lives in the creepy mansion. Since you owe me one, I'd really appreciate it if you'd come with me to question him."

Halen shoulders her bag, and I take note of how she hoists the strap onto her left shoulder rather than her dominant right, and the way she's buttoned her thermal all the way to the top.

Halen expels a breath as she faces Devyn. "I'm relieved my profile was of use to you," she says, "and as much as I want to help further, and I really appreciate all you've done,

Devyn..." She stalls. "I'm off the case. If I go with you, my presence will only hurt your investigation."

Devyn's pursed features convey her dismal acceptance. She shakes her head. "Fucking feds."

Halen gives her a fragile yet genuine smile. "I'll make sure Professor Locke can help you. He'll be of more use than me anyway. It was his expertise that built the profile, so he should be the one to help conduct interviews."

"That's not happening." Alister approaches, all bluster as if the two women standing here didn't just take him down a hundred pegs. "Childs," he addresses Devyn. "I've appointed a few agents to accompany you to your suspect's residence. They're leaving now."

With a guarded look, she nods to Alister. "All right. At least we're moving forward." She touches Halen's arm. "Thank you for all you've done to help."

"Good luck, Devyn." Halen watches her friend head off toward the cluster of suits before she starts to turn away.

"St. James, Locke, a word." Alister pivots, expecting us to follow.

Halen's gaze fleetingly touches mine before she trails behind Alister toward a glass-enclosed office.

After Alister closes the door, Halen removes a printed report from her satchel and thrusts it toward the agent. "Here is the final profile. Any required follow up reports will be issued to you through my department."

Alister accepts the report without looking at it and sets it on the desk. Then he taps his phone screen. A printer wakes and starts scratching out papers.

Halen grips the strap of her bag, uncertain. "As I'm of no more value to the case and my investigation of the crime scene is complete, I'll be leaving today. However"—she glances at me—"Professor Locke should still be considered a valuable asset and remain on the case, as his expertise will be needed to decipher any future crime scenes or discoveries."

"Like the discovery your department sent me just a few moments ago?" he admonishes, rubbing the back of his neck. "Apparently, your investigation isn't complete. Unless your updated profile takes into account the markings found beneath the reed grass. Or was I supposed to receive that update from you by telepathy?"

Halen raises her chin defiantly. "It was my department's discovery," she says, "so it went through the proper channels—"

"What markings?" I interrupt their exchange. "Why wasn't I told?"

Alister turns a riled expression on me. "You were in holding, and are not privy to every update. Only the ones I sanction."

"I wasn't talking to you." I give him my back, turning toward Halen. When she doesn't respond, I nod. "Because of the engravings. Turnabout's fair play, then."

She expends a lengthy breath. "I'm not that petty to risk lives. As Agent Alister stated, you were in holding, and I had already been removed from the case."

"You're no longer removed," Alister butts in. "I have a team of field agents already en route to the killing fields to start removing the reeds so the markings can be processed properly." He glares between us, giving us each a stern, reprimanding look. "Forty-eight hours. I want a goddamn real suspect, and you both have forty-eight hours to give me a name."

Glancing at the floor, Halen battles some internal struggle, then meets Alister's scowl. "Yes, sir."

My insides flame with the primal urge to make him bloody. She's not subservient to him.

As Halen heads for the door, he adds, "Oh, Dr. St. James, one more thing." She hovers in the doorway. "Since Dr. Verlice has given his notice and has officially quit the unit, you've been assigned as Locke's psychiatrist."

"Agent Alister, that is not my area of special—"

"Do you not have a doctorate?" He cuts her off, issuing his rhetorical question before he turns toward the desk printer. "Then put it to use. With the urgency of this case and time constraint, as you yourself underscored, we're utilizing all our resources."

Alister holds out the printed pages to us, a thin stack in each hand. "So we're all on the same page, here's the Bureau's official lab results."

Resigned, Halen accepts the report and exits the office, not giving Alister the opportunity to bark another command. I take my copy and curiously look it over.

• Organs and body parts were removed from bodies within forty-eight hours of discovery of the crime scenes. No signs they were stored or frozen. Denotes offender is holding victims in nearby vicinity of the crime scenes.

• No drugs or foreign substances discovered in organ and skin tissues.

• Stag/deer analysis. Inefficient volume provided and/or corrupted saliva in discovery for testing purposes. Casts prepared of teeth imprint to search in databases.

• Hemlock. Confirmed species: *Cicuta douglasii.* The cicutoxin results in delirium, abdominal pain, nausea, convulsions, vomiting, and severe seizures within less than an hour of ingestion, most often leading to death.

"You got something else to add, Locke?" Alister asks.

I fold the pages and slip them into the inseam of my suit blazer, then I let my facial features rest in their natural, callous state. Alister notices the difference in the shift.

"Why not spotted hemlock, the species of hemlock that killed Socrates?" I ask, reasoning. "Would be more historically accurate and true to the offender's theme."

Alister only stares blankly at me. "I'm not a botanist, Locke."

I nod slowly. "This species of water hemlock? It's the most poisonous, and one of the most lethal in the world." In other words, the offender deviated from his narrative for a reason. "I'd be careful who I offend in this town, Alister. After all, the suspect is most likely a local, and the locals are the ones preparing your meals for the time being."

His face flushes, anger protruding the veins in his neck. "You think you're smarter than everyone else," he says, gauging me with narrowed eyes. "I see how you look at her."

A current of rage simmers in my bloodstream, and I drop all pretense. "I see how you look at her, Agent Alister."

His jaw sets, nostrils flaring. "Get the hell out of my office."

I hold his incensed gaze with a smug smile. Then I leave, knowing we're far from done.

I reach the front doors of the building in time to catch Halen's low ponytail disappearing into the crowd of media camped out in front of the police station. She weaves a path through a throng of reporters, rolling her suitcase behind her.

Carving my way through the crowd, I catch up to her on the sidewalk. "I think I'm in need of a session. I have some issues to work through, Dr. St. James."

"I'm not your doctor," she says, picking up her pace. "That would be unethical."

My dark thoughts are full of how unethical we could be together.

I turn my thumb ring a few times, then: "Your profile didn't have any mention of The Three Metamorphosis." I glance over at her, she walks faster. "You didn't give the locals any of the details."

"They don't need all the details. That would only muddle the facts. They just need to know the description of the offender to locate a suspect."

"Aren't you curious about this suspect?" I ask, my stride matching hers.

She reaches the paint-chipped door of the hotel, and I open the door for her. She hesitates a moment before walking through. "Devyn is smart and capable," she says. "If the hermit is their guy, she'll know what to do."

"If it is him, he won't be at the mansion. You know this as

well as I do. He's already descended from his cave, he's walking in the steps of Zarathustra. There's only one way to draw him out."

"I'm not interested in any more of your methods."

"Because you're scared to confront the truth of what's between us."

Halted at the stairs, Halen stares at the patterned, threadbare carpet. Then she says, "There's nothing between us," as she picks up her suitcase and starts up the steps.

I wait until we reach the landing before I challenge her. "The taste of you lingering on my tongue says differently."

Her beautiful face flushes with the palest hue of pink. "I know your ego won't allow you to accept this, but you're not special, Kallum," she rebounds. "I've gotten carried away before while putting myself in the mind frame of an offender. And that's all last night was."

"You really do lie so pretty, sweetness."

Her features draw into a serious expression. "It was your goal to debase me," she says. "You wanted to see me squirm and to humiliate me. You got what you came here for. I got what I needed to finish the profile. So let's drop the acts now. We're working this case for another forty-eight hours, then it's over."

"Then you can run. Before that, though, maybe we should check out the markings at the crime scene. The ones you kept from me."

She turns toward her hotel room. "You can do whatever you want, Kallum. I'm going to get some sleep."

"And where are you going to do that?"

She reaches into her pocket for the key, muttering with a breathy curse she'd already turned it in at the desk.

I lean against the doorframe and hold up the room key I swiped from Stoll. "I have your key right here, roomie."

She directs a glance down the hall, as if considering her options, a weariness sinking her shoulders. Then she snatches the key from my hand. I enter my room as she enters hers, meeting her in the open, adjoining doorway.

"I prefer to fuck with the lights on," I say. "What's your preference?"

Hand braced to the doorknob, she says, "Goodnight, Kallum."

As she swings the door shut, I catch it, keeping it wedged open with my shoulder. A smile curls my lips. "Sweet dreams, Halen."

Heated tension gathers in the narrow doorway before I allow her to close the door. I hear the rattle of the chain as she slides the lock into place.

12

BRIDGE TO REBIRTH

KALLUM

I t may have been Chaucer who first penned the derived maxim on the devil making use of idle hands. After hundreds of years, the wordage has altered, but the meaning remains unchanged.

We're still blaming devils for our bad deeds.

While Halen slept, I occupied my idle hands with pilfering the necessary items for tonight.

Time is always the enemy.

The patience I've been able to afford ran out the moment I reentered my hotel room and Halen's sinful fragrance took a cheap shot to my gut.

The scent of her shampoo infuses the air like a toxin invading my bloodstream. Lily of the valley alluringly drifts under the doorway. Ylang-ylang wraps my senses in a chokehold. The violent assault grips me in a blind fury until

I'm forced to shoulder the conjoining door open, snapping the chain bolt off the hinge.

My chest heaves as I loom over the threshold, the sinew cording my bones stretched tight and muscles on fire as I try to rein in the vicious craving.

The bathroom light spills into the dark room, bathing Halen's curled figure underneath the sheets like a fallen angel.

With marked restraint, I throttle my craving and seat myself in the corner chair of the room. Hands braced on my thighs, I watch her sleep, listen to her breathy exhales. Her legs twitch beneath the covers and she flinches, releasing a soft moan. Her mind won't let her rest, even when her body is vitally desperate for it.

"Kallum…"

My whole body tenses at my name on her lips.

The wicked temptation to peel those covers away and slide between her thighs tears a destructive path through my mind, making me question my fucking sanity.

It's the lovely bad things that steal into our thoughts in the middle of the night and tempt us across the line between good and evil. Those torturously beautiful sins that provoke our deepest, most deviant desires. It feeds us in the dark, stoking a frail flame into an inferno we can no longer resist.

She is my flame.

And I am all but pleading for my muse to burn me alive.

As my senses run wild, I can taste her saccharine fear. Her muted scream rakes nails down my back. I can feel her pulse kick against my palm. My need for her is tangible. She's carved into my goddamn flesh.

The longer I watch her sleep, the stronger the urge to make my desires manifest.

My fingers dig into my thighs as I hold myself back. The slightest abrasive rub of my jeans over my raging cock damn near sets me off.

So when her eyes flutter open to remove the devious temptation, relief slams my body.

She doesn't react to my presence by flinging herself out of the bed or screaming. Even coming out of a fitful sleep, she's soft and pliant when she first wakes.

Her hazel eyes track over me as she becomes fully conscious. "How did you unchain the door?"

The tension ebbs from my constricted chest on a forced exhale. "A slab of wood won't keep me from you. What were you dreaming about?"

Sweeping the tangle of hair from her forehead, she eyes me with severe suspicion. Then she glances at the door to see the broken chain lock. "Sigils," she says, her voice a throaty rasp from sleep.

I inhale her punishing scent, nostrils flaring at her admission. "Keep going."

"A symbol started appearing on my body," she says. "All over. I don't know why or what it meant. Vague, like all dreams."

She pushes herself up against the pillow on the headboard. Her nightshirt stretches tight over her breasts. A sliver of her pink panties peeks above the sheet. My heart thunders inside my chest at the sultry sight of her.

"Where did the sigil first appear?" I ask.

A hesitant arch of her fine eyebrow, then she daringly draws the sheet down. My breath stalls in my lungs as she guides my gaze with her fingers. Across her belly, over her hip. My lungs burn for oxygen as she parts her legs and her fingers settle on the enticing skin of her innermost upper thigh.

"Here," she says.

Whatever control I had mustered snaps.

I'm out of the chair and stalking to the edge of the bed where, when I reach her, I have to fist my hands to keep from touching her. My breaths saw my lungs to escape.

An ember of fear sparks in her eyes, but it's not strong enough to snuff out the dark swirl of emotions fighting for dominance. Lust. Anger. Yearning to submit to the danger.

Resistance only heightens the hunger. The constant battle to keep our desires in check is a weary one, and when that sweet surrender finally takes us, the rapture is divine.

"What did the sigil look like?" Restraint coils tense muscles around my bones.

Her phone lights up to briefly steal her attention. She reaches for the device and reads a message. "Devyn says they can't locate the hermit suspect. She really could have went with a better moniker. But Alister's team has gotten onboard with the search."

I remove the phone from her hand, toss it on the bed. "You knew he wouldn't be found. You also know how to find him."

Her strained swallow drags invitingly along her throat as she pins me with a searching look. "I'm not playing these mind games with you, Kallum." She throws the covers aside and scoots toward the other side of the bed.

I grab her ankles and tow her back toward me, then flip her onto her back. A savage craving fires through my veins as I collar a hand around her throat. Fingers braced to the back of her neck, I press my thumb to the soft curve under her chin and, in one fierce move, draw her up toward me, angling her face right below mine.

Balancing on her knees, Halen releases a shaky breath. Her body trembles as I keep her where I want her.

"What did the sigil look like?" I demand this time, my voice fire over brimstone.

She blinks, her gaze flitting over my hardened features as her pulse riots against my palm. Tentatively, she brings her hand to my wrist and slips my sleeve back to reveal an inked design.

"Like this," she says, her voice strangled by nerves. "But there was a line through it. And I've seen your tattoos. I'm overly tired and stressed." Her swallow teases my palm. "Even if I wanted to know the meaning, you can't remember."

I use my free hand to unfasten the buttons along the placket of my shirt, effectively silencing her excuses. As I stretch the shirt open, her eyes drop to the tattoos, and her fragile breath caresses my skin.

Her shocked silence intensifies my hunger, and I bare my teeth as I clasp her hand and press her fingers to the sigil carved into my left pectoral—the design she saw in her dream.

She has seen most of the tattoos marking my body. Her

dreams could be a manifestation of her obsessive desire to name me the Harbinger killer and her overworked psyche. A rational analysis.

Yet, when our suppressed desires fight to surface, they seek to take shape within any outlet, like the destructive force of water as it creates a new channel toward the ocean.

"I carved this into my skin the night of Wellington's murder," I say. "I know the meaning and the purpose, because every fucking day it won't let me forget."

Her curious gaze burns through me as she surrenders. "What is the mark?"

"The sigil for my muse."

Her mouth parts, her hesitancy clogging the air between us. She doesn't probe further. Because if she asks, then she has to decide what to do with the answer.

Before I release her, I take something for myself.

Slipping my hand from hers, I roll her sleeve back. I keep her braced in my hold as I push the cuff up her trembling arm. This time, she doesn't deny me.

My fingers graze the rough, beveled scar tissue, but the injury she sustained during the wreck isn't what has my heart thrashing my rig cage.

The scripted words tattooed over the scar read: *One must cultivate one's own garden.*

"It's Voltaire," she says, the soft cadence of her voice spilling into my head. "But you know that, I'm sure. It reminds me to stay in the present."

I know the line quoted from *Candide*—and I also know what that line means to her, and why it was imperative for her to brand it on her skin. To recite the mantra to herself every day.

Her dread is so tangible it scorches the back of my throat.

"If there was ever a philosopher to imprint on your body," I say, lightly tracing my fingers above the raised words inked into the scar, "this would be my choice for you."

Something daring flashes beneath her gaze, and I swear if she continues to look at me with those large pixie eyes, with the goddamn hypnotic rhythm of her pulse enticing me, I won't be responsible for the carnage I commit.

I move my thumb from under her chin and sweep the pad along her jaw, savoring this moment.

"Last night," she says, "when you said what you did…" She swallows. "Don't mock my pain, Kallum."

With my free hand, I lower her sleeve, letting her shelter this part of her grief, but I flip her necklace out of hiding from beneath her shirt. Then I trail my finger over the concealed bite mark on her shoulder. "Don't hide your pain from me, and I'll never shame you into hiding it."

Raw vulnerability leaks into her features. She rests her hand against my chest to regain balance. "You derive pleasure from my pain."

It's as much a question as it is an accusation.

A dangerous smile slants my face. As I tighten my hold on her once again, I lower my mouth next to her ear. "Don't psychoanalyze me, doctor." I pull back and drag in a searing lungful of her scent before I push in close to her lips to taste her broken breaths. "The very, very bad things I want to do to you…we'd both derive pleasure."

A shiver rocks her body and she licks her lips. The demanding urge to pin her to the mattress threatens to annihilate my feeble control.

Sensing the danger, she traps my gaze. "I can't tell what's real anymore."

I release a tense breath. "There has never been any *act* between us, little Halen. That is real. Everything between us…nothing has ever been more real."

The visceral lure of her gravity ensnares me, her pull too powerful. If she demands more, I'll open a fucking vein and let every truth bleed out—but she's still wary enough to know when she's teetering too close to the hazardous edge.

Fear crests above the depths of her silvery gaze and, dropping her hand, she removes her touch. I feel the force of the severed connection all the way down to my roiling marrow.

With a guttural curse, I tamp down the clawing hunger and release her. Taking a forceful step back, I button my shirt closed. The darkness of the room presses in.

"Less than forty-eight hours," I say, reminding her of our limited time.

She lowers herself to the bed and pulls her legs beneath her, offering me a tantalizing view of her panties to further wreak havoc on my pulse. I can still taste her from last night. That flimsy barrier dares me to tear through the material and claim what's mine.

I've all but scratched away her surface. Only a sheer veil remains.

She touches her neck, her thoughts pulled inward, before

she grabs the phone and taps the screen. As if flipping a switch, she slides into her comfortable persona where she believes her erected walls protect her from me. Then she aims the screen in my direction.

"An analyst in my department pointed out a shape in the reeds," she says, offering me the information I accused her of withholding. "A circle."

And like that, she slips through my fingers all over again.

Leashing my frustration, I give my attention to the image. It was photographed from an aerial view. The circle is clearly defined where the reeds have been broken to mark the ground.

Halen toggles to another screen, her demeanor growing impatient. "Alister's team posted an update confirming it's a ritual circle, carved in the earth by an unspecified object."

"A thyrsus," I say, giving her the specified answer. "The staff associated with Dionysus and his followers. It was used during ceremonies and rituals. So safe to assume your suspect made use of it, too."

She closes the tab on her phone and sets the device aside. "Could it have been used to string the eyes to the trees that high up?"

She's still reaching for logical explanations, a way to piece together the inexplicable and bizarre. Because that is what she used to do, who she used to be, before the solid earth beneath her feet crumbled.

"Halen, anything is possible." I smirk, recalling her claim during the trial. "Didn't you once state that?"

Her gaze darts away, a fragile awareness creased in her stressed features. She tucks the white forelock behind her ear and throws her legs over the side of the bed. "Then there's nothing left at the crime scene to connect."

I roll my sleeves up my forearms, my body still tense and flesh overheated. Caging my obsessive thoughts, I attempt to lure the spider with enticing prey.

"His narrative," I say, and she looks at me with a furrowed brow. "Connecting his story, that elusive motive. Isn't that what you look for in the scenes?"

Her gaze tapers warily. "I think I've already uncovered enough of his motive," she says, and I don't miss the double entendre directed at me.

I spin my thumb ring a few times. "An unhinged mind doesn't think linearly," I say. "He's moving through the stages by his own design. He'll be feasting soon."

Escaping my reach, she snatches the phone off the sheets and stands near the foot of the bed. "The locals know their suspect better than anyone else can." She scans through her messages, then grabs a pair of jeans out of her open suitcase. "Maybe it's time to follow their lead."

"Where are you going?" I demand.

She opens the adjoining door, the broken chain knocks against the wood. "I'm going to help with the search." She points through the doorway. "And you're going to your own room."

In less than two days, I'll be back at Briar. And she'll be out of my reach.

I reseat myself in the chair, earning an exasperated breath from her. "Kallum—"

"He stared into the abyss," I say, the gravel in my voice

reflecting my shortening fuse. "The narrative stems from the ritual ground. That's where *we're* going."

"Then go." She hastily runs her fingers through her hair. "Because if you have some information you're not sharing with me...either say it, or otherwise I'm going to help Devyn. I owe her."

A rush of heated fury zips through my veins. My jaw tightens as I watch her slip her legs into her jeans. She needs to be corrected about who she thinks she owes.

My gaze lingers on her sexy ass as she buttons her pants, and I drag in a searing breath to curb my impatience. "He gazed into the abyss," I say. "He stared death in the eye. Realizing this is all for nothing, that anything we do is pointless because it all ends."

She turns to face me. "Everyone realizes that at some point," she counters. "Not enough of a reason to justify a dissociation of this grandeur."

"But do they really?" I force eye contact with her. "We all have a vague recollection of our end. But how many of us truly face our mortality on a candid level where, once we know—once it infects our entire state of being—we cannot simply return to life as we once were."

She seems to take my words further inward, and the sudden worry of her slipping too far out of reach stalls my breath. "How does it end for Zarathustra?" I ask, shifting her thoughts.

"It doesn't," she says, reasoning. "At least, it doesn't end in a literal sense. He overcomes his final sin. Compassion...

pity. Then there was a lion and a lot of the author's vanity leaking into the prose."

My mouth tips into a slanted smile. She's not wrong; Zarathustra is a divine depiction of Nietzsche. Philosophers can't resist feeding their egos. But logic and rational deduction will only serve to frustrate her further. And it won't serve me at all.

It's time to start lowering the veil.

"Nietzsche advocated instinct over reason." Elbows braced on the armrests, I steeple my fingers together. "The 'will to power.' The belief that, essentially, our will alters the universe. Amid your offender's crippling fear of his end, his weakness of the flesh, he will cling to this belief."

She sits on the edge of the bed, dropping her head in her hands. "We're going in circles, Kallum. When I first read *Allegory of the Cave*, it was like falling down a rabbit hole. Yet he's incorporated every symbolism into his delusion." She blows out a breath and pushes her hair back, linking her hands behind her neck. "Everything connects. As if I already have the answers, all the pieces, but finishing the puzzle is like trying to link together over a million intricate pieces."

"Synchronicity," I state.

"But now I'm just exhausted." She rests her hands on her thighs. "No more rabbit holes, no more existential meanderings. I need facts. Or...I need to leave and let the case solvers do their job."

I narrow my eyes on her. "Running away is your default."

"You don't know anything real about me."

"I know things that would make your head spin."

"I'm trying to rationalize how to save these people—"

"You rationalized renting a car when you were leaving today," I say. "To go where?"

My question gives her pause. She looks to the door. "I wasn't sure," she admits.

"Neither of us have a place we belong." I cock my head. "Aren't we a fucking pair."

She releases a derisive breath. "Yes. A crazed, murderous fiend, and an apathetic profiler who lets him go down on her in the middle of an urgent case with lives at stake." She shakes her head, disgust evident in her drawn features.

I can't help the devilish smile that teases my lips. I stand and walk toward her. She keeps her gaze aimed on the floor, so I lower myself to my knees and cup her face.

"Falling through suffering is a descent into chaos," I say, savoring the feel of her soft skin. "It's the darkest obscurity, the ultimate terror. But the ascent out of the abyss reveals itself in the most tender moments."

Her gaze alights on me, and a kernel of hope—that rare emotion always so elusive amid true despair—flares in her eyes. If I could bottle the awe in her face, my ego could feast and never starve. But it's not her soft underbelly I'm a glutton for.

I sweep my hand to the nape of her neck and sink my fingers into her hair. I grip her hair and force her head back as I rise to my feet. Staring down into her face, I drink in the emotive fear crashing through her.

I flatten my other hand against her chest, absorbing the violent thump of her heart.

"That day in the quad when I approached you," I say, "you felt your heart race for the first time." Her heartbeat quickens in response. "That's what terrified you."

She struggles against my hold, her nails dig crescents into my wrists. "You twist everything—"

"That fire is really why you became infatuated with me," I press on. "Why you couldn't stop thinking about me, even when your career was in jeopardy."

Her fight stalls. Breaths ragged, she doesn't deny it.

"I could strangle you." I yank her head back farther. "Does that frighten you?"

She doesn't hesitate. "No."

My gaze drags over her features, assessing the truth for myself. "Death doesn't scare you," I say, "because you have nothing left to fear losing. You've stared into the abyss, faced your worst horror, and now you fear nothing at all."

She swallows hard, and the intoxicating mix of her lust and terror is the most potent aphrodisiac.

"Except me." I slip my tongue over my teeth. "You fear everything about me. The way I tempt you to lose control. The way I dare you to rattle the cage of that dark prison in your mind. But most of all, you fear the way I make you *feel*. That terrifies you so deeply I can taste it every time you look at me."

Her heart rate spikes, slamming against my palm.

"What do you fear, Kallum?" she asks, her voice breaking on an exhale.

My smile falls. "As if I'd give you yet another power over

me, sweetness." I *tsk*. "You'll have to solve your own riddles."

I remove my hand from her chest and touch her face. I run my thumb over her full lips with a reverent yearning so intense, my teeth grit against the need.

"The more you suffer, the deeper your pain, the more intoxicating your rapture." I wet my lips. "That's why the frenzy was so seductive to you last night, Halen. You've experienced hell. Anything above that is sheer, transformative ecstasy. It's Nietzsche's *rausch*. The path to the philosopher's stone. What your suspect so desperately desires."

"You are certifiably mad," she says.

"*Want* will drive you right into the maddening depths, I assure you. But you have to want with a fire, with a passion. The day you stop wanting, is the day you decide to die." A tense beat settles between us, the air thickening. "I know this, because I believed I'd never find my muse. Unfulfilled until the end came for me. Bored. Apathetic. Uninspired."

Worshipful, I trace my finger across her cheek. "But then there was you—and you sparked a ravenous desire, one I will drop to my fucking knees and grovel for."

The fear within her peaks, her defenses erecting to close me off. "You need help, Kallum," she says. "I should have left you in that hospital to rot."

A deep chuckle escapes, and I fasten my hand to her jaw. "Oh, you couldn't hop on that plane fast enough to get to me. You're in thrall to your obsession just as I am. There's nowhere to go, little Halen. No one else can give you the answers to the questions plaguing you."

The veracity of my words penetrates her obstinate defenses, and her expression opens.

"And the answers will be delivered my way because *you owe me*." I seethe the words, dropping them against her mouth.

With what restraint I have left, I release her, and she pushes away from me.

"Now, are you coming willingly? Or am I throwing you over my shoulder, gagged and bound?"

Her anger is a fiery whip as it lashes out at me. "I don't know if you're really insane or not, but you're a fucking sadist." With derision in her heated gaze, she grabs a hairband and ties back her hair in a low ponytail, then grabs her mud-covered boots from beside her case, decidedly making her choice.

Good girl. Although I'm admittedly disappointed we're not going with the former option.

As I head to my room door, I say, "Trusting my methods has gotten you this far. Dare to go all the way, little Halen."

"All the way down to the pits of hell with the devil himself." Her slitted pixie eyes slice me. "You asked me which one of us was selling our soul. I think you now have your answer."

A smile forms as I hover in the doorway. "The ninth circle welcomes you, sweetness."

She slips her feet into her mud boots. "You truly believe everything you say." She assesses me coolly, logically, through the lens of a psychologist.

"I've had some time to work through my struggle with

faith and trust. If you can't trust your own mind, then what can you trust, Halen?" I leave her with that as I dip into my room to gather the supplies.

The suspect and I have at least one thing in common: We both need a bridge.

For him, in order to overcome his pity for the higher men and do what's necessary to feed his unrelenting desire for self-deification, he must sacrifice them. Those he painstakingly selected. Those he may even love.

They are his bridge.

For me, I'm not here to save lives or this town. I'm not here to serve justice. I don't need a fucking bargaining chip.

My muse owes me.

And I'm here to collect.

My bridge will be built of blood and bone. Fear and unadulterated lust.

We sacrifice that which we love to obtain our passions.

Before I meet Halen in the hallway, I use a butterknife to remove the plastic covering of my ankle monitor. Breaking the circuit is what gives off the signal to send an alert. I bypass the circuit and unscrew the pins. I remove the band and set the bracelet next to the receiver on the dresser, giving myself free roam until the morning.

We're silent as we descend the steps of the emergency stairwell and exit on the backside of the hotel.

Halen removes the car keys from her pocket. "Once you finally tell me the truth," she says, stopping at the driver-side door of the rental car, "you're not simply going to hand yourself over."

I hold her gaze across the roof of the car. "The truth sets you free."

Mouth pinched in a hard line, she nods slowly. "Right."

She has never appreciated the honest answers I offer her.

"Here's one more truth for you to puzzle over," I say as she opens the car door. "Your suspect needs to feel threatened someone else is more worthy than him of ascending."

Tossing her bag in the backseat, she says, "And who would be more worthy...?" Her voice falters as the whole picture starts to come into focus.

With the crescent moon hanging in a sea of fiery stars above her, Halen touches the diamond at her neck as understanding dawns.

"You have to perform the rite," I say, confirming her suspicion. "Invoke Dionysus. Descend into the depths. Make your suspect believe you're closer than him to ascending into the overman. This will lure him out of hiding far faster than a search party."

It can only be her. Her pain and suffering is a siren's song to the lost. Her insatiable frenzy to reach divine madness elevates her to a celestial temptress.

"What are you going to do to me, Kallum?"

"I'm going to bathe you in a libation," I say, my blood heating at the mere thought. "I'm going to make you the ultimate temptation."

"You're going to sacrifice me." Her breathy allegation slips over my skin.

To effectively give us both what we desire, I will make Halen into a pagan goddess. Adorn her head with a crown of bone, pose her against a barren tree, right under a ring of moonlight, where I will bathe her in blood and worship her body before I devour her.

Seduction of the mind, body, and spirit. The sacred trinity. At the height of frenzy, I will take all of her.

This is *my* ritual.

The time has come to awaken my muse.

"No, sweetness. I could never sacrifice you. I'm far too covetous over my desires." I lick my lips with aching hunger. "You're going to ascend."

13

AWAKENING

HALEN

There is an abyss for us all.

Every walk through life shapes a chasm where our darkest fears and deepest regrets erect the walls of our tomb. Not the physical place where we'll lie and claim peace, but the void of our despair. It's far darker than any grave, and more terrifying than any physical death.

It's the utter certainty of our aloneness.

For all the love and happiness and connections we cleave to in life, such rare, blissful moments can only be experienced because of the suffering we bear. This was Nietzsche's core belief, and it's one I painfully accept.

Our abyss tears at our lives like demons ripping apart souls in the bowels of hell. That helpless pain is a torment so unbearable, we may even plead for the oblivion of death to end our anguish.

The suspect is weak in my eyes because of his fear—because he clings to his life, striving to avoid pain, so fearful of falling into obscurity.

But Nietzsche believed that self-overcoming could only be attained by suffering and solitude. There is no path to enlightenment but through pain.

His method to overcome his fear and pain was his own personal descent into the abyss of his mind—one which he never reemerged from, where he languished in the depths, his mind lost to madness.

Or was his madness an escape, a form of true enlightenment where he found a higher wisdom?

Reality is subjective.

I can't pose any elevated argument, but I can claim with cold, clear logic that acceptance of our demise is not a strength. Overcoming fear of death is not courage. It is not looking the monster in the eye and overpowering our fate with bloated ego to immortalize ourselves.

True strength is having the fraught will and calm surrender to accept our heartsickness, to awake every day and feel our pain, embrace our suffering, and choose to live in spite of our great losses.

I've stared into the face of death.

I've fallen to my knees and wept before the monster.

I've sank into the darkest chasm.

But it wasn't my death that frightened me; it was the loss of those I have loved most in this world that tore me into an endless, yawning abyss.

All the broken fragments of my life are filed sharp. The more I tried to piece them together, the larger the seam I tore.

My darkness stretches into an infinite void.

And that dark void of my soul is what beckoned Kallum to the jagged crags of my cliff. It called to him. He looked right into me and slithered inside.

I thought I was lost until the devil found me.

I crave the respite he offers from the pain, the numbing balm I feel in his arms that soothes the unbearable ache in the middle of my chest, and the blissful forgetting his touch brings, surrendering my torturous thoughts to the nothingness.

That is his sinful seduction.

And my sin is the desire to be seduced.

His evil calls to mine.

The temptation to *want*, to *desire*, to be alive with *passion* will stir my soul with frenzy until I succumb to his madness.

But, madness is more bearable than pain. Maybe that's the only wisdom Nietzsche uncovered.

And maybe that's how I allowed Kallum to slip in unnoticed, like a demon slipping into a dream and turning it into a nightmare.

That waking nightmare is all around me as I move from behind a tree and enter the ritual site.

The night sky is a soulless black that strangles the fiery embers of stars above the killing fields.

The reeds have been cleared away. Markers flag the perimeter of the circle. A ring of fire crackles in the center. The firelight dances on the planes of Kallum's face, shadowing the contoured hollows.

He is the grim reaper bathed in beauty and illusion.

Yet, as much as I'm remaining on this case out of the desire to do good, I'm not a martyr.

I *envy* the suspect. I am *jealous* of his delusion that offers even a moment of peace. If the option was presented to me to sacrifice one life to bring back my family...

My parents. Jackson. Our baby.

The damning truth is, I'm not sure I would make the selfless choice. I'm not standing in this field to save thirty-three victims from the abyss.

I am the fucking abyss.

I'm here to slay the demon taking up residency in my hollow soul.

I pull my bundled clothes to my chest as I walk toward one of the evidence tables. I feel Kallum's intense stare tracking me, then hear the rustle of his footsteps. I touch the diamond at my neck, close my eyes to take one moment of solitude, then I reach behind my neck to unfasten the clasp.

The abrasive feel of Kallum's fingers brushing my nape sets off a riot in my pulse. Hands shaking, I drop my arms and wait for him to remove the necklace.

The chain slips along my collar and, as he turns me around, he brings my hand up and drops the necklace into my palm. It hasn't left my neck since I placed it there after Jackson's funeral.

After the pitying stares, after the gossiping, hushed rumors of when I'd finally remove my engagement ring.

I curl my fingers around the diamond that's still warm from my body heat as Kallum regards me with heated eyes.

"The robe's not purple," he says, "but this will do. For now."

The white threadbare robe from my hotel bathroom loosely drapes my body, the belt doing a poor job of cinching it closed at my waist. The chilly night air touches every exposed section of my skin, clashing with the heat of the fire and torrent blaze in Kallum's gaze.

I turn to place the necklace on my folded clothes. "And when we're finally done..."

The snap of the fire cracks through the tension. He turns me to face him, lifting my chin and gaze. "Then we can both leave here satisfied."

His eyes are dark as flint. He embodies all that is unknown and feared in the night. And as he drops in closer, his woodsy cologne mingles with the scent of the fire to overload my senses.

His mouth hovers far too close to mine. "Are you ready?" he asks.

I only nod because, somewhere beneath the turmoil and unease threading my spine, I can feel the electric buzz—that same sensation I pick up on when I first enter a crime scene, like a nest of swarming hornets. The perpetrator leaves behind an imprint, his presence rooted in the soil and steeped in the air, so thick it's like trying to breathe through tar.

When you're attuned, you can see the stain left behind in time. You can even detect the vibrations of emotions, the way Kallum senses me, my pain a feast for his dark soul.

The vibrating current of the marsh wilts in comparison to the charged spark arcing between our lips. There's a force between us that is too strong to deny. I just don't know what it means, or whether I'm strong enough to resist its destruction.

I lick my lips, tasting Kallum in the smoky air, and his dark energy crushes against me as he watches the action with savage hunger.

He laces his fingers around mine, then leads me toward the center of the circle where the fire licks a seam between two realms. One a reality I've trusted my whole life, and the other a world of duality, where creatures of the night don masks and commit acts of debauchery to satiate their lust.

As Kallum releases my hand, I draw my robe tighter. The coarse material gives me something stable to hang on to as Kallum stalks to the gathered provisions.

The items he collected.

Proving he knew the outcome of tonight before he entered my room.

He may have even known the outcome before I sat down at that visitation table.

Once he told me his intent for the ritual, I could have ran. I could have filed the paperwork to send him away. I could have even told Agent Alister of my location, set my phone to record, and waited for agents to descend on the site.

And the only reason I can logically grasp why I did none of these things is the furious beat of my heart. The awareness that, one way or the other, after tonight, nothing will be the same.

For someone who has existed in a perpetual state of limbo, change is the most frightening idea…but it's also the most enticing.

I close my eyes and inhale the smoke-filled scent of burning reeds.

When I open my eyes, Kallum has the stolen necessities arranged on the ground around us. Carving knife. Bottle of merlot. The circlet made of the bones of a stag.

I stare at the circlet of pale bones. Woven by a vine of ivy, the brittle shards of bone form the base where the delicate and slender antlers of a fawn are twined.

The antlers Kallum took right off the wall of his hotel room, and the stag bones I passed every day that I trudged to this scene, never realizing until tonight they were always intended for me. Just as I never realized that, all those months ago, staring into the startlingly beautiful eyes of a madman, he was bound for me in the end.

Placing my phone next to the knife, Kallum increases the volume on the small speaker, imbuing the night with a rhythmic drumbeat. The languid flames roar to life in response, as if summoned by a kinetic force I'm too dormant to sense.

As Kallum rises to his feet, I feel the shift in tide. His gravity encapsulates every molecule, dominating the elements with his commanding presence.

He turns toward me and unbuttons his black shirt. His eyes are molten, reflecting the stirring dance of the fire. He removes his shirt in a vigorous yet effortless manner that rockets my pulse.

My gaze is drawn to his tight definition, to the leanly carved muscles mapping the planes of his striking body. As he moves closer, my gaze traces the ink that held me captive in the room tonight.

The skull of a stag resides in the center of his chest. The swirled antlers coil up his collarbone and crest the lower half of either side of his neck. When first I stared into those empty sockets, it was like the inky blackness of Kallum's soul was bleeding into mine.

But as he advances toward me now, my gaze isn't drawn to the stag—I'm breathless at the sight of the sigil for his muse, the design inked into the flesh over his heart.

Kallum pitches his shirt to the freshly upturned earth and grabs the bottle of red wine. His features are sharpened by the shadows as he approaches.

Uncorking the bottle, he commands, "Drink," as he tips the rim to my mouth in the same way he did at the party.

I tilt my head back as he pours. The tart flavor of fermented grapes slips over my tongue. I close my mouth to swallow and the wine spills down my chin. Using his thumb, Kallum wipes the maroon liquid from my chin and brings it to his mouth.

I blink back the memory of him tasting the blood from my lip. A turbulent mix of unease and heat swirls in my belly as the memory of dancing with him fuses with this moment in time, as if layering one on top of the other.

He licks the wine from his thumb, his gaze boring into mine. "I once thought your sweetness would dribble down my chin." He pushes in closer and grabs hold of the robe. "But it's more delectable on you."

I'm naked beneath the robe, a fact I'm made very aware of

as his hand slides along the thick collar and slips beneath. The backs of his fingers graze the curve of my breast, sending a sharp pulse of arousal between my thighs.

He pushes the garment off my shoulders, disrobing me in a sensual manner meant to imitate a ceremony. If not for the burning ember of lust in his eyes, this moment would feel sterile. He takes a step back, bottle held in his hand, to allow his gaze to fully—and shamelessly—wander over my naked body.

The feverish brush of heat everywhere his gaze touches sends a buzz to my head that has nothing to do with the alcohol rushing my system.

"I'm trusting this is how the rites were performed," I say, shivering against the chill raising the fine hairs along my skin.

"Don't," he says, his gaze tracing a deliberate path up my body. "I've never witnessed the rites. They're thousands of years old." As his gaze roves up to touch mine, his mouth steals into a smoldering smile. "Fuck, you're beautiful. A goddess to worship."

"You're making this up as you go," I say, accusation strengthening the weak tone of my voice.

He takes a step toward me. "I am, as should you. There are only carvings to demonstrate the Dionysian dance performed during rituals. No one can recreate it authentically. It's not about the steps or mimicking the rites; it's about embracing the madness. Surrendering to the frenzy. Experiencing the passion. Such as with chaos magick, no practice can be done wrong. It's the conjurer's belief in the power that charges the sigil."

Turning toward the fire, he gives me a moment to collect my thoughts. All this I knew about him prior to placing myself in this vulnerable position. What's more distressing is the uncanny sensation of eyes watching.

At any moment, an assembly of special agents or a media crew could wander up to the crime scene. But no—that's not a real worry. That would bring a host of uncomfortable questions, but I've faced far worse.

This is an eerie sensation I can't place, like the feeling I got when I first saw the creepy trees in the marsh.

The trees have eyes…

The proverb heightens my senses until the wine slides into my veins. My head sways with the heady rush of alcohol and steady drumming. And when Kallum returns carrying the circlet of bones, an intense perception of being outside myself comes over me.

I've felt this before. Similar to the start of a panic attack, but without the comfort of knowing it will soon pass.

"Wait—" I hold up my hand, then cover my breasts with my arms. "I need a minute."

I take three centering breaths, then scan the dark field. I can't discern any shapes past the hazy glow of the fire. The blackness engulfs the distant backdrop, making my heart rate climb.

He cups my face, pulling my gaze up to meet his. His breath steals across my lips in a tantalizing stroke that holds the threat of the unknown at bay.

"I won't let anything bad happen to you," he whispers over my mouth.

I swallow the forming ache. "You are the bad thing."

A crooked smile hitches the seam of his mouth. "And you are the loveliest bad thing." He drops a tender kiss to the corner of my mouth.

The wild beat overtaking my soul flays my defenses like the knife strapped to his leg.

With the pale crescent moon above as his guide, Kallum adorns my head with the crown of bones. He brushes my lock of white forward, his fingers sensually grazing my cheek. The weight of the bones and antlers bears down on me, the ivy tangles my hair.

Kallum wanted a pagan goddess for his offering, and that's what I've become.

"Antlers are worn by the initiate to make you more than human," he says, the steel blade flashing in the firelight as he brings it between us. "The higher you are to the sky, the more godlike you become."

I can't focus on what he's saying over my attention fixed on the knife in his hand.

"This whole scene is a sacrifice," he continues. "The deer is a sacred offering to Dionysus." He glances at the gnarled, barren trees looming overhead. "Trees are hallowed and given in offering. We're amidst a sacrificial monument."

"Just as I'm an offering," I say, covering my breasts again.

He wets his lips, his savage appetite evident as he grasps my wrists and shoves my arms down by my hips. "Our bodies are sacrificed through debauchery and gifted in praise, every carnal pleasure an offering."

Flicking his thumb over the blade, he moves to stand

behind me. A ripple of unease coasts my flesh, but there's also the flaring heat tripping my pulse as his hand brushes my lower back.

"Do I have to keep talking like a tour guide?" His voice dips to a seductive baritone that melts into my skin. "Or can we get right to the good part?"

His hand slips around my waist, and I try to relax against him. Give myself over to the feel of his strong body encasing me, his warm flesh caressing my skin with maddening friction —but I can't escape the image of the knife in his hand.

"When this is over," I say, "whatever you feel I owe you...we're done." My bold words falter as he sweeps my hair aside to expose my shoulder.

The pads of his fingers gingerly trace the bite he stamped there, the sensitized skin hot beneath his explorative touch. "Before this is over," he says, dropping a light kiss to the bruised imprint of his teeth, "you're going to beg me to fuck you right out of your mind."

He flattens his hand along the valley between my breasts and drags my body seamless to his. My body follows his lead as he rocks us in a furious motion to the fever pitch of the drums, coaxing me to dissolve under the swelling tide.

The abrasive rub of his jeans along the delicate skin of my backside is a torturous mix of pleasure and frustration, the hard ridge of his erection grinding into my flesh, straining to be unleashed.

The fire pops and sizzles in the open night air. The smoldering reeds send fiery flakes of ash up in a smoke signal like a warning. I'm swept into his arms in his dance of chaos and frenetic movement, and I realize that, as I'm lured further into the seduction, I was primed for this moment.

Kallum challenged me at the party to give in to my base desires, to let go of my inhibitions and submit to the frenzy.

His frenzy.

His mouth grazes my shoulder in sinful pursuit to reach my neck, where his tongue delves out to taste, teeth scraping in cruel teases as he advances toward my ear. The heavy pant of his breath caresses the shell of my ear, the sound erotic, the sensual feel lulling my eyes closed.

"Everything is connected," he says, persuading my hips to roll obscenely with his. "We're designed to feed and fuck and reproduce. Over and over. The eternal recurrence. But nothing in this universe is more connected than you are to me, Halen."

My heart rate soars, a heavy *woosh* fills my ears. Kallum releases me and walks around to stand in front. I still my body, waiting.

He guides me to my knees, the sodden earth cold against my skin. As he looks down at me, he inhales a deep breath, the skull on his chest rising in the firelight. "Touch yourself," he commands.

My mouth parts as anxiety bites my nerves.

Kallum glides his tongue over the seam of his lips as he openly eyes my naked body. "Either you're going to fuck yourself right now, Halen, or I'm going to fuck you."

He's aggressive, vulgar—and my body should not be responding to his filthy words, but the heat pooling between my thighs flushes my face.

As I tentatively slip my hand down my belly, Kallum

takes a step back to absorb the full view. At the feel of my fingertips descending over my clit, my hips involuntarily rock. Breathing staggered, I keep my gaze aimed on Kallum as I give him exactly what he wants.

He harbors no shame as he brazenly drops the hand holding the knife to his side and proceeds to use his free hand to rub his cock over his jeans. The sight is lewd and it sends a blistering shot of arousal straight to my core.

Undulating my hips faster, I arch my back, my fingers seeking the needy spot between my slick lips. The night cloaks us, enabling these depraved yearnings, and I can't deny how badly I crave his touch—how, when he lowers the zipper of his jeans to free himself, the sight of his thick, hard cock makes me whimper.

I bite down on my lip to stifle the sound, unable to take my gaze off Kallum as he fists the base of his shaft and strokes himself to the tip. My knees dig into the mud as I spread my thighs wider, driving the throbbing ache deeper.

With a feral hunger, Kallum bears his teeth and drops to his knees right before me, making my heart batter my chest. He reaches for the bottle and, tunneling a hand into my hair beneath the crown of bones, he forces my back to arch farther as he spills the wine over my breasts.

He dips lower and licks a blazing trail over my chest, down around my erect nipple, his teeth grazing the sensitive bud. My whole body ignites. Untamed need curls in my belly as I finger myself, his fire singeing my skin everywhere he touches.

"God, you're so fucking beautiful, perfect." His praise

envelops me in a heated current, dissolving all restraint as I become pliant to his will. "You make me fucking crazy."

Bowing my back farther, he tenderly guides a hand down my chest, discovering every aching zone of my body calling out to him. He dips me back, brings me forward, rocking us in a dizzying motion as the pulsing, demanding ache swells with need to be sated.

The feel of his cock grinding against my stomach is torturous, and I'm so wet and swollen my fingers slip and struggle to give my body what it needs.

"Touch me, Kallum. Inside—"

I'm not aware the plea has left my mouth until Kallum unleashes a fierce growl. His eyes blaze hotter than the fire as he draws me upright. Then he's moving behind me and pulling my back to his chest.

He pushes his hand between my thighs. The arched heel of his hand brushes along my slit, and my core clenches around the intense and almost painful ache. My body responds to the erotic sensation as wet heat saturates my folds.

Kallum glides his thumb ring over the sensitive flesh to provoke a moan. His low growl is a primal response to the feel of my arousal, and it resonates in my chest to trap my breath.

"Breathe." He issues the command and, as I drag in a hastened breath to fill my starved lungs, an image flickers across my vision.

Kallum's clashing gaze wide and staring into me.

Blood staining his hands.

Breathe *mouthed from his lips.*

Blinking rapidly to beat back the image, I reach for a stable breath to control the tremor stealing through me. The knock of the drums increases, and a surge of adrenaline rushes my blood. My head goes light, disorienting, as if I'm drugged.

Kallum's hands travel my body in frantic search, touching, groping. Desperate to claim all of me at once.

I roll my head along his chest, trying to latch on to some rational thought. "It's too much…going too far…" I reach up to remove the circlet, but Kallum traps my wrist.

He braces my arm along my hip, then the sudden touch of cold steel on my flesh fires through my body with a jolt of alarm. The blade flattens against my stomach, and my belly flinches with an instinctive tremor to contract my muscles.

The intense, resulting pleasure that clenches deep inside almost shatters me.

He releases my wrist to bracket his arm across my chest. Slowing our movements, he drags the blunt edge of the knife across my midsection. My adrenals flood my system with panic.

"Primordial pain unlocks our will," he says, his breath hot against my ear. "But fear exposes our most base desires."

The pressure of the blade is suddenly gone as Kallum holds the knife out before me. The glinting steel catches the firelight in a hypnotic wave to mimic the undulating flames.

Then, with an abrupt shift in position, he releases his grip on my shoulder and places his hand next to the knife. Clutching the hilt in one hand, he sends the tip of the blade into the palm of his other and slashes a deep-red seam across the center of his palm.

As the blood wells, the sight stirs a visceral reaction. My heart crashes into the cage of my chest, frantically beating in time to the climbing drumbeat. Shadows encroach along the edge of my vision and I start to tunnel under.

"Stay with me, sweetness." The command is delivered in a calm cadence that holds me bound.

He trades the knife from one hand to the other and slices diagonally across his palm, splitting the skin to allow a line of blood to flow free.

My lungs plead for air. The edge of my consciousness darkens, wavering as the Cambridge crime scene flickers like the fire in my peripheral.

Only I'm viewing it from the wrong angle. Glimpses of the victim's blood—bright-red and fresh—just as fresh as the blood dripping from Kallum's hands.

He proceeds to slice his palm twice more. Blood coats the hilt. Red trickles down his forearm. A haze of red layers my vision as he gently rests the flat of the blade across the fleshy swell of my breasts and commences to smear his blood.

His hand collars my throat from behind, and the warmth of his blood sinks into my skin. He savagely drags his hand from my neck to my collarbone, then grips my breasts, painting my flesh in his violence as he roves over my body. My skin becomes sheened in crimson that reflects the flames licking against the dark night.

"Kallum—stop."

Before panic can drag me all the way under, he sets me free and he gets to his feet. He walks around so he can admire his work. A beautiful smile overtakes his face and, it's so inviting, so captivating, I cave under its spell.

He leans over and grasps my neck, guiding me up to stand before him. He cups my face with blood-stained hands, and his thumb traces a wet path across my lips.

"We draw blood to feel alive." Lowering his head close, he brushes his lips in an infuriatingly light kiss over mine, sparking a current that demands a connection.

My skin buzzes with an electric pulse as our bodies draw together. "Tell me what you need," he demands.

The seams of two worlds bleed into one, just like our bodies are sealed together by a magnetic force too strong to resist—and the undertow drags me under.

I hear the echo of his voice inside my head. *Tell me what to do.*"

Panicked tears spring to my eyes, my psyche unable to handle the onslaught as it tears an outlet. I clamp my eyelids shut, cutting the tears off. And in the dark, the terrifying images flood in a deluge to assault me. They won't stop.

"Make it *stop*—"

"Beg me..."

"God, Kallum. Fuck me," I say. "Fuck me out of my mind."

A fierce growl tears from the hollow of his chest, detonating on impact as his lips crash against mine.

The kiss rocks through me, leveling my senses. His lips are reckless and unforgiving as his mouth closes over mine with furious, brutal abandon meant to punish me for some sin.

I link my wrists around his neck, yielding to the thrashing desire trying to claw through my chest.

He pulls back and devours me with his eyes. "Fuck... I'm going to tear into you, little Halen." Then he captures my mouth again and bites into my bottom lip.

Gripping the backs of my thighs, he hauls me into his arms. The knife hilt digs into my thigh as Kallum carries me toward the cropping of trees. Rough bark scrapes my back where he presses me against the tree, his body bracing mine.

His fingers seek my heated, wet folds as his mouth searches out the pulse point in my neck. The circlet shifts off-center as I arch against him, lifting my head to give him full access.

As his fingers plunder around my seam, he bites my flesh, drawing forth a throaty moan. I'm lost to the feel, vibrating on a charged current, all fear and illusive images chased into the shadows of my mind. And I let his frantic touches and feverish kisses hold them back like a dam.

My feet are placed to the earth while Kallum kisses me sensually, stealing the last dregs of my breath. I don't realize what's happening until I feel coarse rope bind my wrists... then my arms are wrenched above my head.

My blood careens against my arteries. I struggle until Kallum grips my jaw. His eyes—raging blue and green flames —hold me captive.

"For my protection," he says, and confusion draws my eyebrows together as he places another searing kiss to my lips before he backs away. "Trust me."

I don't. I can't trust him, not ever—but all too soon my

wrists are bound and tied to the tree, and I'm pushing against the tide again. The cuts on Kallum's palms are friction over my heated, sensitized flesh as he worshipfully caresses my breasts. He takes my nipple into his mouth, teeth teasing the bud and sending me back to the safe harbor of my mind.

The surrender consumes me. I'm trembling as he maps every plane of my body, painting my skin like it's his canvas. He lowers to his knees and pulls my leg over his shoulder to spread me wide.

I'm bathed by the moon and fire, wine and blood, adorned in bones—and a soulless demon is feasting on my flesh. But I've never felt so protected, safe, and I give in to the stir of frenzy.

My body rolls with the erotic flow of the current, my mind delving to where base desires flourish in the dark. As Kallum ravishes my body, the torrid flames ensnare me, until I feel the piercing bite of the blade break my skin.

Breath bated, I look down as he wields the knife to carve my flesh. My leg trapped against his shoulder, Kallum marks the uppermost part of my inner thigh right below the seam of my leg. The exact location I pointed out to him.

I moan through the pain. The sharp cuts send a shot of arousal to my core, slicing through the dull ache that encases me. I watch in shocked awe as he shapes the sigil with the tip of the blade—the same design he carries on his chest.

"You're mine," he whispers across the inflamed skin. "Come back to me." Then he licks the wound. His tongue traces the bloody lines of the sigil before he licks a path to the neediest part of me.

I close my eyes, my head falling back against the solid support of the tree. I let the wild emotions tear through me as Kallum licks and sucks and devours.

I grind against his mouth in shameless, brazen undulations of my hips. His fingers push inside me with no preamble, and I suck in a breath at the salaciously full feeling as my inner walls pulse against his expert, rhythmic plunges.

As his tongue swirls torturously over my clit, I turn my head to the side and pant against my arm. An intense pull in my lower back grips me, that delicious tingling webs over my skin, and I clench so hard around his fingers I almost break.

I'm so wet, I can hear the sound as Kallum removes his fingers, and I can't help but look down.

My breath stalls as a cold prickling sensation sheathes me in alarm.

The intensity of Kallum's hungry gaze meets mine as he pushes his blood-coated fingers into his mouth. The earth beneath me all but vanishes.

That's not possible.

I strain to see if it's the blood stemming from his palm or my thigh—but all logical deduction ceases when I see the trail of red dripping down my other leg.

"How—?" My voice breaks around the word.

"You're mine, Halen. You belong with me." His fingers plunge inside me again, his mouth stealing my fear as his tongue flicks over my swollen clit. He laps, sinfully devouring me and feasting on my blood.

Any rational thought is too far out of reach. I can't think about the accident or loss—*so much loss*—or the fact I was never supposed to bleed again. Not when Kallum is taking me to the edge, and not when the eerie sensation creeps through my senses and drags my gaze to the dark field.

His savage growl precedes his advance as he rises to stand, capturing me in a brutal hold as he grips the backs of my thighs. His pants are lowered, the need to be connected so demanding he didn't waste time removing them.

The smooth head of his cock notches against my soaked entrance. My core clenches in anticipation. The ropes cut into my wrists as Kallum lifts me effortlessly and wraps my legs around his hips.

A suspended second where our eyes connect, where I dissolve under the crashing wave of his heated, ravenous gaze, and he sinks inside me in one forceful thrust.

A cry rips from my mouth as he fills me completely, the fullness so intense a shiver racks my body.

"Fuck…you're perfect." His praise rolls into a harsh groan as he pushes deep inside, spreading my walls to take all of him.

The sharp bones of the circlet scrape my arms as I tense, my inner walls contracting to hold him within me.

His heavy breaths fall over my lips as he rocks out and thrusts in once more. His pace speeds, his biceps flexed in stunning taut lines that display his dark tattoos like his body is an art exhibition.

The stag skull moves and flexes with his increased rhythm, and I have the fierce desire to trace the curves, before my mind is pulled under the pleasurable current.

He secures an arm around my lower back, angling me

where he wants me as he fucks brutally, passionately, giving me what I pleaded for—fucking me right out of my mind.

No pain. No apathy. No dull ache burying me under my past.

I'm all blistering fire and honed pleasure and unadulterated lust.

Kallum clamps his other hand around my nape as he searches out the soft junction of my neck where he sinks his teeth. My body grinds against his in desperate need to heighten the friction until we combust.

A slur of profanities escape his mouth on a deep groan, tangled with a string of some old language my mind can't comprehend in this moment. But it does something violent and dangerously erotic to me, and I moan loudly against his ear.

He sucks at my breast, trapping my nipple between his teeth. "You're so goddamn perfect for me," he says, his gaze flicking up to snare mine. "These beautiful breasts were created for me. This fucking perfect pussy—" he ruts into me on a decimating thrust "—mine to destroy. Ah fuck, that's it. Take all of me." His thrusts speed faster, devastating my sanity. "I want to see how beautifully you come for me."

"Kallum—" His name is a desperate plea as heat snakes up my back, and every erogenous zone on my body lights up. My channel pulsates against him with the need for release.

Oh, god. I turn my head to the side, seeking a cool breath to douse the stinging fire—and the flash of yellow eyes amid the dark reeds freezes my blood.

The pending orgasm hurls through my spiraling fear as I

frantically search the darkness. The golden glow of eyes blink in pairs, dotting the perimeter. Then I see the branches move.

"Kallum…"

He grunts, hips bucking aggressively between my thighs to tear any lucid thought from my mind. My inner walls clench around him, driving him into a fury of wild thrusts.

As the branches shift in the reeds, I realize with a satisfying rush of relief they're antlers. Deer rustle in the marsh, their eyes flashing with firelight. Pure relief floods my system, and adrenaline rushes my arteries to send me careening toward the edge.

"Oh, god…Kallum," I cry out as the orgasm crashes through me, and Kallum is there to answer.

"Fucking see god, sweetness. You're mine. Say it," he demands as he stares into my eyes. He's all carnal sin and lust as he relentlessly thrusts inside me.

"I'm yours," I say, my voice broken by a moan as he ruts into me, stealing the last of my breath.

Kallum fucks with a savage frenzy as he claims me. Rock-hard and engorged, his cock pulses against my inner walls, and I feel the moment he breaks. His growl vibrates over my skin, taking me over the edge with him.

He lowers his head to my chest and bites the flesh of my breast, the pain tensing me around him and urging another orgasm as the pleasure peaks.

I ride him with needy rolls of my hips as he thrusts inside me once more, holding himself deep as the last of his orgasm throbs between us.

As I come down, I scan the field of flashing yellow deer

eyes and land on a giant set of antlers. The branch-like horns rise up from the reeds in a slow, eerie progression that prickles my senses.

Kallum's heated breath fans my neck as he pants, his body trembling with aftershocks. I realize I'm shaking, desperately trying to drag in enough air.

The antlers ascend higher above the reeds, reaching into the night sky.

And when I see the body creeping forward out of the reeds, fear tears a wild path through my chest.

"*Kallum—*" I shout, finally gaining a full breath. "He's here."

14

CHAOS OF THE HEART

HALEN

F ear can be a potent aphrodisiac. Fear heightens our senses, sends a rush of adrenaline to our heart. Every nerve in the body is stimulated. The onslaught of rousing heat fires into a frenzied climax.

As my mind comprehends the danger, my body clings to the moment of bliss—the pure, rapturous experience of a suspended moment where I exist on another plane.

"Oh, god damn." Kallum groans as my sex clenches around him. "That's it, sweetness," he coaxes. "Squeeze the fuck out of my cock. Let me taste that sweet fear." His hand collars my throat, cutting off my air supply.

Frightened tears spring to my eyes, and he licks the salty trail streaking my cheek.

Kallum's primal growl hurls me over the edge—even as I cannot take my eyes off the beast of a man advancing toward us. He moves like a disjointed demon. The closer he gets, the better I can discern his severe features. The black thread stitched into his eyelids. The massive antlers mounted to his shaved head.

The rapid orgasm spirals through me so torturously strong, my body trembles uncontrollably as it burns through my muscles. A turbulent storm of pleasure and pain swallows me when Kallum loosens his grip on my throat. I gasp in a desperate breath that shatters me from the inside.

Kallum pumps vigorously inside me to claim the last dregs of my orgasm. His cock pulsates against my swollen channel, and his hot cum spills down my thighs.

Above logic and reason, pain and suffering, all sensation exists in a cosmic vacuum of euphoria....before I'm clawed down into the darkness.

My system overwhelmed, I sag against the tree, my bound wrists on fire. I feel the throb of Kallum still inside me as his climax tapers. His warm breath drifting over my skin, he rests his forehead to mine, his muscles strained and skin heated as our pulses sync.

As Kallum draws back, his devastatingly beautiful eyes seek mine through the chaos. My heart aches from the intensity, from the way his face fills with awe as he gazes at me.

He licks his lips and captures my mouth in a brutally demanding kiss that constricts my heart. He tastes me in slow, sensual caresses before he breaks away.

A devious smile crooks his mouth as he hikes his jeans up

and takes a step back. "I knew he wouldn't be able to resist you."

A cold splash of fear hits me.

Adrenaline blasts my veins, the sounds of the field muffled beneath the roar in my ears. The stagnant marsh air chills my slick skin.

My gaze darts to the horned man. Bare-chested, his gleaming muscles bulge in the waning firelight. His booted feet *clomp* the earth near the fire ring. The skin surrounding his seamed eyes is inflamed. His movements are jerky and off-balance, hindered by his inability to see, but he utilizes his other senses as he progresses with deliberate steps around the sizzling hiss of cinders and heat.

The fine hairs on my body bristle at the inhuman sight of him.

The overman.

Kallum turns to gauge the intruder. "Fuck, he's big."

Yanking my wrists against the binding, I try to loosen the rope. "Untie me," I demand.

He spares me a quick glance before he lowers himself to the ground to grab the discarded knife. Relief uncoils the tension threading my spine as I wait to be set free, until Kallum sets off in the direction of the man.

My heart plummets.

I struggle harder to free myself.

Kallum's cut form stalks in careful, measured steps toward the center of the cleared circle where the dwindling fire provides enough light to make out the horned man's brawny build.

He stands opposite Kallum, towering by almost a foot. The antlers give him another two-to-three feet over Kallum.

He's not a monster, yet he is monstrous. He's a mortal man who believes he's invoked the horned god and has become divine in a bestial form. He exerts power and strength in every flexed muscle of his intimidating physique. His biceps are enormous. His thighs are sharply defined along his jeans.

Kallum creeps toward the offender, wielding the knife in a sure grip. The knife carrying our blood—the DNA evidence that will be left on the perpetrator and traced back to us if he injures him, or worse…

This man could be the only way to locate the victims.

The horned man shifts his attention in Kallum's direction, and my heart flips inside my chest.

"Kallum, *no*—" I shout, futilely twisting against the rope. "The victims."

I cry out as I tear one of my hands free of the rope.

Breath caught in my aching lungs, I watch Kallum take a swipe at the beast.

Angling backward out of reach, the horned man barely evades the attack.

My relief is short as a guttural roar is unleashed from the offender. I shiver, my blood icing my veins. The giant man brings his large hands together to trap Kallum's neck.

Hefting Kallum off the ground, the horned beast lifts him into the air by his throat with inhuman strength. The knife never makes contact as the offender throws Kallum to the ground with such force, I feel the vibration in the soles of my feet.

A scream wrenches from my gut. My vision wavers along the borders as the beast turns his fury in my direction.

Chest rising with my desperate attempt to fill my lungs, I rush to untie my other wrist. My fingers are numb and clumsy as I fight the knot, my wide gaze staying locked on the stitched eyes.

He charges straight for me.

My hand slips free of the rope and I drop to my haunches. Naked and shivering, I sink my fingers into the damp earth. The horned man with no eyes barrels forward.

His feet thump the ground in heavy beats, sounding louder and speeding faster than the distant drumbeat floating through his ritual ground.

As he nears, he staggers off kilter before righting and correcting course. I take advantage of his misstep and glance around in search of a weapon. Nothing within reach, I look down at my fingers dug into the mud…at the rope.

My vision flickers, swapping the sight with an image of another object in my hand.

A tire iron.

A jolt of alarm pierces the disturbing imagery, and I'm yanked back into the present as his roar shatters the nightmare.

I glance at Kallum splayed out on the ground. I'm facing the beast alone and, as he draws near, I don't think.

I grab the rope.

Stilling my breaths, I try to control the tremble of my

body. I don't make a sound as his booted feet enter my line of sight.

Slowly, I track my gaze up his large physique. He stares down at me with those empty, stitched sockets, his bare chest heaving. His nostrils flare right before he sways to the right.

I drag in a quick breath. I grip the rope.

He takes hold of one of the slender fawn antlers on my crown. He traces the curve of the bone with reverent curiosity, then inhales deeply as if he's *sniffing me.*

With a queasy tumble to my stomach, I realize what he's scenting.

My blood.

Warmth trickles down my thigh, and I squeeze my legs together. A tremor ricochets through my body, but I try to keep still. Confusion etches the man's chiseled features and he tilts his head.

He sways again and staggers, releasing the antler.

I don't waste time wondering what's wrong—whether he's intoxicated or wounded—I seize the opportunity to wrap the rope around his ankle.

Using the force of my whole body to dislodge him, I fall backward and bring the beast to the ground with me. Half his weight lands on my legs, pinning me to the earth.

A savage panic rises up from the shadowy trenches of my mind. The fear of being trapped—*helpless; attacked*—lights a wick of desperation and fury.

Coated in wine and mud and blood, I wrestle my legs from beneath and climb atop his chest like a wild animal. We are two horned beasts battling for dominance.

This man fears death.

That is my only advantage.

His massive body quakes beneath me as his hands flail in frantic search. I hunker low to his torso and secure the rope around his thick neck.

My vision goes dark. The fading embers of the fire cast eerie silhouettes against the veil obscuring my sight like a dreamy shadow play.

The obscured face below me flickers to the distorted crime-scene photos of the Cambridge murder. Like two movie reels have been spliced together, the scenes flip between two faces.

Villain and victim.

The rope gripped in my hands morphs into a tire iron.

Blood...so much blood.

I'm thrust out of the vision as I feel a large hand clamp my throat. I tighten my grip on the rope until my palms burn, and his roar rattles my eardrums. His hands throttle my neck, cutting off my supply of air. Pressure builds at my temples, my eye sockets ache.

Panic fists my lungs until I lose feeling of the rope in my hands—and I know I'm going to die.

I've never feared this moment. Even yearned for it when the heartache threatened to destroy me. So I don't understand why I'm struggling so violently against it now, terrified of never taking my next breath...

Cast by the waning embers, Kallum's shadow moves into my line of sight. Relief sails through me so fucking powerfully, tears spill over my eyes.

I search for him on the perimeter of my dwindling vision, and when our gazes connect through the strobing reel of my life, hope is strangled from my veins.

Kallum stands over the struggle with a calmness that chills my blood.

He's going to let me die.

The longer the seconds stretch, the more my vision blacks, the more I accept the outcome and the totality of my life. Then the flickering reel flashes a terrifying scene in such startling clarity, a muted scream claws its way past my constricted throat.

Kallum moves. Looming over me with features carved in brutal fury, he raises his foot and brings it down on one of the beast's antlers. The *crack* vibrates in my bones.

Dropping to his haunches, Kallum grabs the point of an antler and meets my eyes through the darkened haze. He thrusts the weapon into my hand.

One second where I register the weight of the bone in my palm, then the next I drive the point of the antler into the beast's jugular.

His hands fall away, and arms band my waist. I'm pulled from the mountain of the overman.

Legs thrashing and air raking my lungs, I search for a stable place to land. Pain radiates in my head to split my brain in two.

Kallum's arresting features materialize through the blinding pain. I cough and fall to my knees, where Kallum follows, his hands searching my naked body. He's saying something, but I can't hear past the pounding of my heart.

As the sounds of the hushed marsh drift to my ears and I slowly resurface, I draw in the crisp night, recognizing Kallum's touch.

"Breathe," he says. His bloody hands cup my face, and the feel of the cuts on his palms grounds me in the moment.

With concern slashed across his brow, he searches my eyes to make a connection, then he wraps his arms around me in a consoling embrace. I feel safe for a fleeting moment, until the memory shatters the illusion.

The memory of when Kallum first told me to *breathe* is so sharp, on reflex I push away.

In my mind's eye, I see Kallum standing in the dark. The dim light from lampposts illuminate his profile. He's holding my face between his palms, his clashing gaze trying to break through the fog.

There's a body.

My throat raw, I strain to talk. "Oh, god." My head whips around, the sudden fear of what I've done crashing over me.

Splayed on the muddy ground, the man's giant body is racked with tremors as he holds the broken antler lodged in his neck. The antlers that terrified me as they rose amid a field of deer spear the earth as he sputters and coughs. A foamy white substance bubbles in his parted mouth.

"I strangled him. I stabbed him." Acute terror punches my chest. "I *killed* him."

"No, you didn't." Kallum's sure voice draws me further out of my confused sate. "He was seizing before you attacked him."

The vile substance that leaks from the man's mouth

matches Kallum's claim. I drive my hands into my blood-matted, tangled hair. The circlet of bones lies on the muddy earth next to the convulsing man. I'm filthy and covered in dirt and wine.

And blood.

I still feel Kallum inside me. He's still so deep beneath my skin.

The present slams against the images in my mind, shaping a macabre scene that pitches my stomach.

Thoughts racing as fast as my heart, I lower my hand and stare at my palm, dazed as the memory of my nightmare crests above the ensuing anxiety. *The tire iron was in my hand.*

"He was as good as dead before you impaled him," Kallum says, ripping me out of my tunneling vision. He climbs to his feet and then hunkers near the suspect. "You're fierce, sweetness. But this brute is next level."

As I study the foamy substance coating the suspect's mouth, only one logical explanation breaks through my spiraling thoughts. "Hemlock poisoning," I say.

Kallum turns a guarded look on me. "That'd be my guess."

I stare into his eyes. "You..." I swallow hard. The tightness in my neck feels like hands still throttle my airway. "You made me stab him."

He hikes an eyebrow in amusement. "You're welcome."

He saved me. But first, he watched me nearly die.

Kallum stands and grasps the back of his neck. "Fuck, he shook me like I weighed nothing."

As my body accepts I'm no longer in danger, the adrenaline coursing my bloodstream begins to ebb, leaving me painfully aware of every wound and bruise.

Converging memories still fight for control in the space of my head. The two timelines bleed together until I'm forced to ask: "What is wrong with me?"

Turning his full attention on me, Kallum absorbs my entire state of being before he walks away, saying nothing.

I look down at the man again. He's no longer seizing. A ribbon of foamy saliva streams down his thick neck. His face is twisted in a horrific expression. He looks every bit a monster.

I recall when I told Detective Emmons that I'd seen a lot.

I've never seen or felt anything more terrifying than what I'm experiencing in this moment.

"He's dead," I say. Uttering a curse, I swipe a hand over my face. Every nerve ending in my body fires at once, eliciting a prickling sensation beneath my skin.

I can't process the ramifications right now. This man is the potential suspect Alister's team is searching for. And he's dead. Possibly poisoned by his own crop of hemlock. The victims are still out there.

Panic scrapes its talons down my spine.

I'm here, I tell myself. *I'm here in this moment.*

The sudden onset of the panic attack grips me in a vise, crushing my chest. My head is light and dizzy, and nothing feels real.

I touch my forearm. Feel the scar. Look at the script.

Reciting the mantra over and over inside my head, I start to feel my heart rate calm.

Focus on the present. Tend to my garden. Do the work.

He could have a clue on his person.

I swallow the painful ache in my throat and try to examine the suspect, taking note of his missing ear where a leather strap has been stitched to secure the antlers. The stitching on his eyelids is sloppy. Something feels off.

No—*everything* feels off.

Coarse material touches my shoulders, and I flinch. Kallum drapes the bathrobe around me. I didn't realize until just this moment how badly I'm shaking.

Because, even as I try to process being attacked by a terrifying beast-man, there is something far more sinister vying for my attention.

From the second Kallum sliced his palms and bathed me in his blood, flashes of another life—someone else's memories—started assaulting my mind.

I cross my arms and turn to face him. "Why am I seeing your memories of the man you murdered?"

It's Wellington's bloody and mutilated face that keeps surfacing to drag me under.

"Not my memories." Kallum stands before me, his expression grave. "You purged it from your mind."

A cold weight bears down on me. "For once, Kallum, I need you to be clear. To tell me the fucking truth. What the fuck have you done to me?"

"I said I'd be an open book to you," he says, his tone too calm. "I've never told you a lie."

Fury ignites in my chest. "Maybe you even believe that," I say, shouldering past him. "I need to call this in—"

As I take off in search of my phone, he grabs my wrist. "You asked me to charge a sigil on your body, Halen." The conviction in his voice draws my gaze to his. "I put it right here." He grazes the pad of his finger along the curve of my shoulder and neck. Right over the bite mark.

My chest rises and falls in frantic rhythm to the fierce drumming of my heart. "Your delusions have escalated." But even as the accusation hits the air, the images are taking shape in the dark hollow of my mind.

I shake my head, trying to force the imagery out. "You drugged me," I accuse, pointing to the discarded wine bottle. "You...somehow planted this absurd false memory in my head. You've done something to me."

Only the sharply filed pieces of the puzzle won't stop snapping together. They form so quickly, coming together to create a terrifying and morbid picture I can never unsee.

Kallum keeps hold of my wrist, his fingers pressed to my pulse point. "This happened to you, Halen. I was there."

My mind tunnels as the vision overlays the dark world around me. From a grainy black-and-white film, to a crisp, full-color motion picture with surround sound, it plays back in cruel clarity.

I swallow the acid burning my throat. "There's something missing," I say, my voice quivering.

"But you remember enough."

Glancing at my hand, I envision the tool from Wellington's car. The lug wrench from the backseat.

As the world tilts, I find Kallum's clashing eyes. *This isn't real.*

He lifts his chin, the contours of his face cut in serious edges. "I'd never seen a more beautiful creature. All fury and frenzy and passion."

"But how?" I demand. "How could you see me?"

"I'm the one who helped you stage the scene."

The flash of memory attacks. The blood on Kallum's hands. I blink it back, and the images flicker between the cuts he administered tonight and the red staining his palms in the dark…after he severed the head.

"Oh, god." I touch my forehead. My head is splitting in two.

Stomach roiling, I squeeze my eyes closed and wrap an arm around my waist, as if I can stave off the sickness.

"No. *No.*" I repeat the word, not believing my own mind. Everything is off. This is a dream. A goddamn *nightmare.* I bled tonight. I was *bleeding*, even though a doctor told me I never would again. "This isn't happening."

"What happened that day, Halen? The day you left the crime scene?"

His question reaches beyond the bounds of my anxiety and plucks the memory from the furrow of my psyche.

"What happened on that day in particular," Kallum continues, "to make you get in your car and drive twenty minutes away from your case and attack a stranger?"

The calming cadence of his voice centers me, and it feels like he's waited a long time to ask me this.

Despite my reflexive impulse to deny the allegation, I think back to that moment in time.

I was buried in the Harbinger case. I was *breathing* it. Delving deep. Because the alternative was to suffer the debilitating guilt of not visiting my parents' gravesite on the anniversary of their death.

But it had only been four months since I lost Jackson. And I was more alone on that day...more heartsick than at his funeral. I was raw. Bitter. Angry. And I couldn't escape. Everything was a reminder of what had been stolen.

Their alma mater was only a short drive away. I remember I had thought... I could visit their college, at least. That would be less painful than seeing their graves. They had met at a concert—a Van Halen show—and then discovered they'd been attending the same school for three years. That was their story. Their meet cute. The reason for my name.

I had thought of driving to the university—but I never went. I remember the gnawing guilt because I was relieved to be buried in the high-profile case.

Then the next day, I got the call about the Cambridge murder. A scene that would forever taint my memories of my parents and embolden me to take the stand against the murderer.

The memory is faded and fuzzy around the edges. I blink it away, finding Kallum's eyes. I shake my head, refusing to play into his psychosis.

"I didn't drive anywhere," I tell him, controlling the tremble of my voice.

A wisp of something dark and violent fumes in his eyes.

241

"You lie so fucking pretty, sweetness."

A chill coasts my skin, but then he draws me close to him. Despite the panic still flaring within me, I don't fight. His body heat is real, and it shields me from the frigid early morning, where I fear the daybreak more than the darkness.

He touches my face, gently stroking his thumb along my jaw. "You killed a man," he says, his terrifying words clashing with the comfort of his touch. "And then we staged the scene to look like the Harbinger murders. It was your idea. Out of fear or guilt or desperation, you pleaded to forget. I knew how to help you forget." He releases a heavy breath, his gaze absorbing me, his hands clasping my face. "Come back to me, Halen."

A collage of memories assault my mind, dragging me back down to the abyss…and I break out of his hold.

"I can't…" I swallow down the bile coating my throat. "This is…no."

I look at the dead suspect as a fresh wave of panic rises. "I have to call this in. I have to contact Alister." I lift my gaze to Kallum, my next words dredged from my soul. "And I don't know what the hell is happening to me, but I have to report this, too."

"No." Kallum issues the command with flashing eyes. "I didn't serve six months in a goddamn insane asylum for you to do that now."

I pull the robe tighter around me. My skin flames and pulses with every scrape, bruise, cut, and bite. I'm a walking map of evidence—evidence of Kallum and I together.

"Why would you?" I ask him, incredulous. Confusion

draws my brows together. "God, if you believe this, why wouldn't you tell anyone? That, right there, raises every doubt, Kallum."

He lifts his chin defiantly. "I wanted to protect you," he says, then he gingerly touches the sigil inked on his chest. "I had to trust that, if my will brought you to me the first time, it would bring you back. I had to have faith in the course. No matter where it led."

A startled laugh falls from my mouth. "That is insane. *You're* insane."

A snap of anger tightens his jaw. "And those who were seen dancing were thought to be insane by those who could not hear the music." He stalks right up to me and clasps my face. "You brought me the music, little Halen, my beautiful muse. And now you hear it, too."

I latch on to his wrists. "No Nietzscheism is going to explain away this madness."

He refuses to release me, and panic wells in my chest. Heart slamming my rib cage, I push against his shoulders until he finally relents.

Crossing his arms over his bare chest, he says, "I did what you asked of me. Against my own greedy, selfish nature that wanted to keep you for myself, because—for the first time in my goddamn life—I felt pain. *Your* pain." He eats the distance between us; I can't escape him. "I cut my finger and drew the sigil right here." He traces a design over the delicate junction of my neck. "Blood is a very personal charging method. But it was *your* will to forget."

I rake my dirty nails through my hair. "This is insanity," I whisper to myself. "What you're describing is dissociative amnesia...repressed traumatic memory... Or a damn psychotic break."

"Call it what you want, Halen. The terminology doesn't change the facts."

I look down at the dead body, then stare at the fire pit, where only the pulsing embers remain. The marsh is growing darker.

Darkest before the light.

Reaching for some rational thought, I march to the wine bottle and grab it off the ground, then pick up any evidence I see as I head toward the table. I snatch my bag and push everything inside.

I'll have the contents of the wine bottle tested. I'll have a toxicology workup on my blood. I'll take a fucking urine test —but I won't be pulled into Kallum's delusions.

"And when no reason can explain it away?" he asks, as if reading my rampaging thoughts. He locates his discarded shirt and shoves his arms inside the sleeves.

I meet his eyes—eyes that I willingly fell into tonight, that made me feel safe and worshiped despite drowning in fear. I craved his touch. I wanted his darkness to shelter me. I let myself go so completely...embracing emotions and sensations I've never experienced before.

With anyone.

That's what the darkness will do. Eclipse us in the deepest recess of our mind, where every aching desire and needy, devious yearning is hidden. Sheltered, concealed from our conscious, we give ourselves over to the seduction.

But light is always just moments away from spilling over our aftermath.

The wreck was my fault.

Kallum is my consequence, the ruin of my soul.

I hold his deceptively beautiful gaze with what strength I have left. "There has to be an explanation."

A dangerous edge carves his silhouette against the umber sky. The black eyes of the stag skull on his chest stare into me. I can feel the shift in energy, the tide receding from the shore too quickly.

He looks through me with the callous regard of a soulless monster. "Listen to our first conversation again," he says, a mischievous grin slanting his mouth. "You'll hear it quite differently now."

My blood stalls in my veins.

Dragging in a fortifying breath, I leave him to hunt down my phone. I find the device near the smoldering embers of the fire, retrieving it with trembling hands.

"What are you going to tell Alister?" he says from behind me.

Despite every fiber of my being revolting against Kallum's claims and the images still afflicting my mind, I have to declare everything that transpired here as part of the report. Which means...

"The Cambridge murder investigation has to be reopened and examined to uncover the truth." I light the phone screen and pull up Alister's contact. I tap his name before I lose my nerve.

"He's here." Kallum nods indifferently to the body of the

245

perpetrator. "But where are his victims, little Halen? I doubt he left behind a detailed map with X marks the spot."

Agent Alister answers the call and, as my gaze locks with Kallum's, I hit Mute on the phone. He's not done. He always has something up his sleeve, just like a cunning illusionist.

He advances toward me, his lethal form stalking me like prey. "If you reopen the investigation," he says, "I'll let them die, Halen."

Dread coils my body. Alister's irritated voice sounds from the phone speaker.

"I don't believe you," I say. "I don't believe you know where they are, and I don't believe you would—"

"Then you also no longer believe I'm your devil?"

Phone gripped tight, I glance between Kallum and the dead offender, an internal battle waging.

"You know I can find them," he says, his expression serious. "You'll *need me* to find them."

He's setting a game board where I don't know the rules. All I know for sure is, if he wants this so badly, then he has an endgame.

"No, Kallum," I say, grasping for strength I don't feel. "I won't need you for anything ever again."

"But there's your Freudian slip." He points out with a devious smile. "The locals need *you*. You can't risk the victims by leaving their lives in Alister's hands. And you can't save them if you're gone, awaiting a lengthy investigation. Those lives have little time left."

A searing anger burns my resolve. "You are the fucking devil."

"That you created, sweetness."

I lower my gaze to my phone and end the call. My sight snags on Kallum's ankle—on the ankle missing the tracking monitor.

There will be questions…too many questions I'm unable to answer. My phone GPS is logged by CrimeTech, and I can justify myself. But not Kallum.

I warily look over the crime scene, making a choice.

When I meet his clashing gaze again, I say, "Leave, Kallum. Go to the hotel. Just…leave."

I can't have my mistakes taint the investigation and hinder the search for the victims.

One of us has to fight for a soul.

"I'll wait for you," he says. A glimmer of vulnerability touches his eyes.

"Don't."

I realize that, once Kallum walks off this scene, he could disappear. He could vanish and never be seen again. I'm torn with how that possibility makes me feel—whether Kallum Locke disappearing from my life would be a bad thing or a relief.

Kallum holds my gaze with the severity of that very threat hovering between us.

I turn away and take measured steps toward my clothes on the evidence table and dial Alister again. When I turn back around, Kallum is gone.

15

HIDDEN WISDOM

KALLUM

Day drinking has its benefits.

Like, say, when an infuriatingly maddening scent is embedded in your pores, and the only way to gain a clear thought is to drink your wits away. Ironic.

I throw back a shot of bourbon and breathe out the fumes through clenched teeth, then nod to Pal. I point down at the shot glass on the bar.

Pal—the owner who also bartends at Pal's Tavern—gives the two special agents at the end of the bar top a wary glance before he grabs the bottle with a silver pourer.

"They don't exist," I tell Pal, trying to ease his worries of being reprimanded by the officials.

"Sure, buddy," he says to pacify me, but pours me another shot just the same.

The way I see it, Pal owes me one. This whole damn town

does. The proof of that scrolls across the flatscreen mounted above the rack of liquor bottles.

The ritual mangler of Hollow's Row has been caught.

Caught isn't exactly accurate, but I suppose the complete explanation is too long and complicated for the marquee bar. And honestly, whoever came up with that moniker should be eviscerated.

Pal turns up the volume on the TV when the updated news report starts.

The Hollow's Row task force has officially released the name of the deceased suspect alleged to have been responsible for the two gruesome crime scenes of dismembered body parts discovered in a marshland. The suspect, Leroy Landry, attacked an official while working one of the crime scenes earlier this morning. Landry died of complications during the attack. The official was taken to urgent care to treat injuries and is reported to be in good, stable condition. A new report from the task force announced Landry had the fatally lethal hemlock plant in his system. Further investigation into Landry is underway. There are no new updates on the whereabouts of the victims at this time.

I toss a sluggish glance outside the picture window. News crews from all over the country pack the narrow streets of downtown. Once the story broke, there was no holding back the circus.

Halen has been in a closed debriefing with Agent Alister for half the day. I was questioned briefly and released after the GPS data confirmed I'd been in my hotel room all night.

According to the FBI report I was able to obtain from my

tagalong agents, Leroy Landry, who, besides having an unfortunately boring name for a man that wanted to deify himself, was confirmed to be the local's prime suspect: the Hermit.

Did he become a recluse before or after he started altering his appearance to be so intimidating? The news report left a lot of interesting details out. The feds won't be able to keep the media ignorant for long.

Not only did a sweep of Landry's home prove his wine cellar was filled with wine-making apparatus, his home library housed a plethora of books on ancient Greek philosophy, Nietzsche, Aleister Crowley, and many other esoteric research material which can all be tied back to the profile.

And, besides having no eyes or ears, he was also missing his tongue. Which makes sense now as to why he was merely grunting and growling. Although, I was more impressed when I thought it was part of his dedication to the bestial personification.

Setting the shot glass on the bar, I spin the glass three times. Then I drive my bandaged hand through my hair and expel a breath. "Another," I tell Pal.

This time, however, Pal takes no sympathy on my misery. "You're cut off."

I push the shot glass to the edge of the bar. Just as well. Pal isn't giving me any celebratory drinks, just as the agents aren't buying. I'm not the hero. There are no heroes in this story. But since I don't have access to funds, this drinking session is on Dr. Verlice.

TRISHA WOLFE

I lay Stoll's credit card on the bar.

I'm not deliberately trying to drink her from my thoughts. That would be impossible. Obsessions don't yield so easily.

I'm just trying to learn to breathe without her.

I revel in the burn at the back of my throat, savoring it like I savor Halen's fiery fragrance that sears my senses more fiercely than any watered-down bourbon.

I was quite possibly delusional in my pursuit. I should have locked her up in the basement of my mountain home like a fucking lunatic and rubbed lotion on her skin until she accepted our inevitability.

But when her pleading hazel eyes—so full of anguished heartache—seared through me, she gave me little choice. She owned me in that moment. I sold my soul to my muse, the little fairy creature of myth, and I charged a sigil right on her flesh.

Did I believe it would work?

That she'd vanish into the night and forget all our atrocities?

There was just enough curiosity left inside me to say *fuck it, let's see what happens.*

Here's the truth of it: No matter the method of practice or conjuring—whether you're a believer or agnostic—it all comes down to the "will to power."

Nietzsche's mind over matter.

Or, as Aleister Crowley, one of Nietzsche's most devoted disciples, stated: "Every intentional act is a magickal act."

The mind is the most powerful form of sorcery in this world.

252

And I intentionally acted on my desire to will her into my life.

Maybe I gave the powers that be a helping hand also... But, as I've said, patience is not my virtue. Even the Fates need a nudge in the right direction.

My effort to unblock Halen by utilizing every trick I've picked up from a lifetime of study failed. Sex, blood, saliva, semen—the most potent combination—all employed to charge a new sigil, and yet her mind, and her will, remains stronger.

My muse wants to linger in the dark.

Feeling the burn of alcohol course my veins, I touch the bandage around my hand with a forlorn sentiment. When questioned about how I obtained the injuries, I told the truth— that I'd given them to myself. I am diagnosed with brief psychotic disorder, after all. There's never any reason to lie when people are willing to provide excuses for you.

They want the lie. The truth is too disturbing to accept.

According to the rumors I've been able to overhear from the bar patrons, the story is Dr. St. James was further investigating the crime scene when the perpetrator attacked. The attack left Dr. St. James injured and in a state of shock after she defended herself. Agent Alister noted the task force's efforts to close in on the hermit suspect is what drew him out.

Of course, Alister would take the credit. I'm sure Halen was all too willing to fade into the background. In the end, her profile was accurate, and the locals made the connection to the hermit suspect faster than the feds. Only they didn't realize how vital his ritual site was.

Did I know he'd show last night? No. Not for sure. It wasn't part of the initial design. But when you're asking chaos to answer your prayer, you accept the gift.

I did suspect the offender would be drawn out eventually, as there was one thing Halen overlooked in the tale of Zarathustra.

The sorcerer.

The corrupter of morals.

He presented a challenge to Zarathustra. The suspect would feel threatened by both me and Halen on his sacred grounds.

And yes, I may be the fucking devil incarnate for using Halen's extremely heightened emotions to try to break the seal of her mind, but if she was going to resurface, it had to be during extreme duress, channeling the frenzy.

Just as I'd seen her that very first night.

Walking the university grounds, immersed in her pain, luring me into her entrancing mystery.

Despite what lies she feeds herself and me, little Halen had a reason to be at my university as, on that day, on the anniversary of her parents' death, she was visiting their alma mater in remembrance.

Research is what I do.

I watched her. Followed her. Seeing her take a life brought *me* to life. So call it what you want. I don't care if she's a gift from the gods or the abyss—she's the muse that revived my dead soul.

Of course, at the time, had I known my muse would return and make me the prime suspect, and that I'd be charged with murder... Well, I might not have given in to her plea to help her forget so easily.

In retrospect, I should have left a note in block letters. However I did try to help her by hinting to Wellington's wife as a suspect. Instead, her psyche mistook the intensity of our connection as instinct to point the finger at me.

"I'm going for a walk," I announce.

I leave the bar, knowing the agents will keep up. With dulled reflexes, I dodge camera crews and reporters and true crime fanatics on my route toward the rickety bridge in the town's central park. The hotel is crawling with leeches, and this spot is the only place to get a moment's peace away from the mayhem.

The trimmed, bright-green grass of the common reminds me of the campus grounds I strolled daily in my previous life.

Admittedly, I was bored. With life. My career. Achievements. All of it.

Before she crashed my world, I was even contemplating a way out. Hell, all the greats had their untimely demises. No one fades out, pissing themselves in a diaper bound to a death bed and is remembered.

That's an eternal death sentence.

To be revered, first, you go stark raving mad, then you exit this world in a blaze.

I thought I was nearly to the point of acquiring my madness. Especially when, after the keynote speech where Wellington pushed all my hot, little buttons, I decided to carve a sigil in my chest and beg the universe to either bring me a muse, some reason to wake up the next day, or I'd go out in a blaze of philosophical glory.

Yes, I realize how overly dramatic I was. But unless one has battled the damning confliction of a brilliant mind, then one cannot commiserate the astounding torture monotony wreaks on that mind. I could never achieve that sort of blissful ignorance that comes from a simple life. I needed divine inspiration to exist.

So when little Halen washed up on my shores of despair, all fiery emotional damage and beautiful agony, my heart beat for the very first fucking time.

Passion lit a fuse of obsession.

Everything about her was new. Exciting. Dangerous. She had extensive knowledge. However, not completely surprising when, the very next day, she wandered up on the crime scene as a profiler.

The start of a dangerously intoxicating game. Our very own secret society of two with a shared, hidden wisdom.

Oh, there is more to the story of that night. How events unfolded. Details that will help Halen further shed light on her dark corner—but she will have to be such a good girl to earn those answers. I promised her I'd be an open book, and I have every intention of honoring that promise.

To the bloody, blazing end.

I brace my elbows on the wooden beam of the bridge. The winding stream below flows over boulders, tranquil until it encounters the hardened obstacle in its path. Even the destructive, powerful force of the water is thwarted in its mission at times and has to navigate a new course.

My blood heats as a fiery ember sparks in my veins. I can sense her like the tide senses the moon. Her gravity draws me around and, when our gazes connect, the breathtaking sight of her makes the dead muscle caged inside my chest beat.

A light breeze carries Halen's consuming scent my way to further entrap me, shocking me sober.

She's showered and wearing clean clothes. Her dark hair is styled in loose waves around her shoulders. The pale strands frame the side of her face. She's wearing a light coating of makeup. She had to make herself "presentable" for the meetings.

She looked just as goddamn perfect to me last night, bathed in our essences and covered in filth.

Her gait is hindered as she walks onto the bridge. She's favoring her left leg, her arm wrapped around her midsection. I imagine the number of contusions and injuries she's nursing, and the fierce need to carry her to bed and work her pain into pleasure grips me.

As she draws closer, I make out the bruising along her neck that she's tried to conceal under makeup. Knowing not all of the marks were put there by me sets my jaw. I fought the demand to slit Landry's throat as he strangled her, but that would have interfered.

Gaze aimed on the worn boards of the bridge, she says, "We need to talk."

I suppress the urge to touch her, force her eyes on me. "Let's go to the hotel," I say.

On instinct, her eyes clash with mine, and I see the fear

banked there. She tucks her hair behind her ear. "We'll talk out here."

A bite of anger snaps at my patience, but I relent. I eat the distance between us to bring her as close to me as this setting will allow.

She reactively takes a step back. "Kallum…"

"What's the verdict?" I ask her. "I know you're not scared to go for the jugular, so are we working together to save your precious victims, or—"

"You didn't run," she says, inhaling deeply to stabilize her uneven breaths.

"I don't run," I say. "Especially from what is already mine."

"So I took that into account," she continues, evading my statement, "along with your behavior on this case. Your expertise to locate the offender was valuable, and although that expertise could potentially help to locate the victims—"

"Tear the Band-Aid off," I interrupt her.

Inadvertently, her gaze drops to the bandage wrapping my hand. A hard shiver rolls through her body, and she crosses her arms. The sight of the rope burns abrading her wrists assaults me with a deviant desire. Flashes of her last night— bound and straddled around me—invade my mind.

She nods in the direction of the two hovering agents in the park. "They'll be leaving soon to escort you to the airport where you'll be transported back to Briar," she says in a rush. "Dr. Torres is making the necessary arrangements for your transfer to a new facility, as the contract for your services to the FBI stated."

"And the other?" I probe, my guttural voice raking the air between us.

She shakes her head, refusing to look at me for long. "Once the victims are located, I'll turn myself in and request a full investigation to be launched into Wellington's murder. I would petition the judge for your immediate release, as it was my profile and testimony that was responsible for having you committed—" her gaze pins me "—but your confession as an accomplice, along with the likelihood that the investigation will bring to light that all this is an attempt by a highly unstable person with motive for revenge—"

A harsh chuckle escapes to cut her off. I nod once, wiping my bandaged hand over my mouth. "I understand, Halen. No need to justify your denial to me."

She clears her throat. "It's just best if you remain detained until the full truth is uncovered."

Halen turns to leave, and I grab her wrist. "My turn."

A heated current arcs between us. No matter what muted color she tries to paint our connection, our canvas is splashed in red, and her soul is every bit as dark as mine.

"What about what you feel for me, little Halen?" I ask, noting the acceleration of her pulse against my fingers. "Can you logic that away, too?"

Her breathing shallows. "I can't," she admits. "But it's not an area I'll be exploring further. My feelings have no bearing on this case or the other."

"Then what about my feelings? What I've sacrificed?" I demand. "My feelings for you have no bearing either?"

"You *can't* feel," she says, her words slashing sharp as a

TRISHA WOLFE

blade. "You're a sociopath, Kallum. You're simply feeding off me like a leech. There's a difference."

She snatches her wrist free, and I'm relieved to see some spark of emotion flare in her eyes.

"Why do you think killers kill?" she asks, her voice strained. "To get the adrenaline rush, to break through the desensitized layer shrouding their emotions so they can feel anything at all."

"I've never felt more alive than with you," I say honestly. "And I never contemplated taking a life until *you*, Halen."

She shakes her head repeatedly, her body trembling. "Where's the evidence, Kallum?"

A cruel smile slants my mouth. *Oh, how fucking ironic.* "You're right, Halen. No physical evidence, no crime. Right?"

Her features fall as realization of what she's said registers.

Admittedly, that was a cheap shot on my part. But I have been incarcerated for over six months all because of her profile based on circumstantial evidence.

Let's just say, where Halen is concerned, if there was such evidence tying her to the crime, a certain tenacious person might be motivated to keep said evidence safely hidden.

A well-constructed contingency plan is another thing I hold in high regard.

However, Halen doesn't need all the details right now, just as she stated about the locals not requiring all the details to name their suspect. Details can get muddled. The mind can only process so much at once.

"I want you to think about this." Before I let her escape, I take her arm and purposely graze my fingertips over the

260

sleeve covering her forearm. "You inked your own sigil in script and you recite your affirmation every day," I say. "Where do you think your subconscious picked up on that?"

Her forced swallow looks painful. "Not everything needs a connection, Kallum. Sometimes, it's just our humanity."

I huff a sardonic breath. "There have been too many coincidences in this case drawing parallels to us. That's the universe bringing us together."

"And I wonder how much of those parallels and coincidences are influenced or even orchestrated by you? Six months is a lot of idle time for someone with the means to feed their delusions and obsessions."

"I love your witty devil reference."

She touches my hand, and I feel her fiery current through the bandage. "I think you're sick, Kallum," she says, her silvery gaze bleeding into mine. "But I think I might be sick, too. I hope you'll utilize your doctors instead of torturing them this time around to really seek help."

I am sick for damn sure.

But the only doctor who can remedy this sickness is pulling away from me.

"That's pretty patronizing coming from you, sweetness," I say, "but, you need to believe the lies, just so you can convince yourself that you didn't love every second of fucking the villain." I lick my lips, then push in close. Her broken breaths coast across my neck, and I wonder how long I can stave off the hunger.

"Maybe you're right," she says, putting distance between

us. "But that's even more reason for me to stay the hell away from you, Professor Locke."

As she turns away, I glance at the agents to gauge their distance.

I stalk forward and step in front of her path. Grasping her jaw, I look down into her beautiful face, those hazel eyes wide with fear and want. "You had your chance to walk away from me once, and the goddamn universe brought us back together. Now, there's no way I'm ever letting you go. We are the duality, Halen."

Her lips tremble and, as I grip her to me, I drag my gaze over her, absorbing the tangle of fear and lust inside her with a dark growl. I breathe in her sweet scent, then capture her mouth in a violent kiss.

A moment where she surrenders under the swell, her soft lips closing rhythmically against mine, before she bites into the kiss. The metallic trace of blood fills the kiss and, as she breaks away, I lick my lip and smile.

The agents apprehend me, pulling me away from Halen and restraining my hands behind my back.

"Time and tide... sweetness." I remind her as they haul me away. "And I'm done waiting."

16

THE DUALITY

HALEN

I touch my lips, feeling the hot pulse of Kallum's ruthless kiss. I can still taste his blood on my tongue. My heart beats erratically as I watch him being escorted away from the park by the federal agents.

When Kallum is placed in the backseat of the SUV, I finally haul in a full breath to fill my aching lungs and stagger to the bench before my legs collapse.

Every bit of strength I gathered to face him, to say the words I practiced, was stripped away when he pulled me so deep inside him. If not for the agents, I'd have given into him.

It's taken me until now to understand the draw Kallum has had over me since the moment our eyes collided. I have feared him because of that, because of the logic he drains from my mind like a siphon.

I lose more than rational thought around him—I lose the woman I once endeavored to be.

I can feel his gaze on me, and I purposely stare at the trickling stream until the black SUV vanishes from my peripheral.

Calming my senses, I bring out my phone. The rope burn on my wrist catches my notice, and I yank the jacket sleeve down.

The injuries I sustained were not easily explained during processing. I had to own to my "peculiar" methods of putting myself in the minds of perpetrators while investigating crime scenes.

I confessed to binding my wrists as part of my research into the offender's ritual. I confessed to cutting myself. Bathing my body in wine and blood.

In a degrading interview with Agent Alister, I admitted to using Kallum's blood as a medium to further explore the ritual, to which he drew his own conclusion of our relationship crossing professional lines.

I did, however, deny that allegation. Stating Kallum was a willing participant in my prep work, but he was not to be held responsible for any of my actions as, at the time, I was the psychiatrist overseeing him.

My record will take a hit. I may never be able to have my own practice.

The final result was the FBI director signing a waiver on my behalf, as my method did ultimately lure the offender to the crime scene. And it was Agent Alister's request that I and Kallum name a prime suspect within a tight deadline that prompted my extreme method of investigation.

Alister may have gotten admonished on that one, but he in no way suffered the same level of shaming as I did.

The catch is, I'm to give no interviews discussing my method or what transpired at the scene, and I had to sign a non-disclosure agreement to that effect.

The only small grace is Landry's death was ruled a suicide. The medical examiner concluded Landry asphyxiated due to the convulsions from hemlock poisoning. I'm sure the FBI weighed in on that decision. With the victims still missing, it looks better on officials for the offender to have an uncomplicated death at his own hands.

Even still, there was no measure that could have been taken to save Landry's life from the toxin. I've had to remind myself of this more than once.

Despite the waiver, the director of CrimeTech did dismiss me from my position within the company.

I'm jobless. Suffering delusional memories that haunt me every time I close my eyes. And potentially looking at a life sentence for murder—or being remanded to a mental hospital.

But first, before I leap off headfirst into any more abysses, I need answers.

Which is why I'm seeking those rational answers away from Kallum's influence.

Holding the phone to my ear, I wait to be patched in to Dr. Floris's line. When the doctor picks up, I hesitate a moment before asking her one of the questions plaguing me.

The endometrial ablation surgery I opted for after my

miscarriage was due in part to Dr. Floris's concern for my heavy bleeding, but was ultimately my choice after I decided I'd never become pregnant again.

There was discussions of other treatment methods, as she felt at my youthful age I may change my mind, but I was adamant.

"How?" I ask her on a shaky breath. I need at least one rational explanation to quiet the storm tearing at my mind.

"Halen, we've talked about this," she says. In fairness to my doctor, I was never very present after the accident. "There is a chance you can have lighter periods and even begin regularly in less than a few years."

"So what you're saying is, it's completely rational that I started my period."

Her hesitancy seeps through the line. I'm sure she's confused as to what answer will please me. After all, I did pay for an expensive surgery with the intent to stop bleeding.

"Halen," she says carefully, "you've been through a lot. You have a high-stress career. Your hormones fluctuate. And stress, along with many other factors can—"

"I just need a logical explanation for what happened to me," I snap at her.

"Yes," she says. "It's logical and even normal that you're experiencing a period right now."

The constriction in my chest loosens, and I abruptly thank her and hang up, not giving myself a moment to back out of making my next call. Before all of my authority is stripped away, I contact Joseph Wheeler.

I figure if he can get psychotic mental patients placed as

consultants with the FBI for high-profile cases, then he can help me pull some strings to gain access to Kallum's juvenile file—the sealed file only the judge was given access to during Kallum's trial.

I issue my request, giving a vague reason as to why I require access, and using my doctorate for the first time as a method of persuasion. The chances are slim I'll get that access, but I at least have to try.

As I head to the hotel, I keep my head down and gaze aimed on my phone as I try to avoid the press congesting the sidewalk.

There's another call I need to make, but I'm undecided, worried I'm not yet ready to unpack the answer. I swipe away Dr. Torres's contact and instead pull up my email.

To say it's difficult for a psychologist or any mental health professional to ask for a psychological evaluation is an understatement. And I'm not yet sure if Dr. Torres is the right call in that regard. His stellar reputation aside, I have more questions for him than answers, and I have to be able to trust the doctor.

I have my own theories. Either Kallum drugged me—or I had an acute psychotic episode due to a number of stressors. Recent death of a loved one. Anniversary of the death of loved ones. High-stress work environment. All combined with the severe sleep deprivation I was suffering at the time could explain an extreme episode.

Which, with how deeply I was invested in the Harbinger case, would logically explain the reason as to why I have patchy memories, giving a sociopath like Kallum the opportunity to slip beneath my weakened mental defenses. He had the motive to do so. Yet...

For every logical explanation, there is an equally illogical factor. There is also the fact an innocent man was murdered to contend with—but if I layer on any more guilt right now, I will snap.

I'll face all of my consequences in time.

Time and tide wait for no man.

I will surrender to time before Kallum Locke.

As I reach the hotel entrance, I spot Devyn in a silver Honda Civic parked along the curb. She waves me over, and I pocket my phone before I lean into the open passenger-side window.

"Get in," she says, her face animated and voice clipped.

"What for? What's going on?"

Her dark eyes pin me with disbelief. "What do you mean, what's going—?" Taking a forced breath, she releases her severe grip on the steering wheel. "Halen, if we want to beat the feds to the crime scene, we need to leave now."

A new level of dread tightens my chest. "Which crime scene?" I ask, my words measured.

"The scene discovered less than an hour ago." Her pretty features draw together as her gaze holds mine.

I push away from the car and glance around the town teeming with federal agents, media, crime zealots.

I could walk away right now.

Whatever awaits me at that scene... I don't have to know.

"Halen—"

Her urgent tone heightens my unease, and I duck my head into the window. "What scene?" I ask again.

"It might be another uncovered ritual site," she says, shaking her head. "I don't have a lot of details yet."

The vise around my chest loosens a fraction. That would make sense, at least. My profile stated there may be a number of practice scenes in the killing fields.

"Devyn, I've been fired," I tell her honestly.

She arches a sculpted eyebrow. "Oh, so you're freelance now?"

I stall. "I suppose."

"Okay, then you're hired," she says. "Officially hired by the Hollow's Row Police Department as an expert forensic psychologist...blah blah." She waves her hand impatiently. "However you want to phrase it. Now, get your ass in the car."

I don't think she technically has the authority to hire me, but I fear arguing with her. And despite every muscle in my body aching, a small part of me is curious, even elated. "Yes, ma'am. Oh"—I glance back at the hotel—"wait here for like, five minutes. I need to grab my kit."

I make quick work of gathering my supplies, which were already packed. What gives me pause is the bag I have stuffed in the safe. After a moment to weigh the potential consequences, I shove my anxiety down into the roiling pit of my stomach and remove the satchel, then I meet Devyn at her car.

"I can't believe you haven't heard yet," she says, flipping through radio stations on the dashboard.

"Fired, remember?" I stress. "I spent a good part of the day in debriefing getting my ass handed to me."

"Well, you're the one who had to go and be a hero." She sends me a tight smile, and I appreciate that she's trying to make light of a dire situation instead of interrogating me with invasive—and degrading—questions like others have.

I don't think I could handle lying to her right now.

But the truth of the matter is, there are no heroes. The victims are still missing, with no leads on how to locate them.

We pass a news crew as she maneuvers her car between two large SUVs. "Damn. The feds have already pissed all over the scene."

As she unbuckles her seatbelt, I say, "Wait."

Her brown eyes dart to mine. "Halen, we do not have any more wait time. Let's go."

Pulling in a steadying breath, I bolster my nerves and reach between my feet to grab the satchel. "I know I ask for a lot of favors."

Her abrupt laugh fills the car. "Are you serious right now?"

"Deathly." My pulse quickens as I glance down at the bag in my lap. "I need you to process some evidence for me." When I look up, her expression has sobered. "This would be of a personal nature. The results given only to me."

She hesitates a full three seconds before reaching across and taking the bag. "Keeping evidence from the feds?"

I bite the corner of my lip. "Something like that."

With a lengthy sigh, she pushes a button to open the trunk

of her car. "Then we should probably keep it out of their sight."

Before she opens the door, I touch her arm briefly. "Thank you."

"Don't thank me," she says. "I'm about to work my new expert consultant to death on this case so we can bring the victims home. You sort of work for me now."

A smile lifts my mouth for the first time today. "Lead the way, boss."

As we exit the car and look around the marshland, I realize it's a different access point to the killing fields. There's a boardwalk that leads through the reeds.

"Public hunting," Devyn says to me, reading my inquisitive expression. "Not that anyone is ever really fined for hunting anywhere they damn well please, but this keeps the reports on gunfire down to a minimum."

I nod slowly, my attention being diverted to a group of suits congregating around the entrance of the boardwalk. Agent Alister homes in on me right away.

His facial features reflect the provoked countenance he maintained for the better part of my debriefing. "No," he says, heading us off. "This scene hasn't been processed yet, and civilians"—he sends me a stern glare—"aren't getting access."

While Devyn duels with Alister over jurisdiction, I set my case down and stare out over the marsh, curious about the distance between this section of the killing fields and the ritual crime scene.

Then one word delivered from Alister drifts to my ears, and my whole body ices over.

Blood rushing my veins roars in my ears. Sounds are muffled to a low drone. I touch my chest, recalling too late that I somehow forgot to put my necklace on—and I can't calm my mounting heart rate.

My legs are moving before my mind catches up to my actions. I dip beneath the yellow caution tape and hit the boardwalk at a sprint.

"St. James!" Alister shouts.

His quick footfalls pound the planks behind me.

As I near the taped-off section of the marsh, the sight nearly levels me. I come to a full stop, breathing heavily through the pain tearing into my side. Alister reaches me, but he doesn't say a word. He doesn't touch me.

The crime scene petrifies me where I stand.

Between two gnarled trees reaching toward the sky, the intricately woven string creates a webbing to display severed tongues. They're strung in such craftsmanship, it's obvious who put them there.

The overman.

But that's not what has my heart battering my chest wall, and the terrified, angry tears threatening to fall from my eyes.

I fight the blurring offenders back as I clear my vision to take in every detail of the scene.

A male body has been erected amid the webbing of discolored tongues. The head has been decapitated and placed near the feet in the depressed reeds. The arms of the victim are staged in a manner to represent wings.

The face has been painted in black-and-white strokes to resemble the skull that appears on the back of the death's-head hawkmoth.

"The Harbinger killer," I say, my voice a weak rasp.

Catching his breath, Alister says, "You're no longer employed by CrimeTech, Halen. Therefore, no longer a consultant on this case." His use of my first name so informally states his feelings clearly. "Also, considering how closely you worked the Harbinger case before—"

"Dr. St. James's services were recently retained by the HRPD," Devyn says, cutting him off.

I can't stop staring at the victim…at the face of a skull. I've fallen through a wormhole.

Talk, I mentally will my mouth to move. *Open your mouth.* I can't fall to pieces right here. Not now. Not with what I've done… I can't let Devyn fight my battles.

"The fact that I worked so closely on the Harbinger case is exactly why my expertise is needed here." I inhale a fortifying breath, even as the ground beneath my feet all but gives way.

Devyn arches an eyebrow in satisfaction before she ducks under the crime-scene tape and claims a location to set up.

Bending over, I pull in a breath and close my eyes.

"Halen…?"

"I'm okay," I say, chewing back the bile rising to my throat.

Alister sighs. "It's been a long twenty-four hours. You've been through a lot."

A laugh falls from my mouth. And I realize how inappropriate my behavior is—but last night won't stop playing on a loop in my head...and now I'm staring at a new Harbinger killing...

Pushing the maddening thoughts aside, I thrust my sleeve up and read the words. I read them over and over until my head stops spinning.

I pull myself upright and lick my lips, still tasting Kallum. He's all over me.

Resigned, Alister releases a heavy breath through his nose and crosses his arms. Turning to face me fully, he says, "So we're working opposing sides, then."

I tear my gaze away from the crime scene. "We don't have to be."

My meaning resonates in his light eyes, and the sharp brackets caging his features soften.

"When..." My voice falters, and I try again. "How recent is this scene?"

He shifts his attention to his team marking evidence. "The tongues? Could be as recent as last night, or early morning. The victim...the medical examiner needs to declare that."

I swallow hard. "But likely before Landry went to the ritual crime scene," I say, surmising.

His silence infuses the stagnant air of the marsh, and I can feel the tension of what's not being said. His stance becomes even more guarded.

"What?" I ask, my heart beating around a dull ache in the center of my chest. "Alister. I've been working this case. I deserve to—"

"Landry didn't commit suicide." He hesitates before saying more. "More results are needed to confirm, but it's looking like the man who attacked you was not the main perpetrator. The injection sites found on his body weren't self-administered. Someone else had to inject the hemlock into him."

It takes a moment for this information to process, and I slowly nod. "He was a pawn," I say. Someone set him up.

"Or there's more than one offender involved," Alister says.

I realized something was amiss when I saw the sloppy stitch-work of the suspect's eyes. There was just too much to process, and too much hope. Something I should know by now only clouds reason.

The suspect who designed the ritual site—the person who intricately weaved the eyes to the trees and who has methodically staged the scene before me—would never have done such a careless job on their own eyes.

And that suspect is still out there.

I look up into Alister's wary face. "But that's not all."

With a heavy sigh, Alister reaches into the inseam of his suit blazer and removes a folded page wrapped in an evidence seal. "There's this."

Before I even unfold the page, I already know.

My hands shake as I hold the letter from the Harbinger killer written in block letters. After reading it over quickly, I lower the note next to my thigh.

"The original letter was found on the body." He mumbles something and drives a hand through his hair. "I can't believe there's two of these goddamn psychopaths running around now."

Dread knots my spine. "I think there always was."

"What?" Alister barks, his fuse short.

I shake my head. "There's something wrong with this town," I say, crossing my arms to stave off the chill. "I hate the trees."

He actually laughs. "Yeah, me too."

I slip the copy of the letter into my pocket and step down from the boardwalk.

As I near the victim, I can't take my eyes off the severed head. The face, the skull. But it's the bones protruding from the bald head that stalls my blood inside my veins.

Each antler projecting from the victim's head has been sawn off at the base.

The eyelids have been sewn together.

"He's missing his eyes," I say, sensing Alister's presence at my back. "And his ears."

"And his tongue," Alister confirms. "And he has fucking antlers adhered to his head."

This victim is one of the missing.

You know I can find them.

Forcing Kallum's voice from my head, I swallow down the acid burning my throat. "Has the victim been identified?"

"Not officially," he says. "But one of the local case workers did give us an initial ID."

I turn to face him. "Who?"

"Detective Emmons," he says, fixing his hands on his hips. "He believes the victim is his missing brother."

Oh, god. I look away and stare out over the wasteland of

reeds, at the eerie trees clawing the gray sky. At the evil rising over Hollow's Row.

As gravity falls away, I seek something stable to latch on to, and find Devyn's commiserating gaze across the marsh. She was right.

I brought something worse to her town.

"Thank you for including me in the updates," I say to Alister, somehow finding the strength of will to hold myself together.

The sense of standing outside myself crashes over me, the riptide dragging me out.

Alister nods, but then a menacing glint flashes behind his gaze, and he says, "I'm thinking of bringing Professor Locke back as a consultant."

I shake my head. Not in disagreement, but in disbelief. "Isn't that a conflict of interest with the Harbinger killer?"

His eyebrows draw together in a confused continence. "Locke was never questioned in regard to those murders. He was also found innocent of—"

"Innocent by reason of insanity," I interrupt, hearing the anxiety climb to my surface.

"*Hmm.* And yet you found him to be a necessary asset on my case." He pushes in even closer, his voice a husky, stern whisper. "Or was that just an excuse to fuck him?"

I turn flaring eyes on him. "Excuse me?"

His smile is smug, and he wets his lips. He trails his fingers across the small of my back, out of sight from anyone else. "If that's what you need to solve cases, maybe we can arrange something."

I step away from him, beating down the rising revulsion. "I'll confer with you when I have something to confer," I say, then I head back to the boardwalk.

With numb hands, I call my ex-field manager. Before Aubrey can start with condolences of my layoff or reprimand me for not going through proper channels, I say, "I want all of my files transported to the address I send you."

"Halen, I'm sorry—"

"Aubrey, send a zip file of my Harbinger case files to my email. Right now. Then send all copies of physical files to the storage facility address when I give it to you."

After a lengthy pause, he concedes. "I am sorry for what happened. It wasn't right."

The sound of a plane flying overhead draws my attention to the sky, and my heart constricts painfully in my chest. The sigil carved into my thigh pulses with a searing heat.

I feel his breath on my skin.

I smell the woodsy scent of his intoxicating cologne.

His touch heats my flesh.

Ending the call, I close my eyes. I inhale a calming breath before I march toward my case with my crime-scene tools.

I'm the only one who knows Kallum wasn't in his hotel room all night.

If there is evidence—even a fraction of a particle—I will find it.

I overlooked one crucial aspect of the story: Nietzsche's character that appeared near the end of *Zarathustra* to corrupt the higher men.

The sorcerer.

The liar.

I have never believed in a higher power. Logic is my deity. The universe didn't bring Kallum and I together—*he did.*

When Kallum told me that I had no idea what was within my power, I couldn't see past my pain, my obsession with him, or his beautiful, enchanting web to lure me into his game.

He was right; I had no idea. I showed him my withered petals, thinking I was beyond his sinister reach, that he couldn't inflict any more pain.

I was so lost and wrong. He has the power to hurt me.

That's a power I have to take back.

If Kallum Locke wants to play on a bloody game board, we'll play.

But I'm changing the fucking game.

EPILOGUE

LETTER FROM THE HARBINGER KILLER

The Overman cannot be allowed to ascend.

The Overman is not a gift to humanity but a death knell,
tolling the end of days.

The Overman will not bring enlightenment or peace. The
Overman's rising will commence the doomsday that will
befall every civilization and plunge humanity into an abyss.
This message is to the Overman: I *see* you. I have *uncovered*
you. I will eradicate your higher men one-by-one until you are
fearless enough to *face* me.

~ The Harbinger

Thank you, lovely reader, for reading my work and taking this
journey with me. It means the world to me to be able to share

my words with you. I hope you've enjoyed the start to Halen and Kallum's story. This book has been a labor of love...and madness. As we're revealing the details of a crime in reverse, there are more answers to come, more twists and reveals, and I hope you will enjoy every dark turn along the way.

You are why I write.

I'd love for you to be the first to get updates on the Hollow's Row series. **The best way to do this is by joining my VIP newsletter on my site TrishaWolfe.com**

You can also come hang out in **Trisha Wolfe's lil Monsters,** my FB readers group, where I share all things.

Keep flipping the pages to read a teaser of the *With Visions of Red: Broken Bonds* series.

Read madly,
Trish

Special gift to Trisha Wolfe readers! Click the link to receive a FREE bonus story featuring your favorite dark romance couple, London and Grayson, from the **Darkly, Madly Duet** .

We weren't born the day we took our first breath. We were born the moment we stole it.

~Grayson Peirce Sullivan, *Born, Darkly*

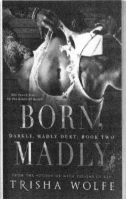

Meet Grayson Sullivan, AKA The Angel of Maine serial killer, and Dr. London Noble, the psychologist who falls for her patient, as they're drawn into a dark and twisted web. The ultimate cat and mouse game for dark romance lovers.

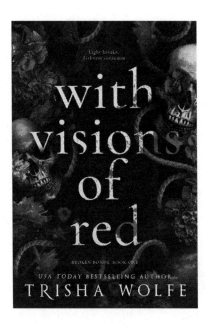

He knows her secrets. Her obsessions. The darkest, most deviant part of her soul. Plunged into a world of torture and suffering, pain and pleasure, Sadie Bonds and Colton Reed balance on the razor-sharp edge of two intersecting worlds threatening to swallow them as they hunt a serial killer.

COLTON

I watch her.

Since her first visit to The Lair months ago, I've been watching. Just watching. And she watches, too.

I assumed she was a voyeur. Only here to feed some curiosity, or feast on the sight of flesh and violence. But the longer I watch, the more I see it in her jade eyes.

She's hungry.

How she even got through the front door, I don't know. Julian must have been feeling charitable that first night. Maybe thinking the same as me—that she was just wanting to settle some curiosity. But here she is again. It's her MO.

I round the bar, tapping Onyx on the shoulder to let her know I'm taking off. Then I duck under the bar top, the beat of the house music thumping in sync to my ramped heart rate.

She hasn't been back for a while. Maybe two weeks. And I'm like a hunter stalking my prey, needing to get a long, lustful gaze at my conquest. Although, truth be told, I have no intention of making a move on her. She's too perfect. I just want to marvel, to watch as she watches, taking in her labored breaths. Her fingers clamped tightly around her flute of champagne.

I lean my shoulder against the wall and fold my arms over my chest and black T-shirt, letting my gaze travel over the room until it locks on to her.

This is just one room in the club. The voyeur. Set up with a stage and plenty of space for the audience to roam and play while each scene is enacted for the members' enjoyment.

I've wondered before if she ever visits the other rooms. If she ever visits mine…if she plays…but I'm trusting my instincts on this one. That, and the fact Julian has confirmed he's never set her up with a Dom or Domme.

Okay, fine. I've asked about her. Even against my better judgment and Julian's unwelcome probing into my life.

All my thoughts cease as the scene on stage begins. The music dies down, and in the sudden, stark silence, a low and melodic beat starts. The dungeon master walks a blindfolded woman onto the stage and commences strapping her to a St. Andrew's cross.

It's a classic scene, one that the sub requests each week. She likes to be flogged while a Dom frees her from her daily monotony as a CEO of some company. Then she prefers her master to go down on her as she climaxes.

But it's the first time *she's* been witness to it. And I move a bit closer, needing a clear view of her face as she watches. My heated breath coasts past my lips, slow and measured, as I spy her vivid eyes trained on the scene. Her lips parted, black dress clinging to the curves of her slim body.

Her chest rises with her sudden and deep inhale. The V of her dress teases me, the creamy skin of her chest hidden beneath a scarf, the round swells of her breasts just below, inviting.

From the corner of my vision, I see the flogger make contact across the sub's tits, and my pants tighten painfully as my target's hand goes to her chest. She caresses her smooth skin beneath that infuriating scarf as if she's been struck.

I slide my tongue over my lips as she crosses her legs. I imagine her thighs pressing together tightly, putting needed pressure against her clit, her panties wet. *Fuck*. I reach down and adjust myself. This is getting ridiculous, how much I crave this stranger, but she's not like the others.

So many tempting beauties occupy this scene, and though I've played with my fair share, and it was satisfying on a carnal level, I've never been entranced the way I am when I watch her.

What would it feel like to tie her down and discover what

she desires? For her to let me in and reveal her darkest fantasies? To extract her fears and inflict them on her, making her tremble, scream, *ache*. Then fall to my knees and gratify her as I worship my goddess.

The muffled cry from the stage cracks into my musings with the strike of the flogger, and I'm awoken from my trance, only to fall into my own form of torment.

I watch as my goddess becomes bold as the other members play around her. She snakes her hand up her parted thighs, under the hem of her dress. Her eyes shut against the scene as she touches herself.

Fucking hell. I'm going to come undone.

Yes, beauty. Rub that slick, swollen clit.

I reach down and run my palm over the rock-hard bulge pressing against my jeans. I feel the connection to her as she pushes her hem up enough for me to witness her sliding her panties aside, then I envision her trembling finger sliding into her warm flesh. Her eyes are clamped closed against the darkness, her breasts straining against the taut fabric, her nipples peaked.

I want to be there with her. Right there, when she comes. I'm tempted to yank my cock out this instant and beat the fucker off.

But my hand stills, my breathing catches in my throat, as a guy moves in front of my line of vision. Dammit. I'm already stepping closer to get around him when my feet stop. I watch as he lays his hand on her shoulder, then bends over to whisper in her ear.

My hands curl into fists.

If she welcomes his advance, I'm going to lose my shit. I won't be able to stand here and watch someone else give her what I know she needs. Fuck him. He hasn't watched her for months; he hasn't logged away countless hours discovering what she yearns for.

And he sure as shit doesn't know that she doesn't want to be touched. But I do—and I'm two seconds away from breaking his hand.

I keep watching, regardless. If she's ready to play, finally, I'll make sure she's safe. I'll watch over her, protect her.

She's shaking her head, trying to get away from him. She's rattled. He's not what she wants. She's here to watch, not play. She's not ready.

Relieved, I slowly back away. I'm pissed hot that he interrupted our moment, but there will be another. There's always another. She's getting bolder.

And so am I.

Only when I glimpse the distress on her face, her panic mounting, I immediately stop.

The guy touches her again, this time on her waist. He's leaning over her, trying to persuade her to join him. He grips her around one thin wrist and forcefully pulls her against him.

That's breaking the rules, fucker.

I'm storming toward him before Onyx can alert the bouncer.

His hand slides around her stomach as she pushes away from him, fear marring her gorgeous face.

"She said *no*." Towering over the guy, I bring all of my six-foot self forward, a dominant shadow cast over him. I haven't touched him. Yet. But my fists are locked, every muscle corded tight.

The guy—who's wearing a dark-gray business suit—straightens his back to bring himself fully before me. "She wants it. She's just shy." He glances down at her. "Needs a little persuading."

Hot breaths saw in and out of my nose. "The lady wants to watch. No means *no*, asshole. In any establishment, but especially here." Hiking my thumb over my shoulder, I say, "I think you've played enough for tonight."

His eyes narrow, but he shrugs, deciding it's not worth the consequences if he wants to take this matter further. He gives me a once over, sizing me up, before he walks around and leaves.

Releasing a strained breath, I let the adrenaline ebb, gaining my composure before I look down at her.

When I finally do, my muscles go lax. She's mortified. I can see it painted clearly all over her beautiful face, splashed with red, even in the darkness.

I kneel down, my whole body strung tight with the need to touch her. I've anticipated this moment—when we'd first look at one another; when I'd hear her voice—but I hate that it's like this. With fear in her deep-green eyes. At least, fear that I didn't put there.

"He's a douchebag," I say. "Are you okay?"

Her burgundy layers fall to conceal her face, and I want so badly to push them aside. It's a wig—I realized this before now. I've imagined what her real hair looks like; dark, to match her eyebrows. Soft, silky, long. I want to strip her of the fakeness and curl my fingers around a thick hank of her real hair. Pull her head back, look down into her eyes. I push the enticing thought away.

She nods a couple times, her movements jerky. "I'm fine. Just embarrassed, I guess." Lifting her chin, she fixes her penetrating gaze on me. All logic flees my brain. "But what did I expect? I mean, look at where I am. I overreacted, that's all."

Blinking hard, I break the hold she has over me, searching for the right words. I need to please her in this moment, but god, I'm already so lost to her.

"You should expect members to behave appropriately, at the very least," I say. "You're not doing anything wrong by being here, watching. That's what this room is all about. He knows the rules." I nod my head toward the black wall, where submissives are lined up in knelt positions. "You're not on your knees. You're not asking to be dominated. There's always a bad apple, and it just looks like one found you."

Long eyelashes frame her widening eyes. She's staring right into the depths of me. "Don't blame the victim," she says, her voice throaty. "I know that by heart. You'd think I'd believe it by now."

I feel my brow furrow slightly. It's as if she's talking more to herself than me, but I tuck this interesting morsel of information away. "That's right. Now," I say, moving a fraction closer. "I'm technically off work. So I'd like to help you get back to enjoying yourself."

The slender column of her throat bobs on a swallow. "I'm not into…"

"Shh," I say. "I won't lay a hand on you. I won't touch you. And I can leave…if that makes you more comfortable." I pause, praying that my goddess doesn't send me away.

When she doesn't speak up immediately, I push on. "I only want to see that look in your eyes, that passion on your face—the one you wore just moments before that rude interruption."

I watch as her breathing quickens. The tremble of her red, red lips. "No touching?" she questions.

My pulse speeds. "Only if you ask. *Always,* only if you ask."

She continues to stare at me in guarded fascination, the seconds suspending us in our own sphere of heat and caution. When she gives a sure nod, I'm lit with fire.

As she swivels her stool to face the stage, I peer down at her, amazed at this stunning creature I've somehow discovered. I pull another stool up close behind her and take my seat.

Her shoulders tense as my thighs and body cage her in from behind. I can feel her body heat radiating off her, caressing me, beckoning me. Her fragrance of sweet-scented shampoo and body lotion fills my senses, tantalizing.

Slowly, carefully, I lower my head next to hers. As close to her as I can get without touching. With difficulty, I aim my attention toward the stage. The Dom is placing nipple clamps on the sub, her high-pitched moans piercing the charged air between us.

"Do you know why he connects the chain to her mouth gag?" My words slip past my lips in a whispered plea.

She remains silent, her gaze steady on the scene. A slight shake of her head invites me to continue, and my dick swells.

"It heightens her desire. Her awareness." I breathe her in, a glutton, needing to satisfy my senses. "It also heightens her suffering, increasing his pleasure."

As the flogger makes contact against the sub's stomach, she jerks her head, pulling the chain taut. "He's punishing her for moving," I continue, "but that sharp spike of pain gives her so much pleasure, that she can't help but be disobedient. She needs the punishment almost as much as she needs the release, the gratification."

My gaze flicks lower as my goddess squeezes her thighs together. I bite down on my bottom lip, inducing a slight pain to keep my emotions in check, my head clear.

The need to slip my arms around her and hike up that damn dress…spread those legs wide…is almost unbearable. I grip my jeans near my knees, clenching the rough material, to keep my hands from roaming.

This—it's not nearly enough. But as the wisps of her hair caress my cheek, hinting at her trembling body, I revel in this profound moment my goddess is gifting me. To indulge in her —to enter into her sanctity. She's my temple and I'm her slave, willing to kneel before her on command.

And as she tentatively runs a finger along her thigh, drawing up the hem of her dress, sliding her hand between her thighs…god, the anguish is pure hell. A torment so divine, I nearly come undone.

I will beg for more.

I'm not ashamed to own it—to confess what I've been craving for months.

"Can you feel what she feels?" I ask, my voice husky with restrained want.

I watch her tongue slip out to wet her lips as she gazes at the scene, and I grit my teeth. The sub—now sated from her penance—throws her head back in bliss. The Dom hikes one of her legs over his shoulder as he kneels before her, devouring her, taking her into his mouth with unguarded vigor.

"She's stripped raw, laid bare," I whisper. "She's utterly vulnerable to him. Having submitted her whole being over to him, she's now free to indulge in the ecstasy which comes from that liberating relinquishing of control."

She shudders next to me, and my eyes follow the trail of her hand upward. Farther and farther—so painstakingly slow —until she's there. Her head lolls to the side, her eyes close, and we're lost together as she caresses herself through the thin barrier of her black panties.

"I wish I could have that," she admits, so low, and my whole body is piqued, awaiting her next admission.

"What do you need?" I ask, my fingers curled so tightly around my jeans they ache, could shred the fuckers. My dick is so hard, I swear, it's going to rip straight through my jeans.

"To be free," she whispers.

I squeeze my eyes closed against the severe quake that her softly spoken words elicit. "Slide your panties aside."

I'm just in control enough to open my eyes and witness

her obeying my order. A primal need to throw her down and ravish her—right here; right now—barrels through me.

"Push inside. Deep. Until it aches." God, but she does. Holy hell, she spreads those sweet thighs and sinks her finger inside until I hear her desperate moan. "Fucking move your hips. Go deeper…"

A shrill moan resounds around us, and the spell is broken.

Her eyes fly open and she stares at the stage, to where the sub is coming with fierce and quivering pleasure as she pulls at her restraints.

"Relax," I say, restraining myself from touching her. "Let me be the one to take you there. Just like that. Let me—"

She sits forward. Pushes her dress back down her legs. "Shit. I need to go."

"Wait." I almost reach out for her, but I stop mid-air. My hand balls into a tight fist. "Don't run. This is what comes next. Let yourself experience it."

She shakes her head, shame creasing the tight corners of her eyes. "It always pulls me under," she says. At my confused expression, she clarifies, "The darkness. It's always there…with the cries. I don't deserve the freedom you're offering. That's not why I'm here."

Then she's gone before I can demand to know more, my beautiful goddess vanishing as quickly as she appeared.

And, oh—I'm so tempted to give chase and beg her to welcome me into her darkness.

The desire to follow her thrums through me with vicious abandon.

I close my eyes, slip my hand into my pocket, and caress

the rough cord of rope to drive away the coldness encasing me in my own dark, hollow space.

She will understand soon there's no reason to hide from me, no reason to be ashamed. I understand her; I appreciate her fear more than any other soul.

Soothed, I open my eyes. I won't be able to wait until she appears next in my world before I see her again.

ALSO BY TRISHA WOLFE

All Trisha's series are written to start at any point and pull you in, but here is her preferred reading order to introduce worlds and characters that cross over in each series.

Broken Bonds Series

With Visions of Red

With Ties that Bind

Derision

Darkly, Madly Duet

Born, Darkly

Born, Madly

A Necrosis of the Mind Duet

Cruel

Malady

Hollow's Row Series

Lovely Bad Things

Lovely Violent Things

Lovely Wicked Things

Dark Mafia Romance

Marriage & Malice

Devil in Ruin

Standalone Novels

ABOUT THE AUTHOR

From an early age, Trisha Wolfe dreamed up fictional worlds and characters and was accused of talking to herself. Today, she lives in South Carolina with her family and writes full time, using her fictional worlds as an excuse to continue talking to herself. Get updates on future releases at TrishaWolfe.com

Want to be the first to hear about new book releases, special promotions, and signing events for all Trisha Wolfe books? Sign up for Trisha Wolfe's VIP list at TrishaWolfe.com

Connect with Trisha Wolfe on social media on these platforms: Facebook | Instagram | TikTok

ACKNOWLEDGMENTS

Thank you to:

My amazingly talented critique partner and friend, P.T. Michelle, for reading so quickly, giving me much needed pep talks and advice, wonderful notes, and for your friendship.

My super human beta readers, who read on the fly and offer so much encouragement. Melissa & Michell (My M&M's), and Debbie for offering me so much helpful insight as always. All the girls in the lil Monsters reader group for reading the ARC, your support and encouragement, and for all that you do. You keep me going! I really can't express how much you girls mean to me—just know that I couldn't do this without you.

To all the authors out there, my kindred, who share and give shouts outs. You know who you are, and you are amazing.

To my family. My son, Blue, who is my inspiration. I love you. To my husband, Daniel (my turtle), for your support and owning your title as "the husband" at every book event. To my personal assistant, my PA of freaking amazing, Meagan, who rescued me from the cliff and became my family. I have no idea what I'd do without you, and I hope to never find out.

There are many, oh, so many people who I have to thank,

who have been right beside me during this journey, and who will continue to be there, but I know I can't thank everyone here, the list would go on and on. So just know that I love you dearly. You know who you are, and I wouldn't be here without your support. Thank you so much.

To my readers, you have no idea how much I value and love each and every one of you. If it wasn't for you, none of this would be possible. As cliché as that sounds, I mean it from the bottom of my black heart. I adore you, and hope to always publish books that make you *feel*.